THE HATE YOU DRINK

N.R. WALKER

Copyright

Cover Art: N.R. Walker
Editor: Boho Edits
Publisher: BlueHeart Press
The Hate You Drink © 2019 N.R. Walker
Second Edition 2025 - Discreet cover

All Rights Reserved:

Warning

Trademarks:

BLURB

Erik Keston, son of the Keston Real Estate empire, knows what it takes to be successful. Despite his inherent wealth, he holds his own. He works hard, he's grounded, he's brilliant. He's also secretly in love with his best friend.

Monroe Wellman lost his parents three years ago and never grieved, never recovered. Inheriting the family company and wealth means nothing, and his spiral of self-destruction is widespread and spectacular. Dubbed Sydney's bad boy, he spends more days drunk than sober, and the only person who's stuck by him through it all is his best mate.

But when Monroe hits rock bottom, Erik gives him an ultimatum, and his entire world comes to a grinding halt. It's not until the haze lifts that Monroe can truly see what he's been searching for was never in the bottom of a bottle. It's been by his side all along.

An 80,000-word friends-to-lovers story about fighting the demons within and trusting in the love that takes its place.

"Because when all you drink is hate, that's all there is inside you."

THE HATE YOU DRINK

N.R. WALKER

Chapter One
Erik Keston

Monroe Wellman, 27, sustained minor injuries in a single vehicle accident last night on North Head Road. Wellman was taken to Rose Bay police station where he underwent drug and alcohol testing. Wellman returned a negative drug test result but was later charged with high-range PCA, his blood alcohol level three times the legal limit.

Wellman became the sole beneficiary and CEO of Wellman Corporation when his parents, Johnathon and Petra Wellman, were killed in a light-plane crash in Macau, China, three years ago. Wellman has had multiple alcohol-related incidents since his parents' death.

*He refused medical treatment and was later
released but will face court next month.*

I didn't need to see the photographs of the wrecked car or the glass and metal strewn across the gutter. I didn't need the reminder of how close it had been this time. I closed the newspaper, folded it in half, and slid it across the counter and let out an exhausted sigh. I didn't want to meet Jeffrey's disappointed gaze. I knew that look. I'd seen it more times than I could count. Jeffrey Kwon, a distinguished Korean-Australian man with short greying hair and a kind face, had been a close friend of Monroe's parents as well as their trusted lawyer for thirty years, and Jeffrey assumed the same role for Monroe when his parents died. He was no-nonsense and astute, but he had a heart of gold and everyone knew Monroe would be lost without him. Well, everyone but Monroe.

"Where is he?"

"Still asleep," I replied. I walked over to the nearest couch and all but fell into it, my head in my hands.

"You haven't been to bed yet?"

I was too tired to even scoff. "Nope. It was after three by the time we left the police station. And then I had to get him into bed." I didn't tell him that I'd sat on the end of Monroe's bed when he'd passed out, trying to calm my anxiety. How many nights had I got a phone call from him, drunk, needing help or a lift, to pick him up from a bar or the police station? A quick glance at my phone told me it was just after eight. The morning sun was up and glaring angrily over the Pacific like it could feel my mood. I scrubbed my hand over my face, feeling the minutes of sleep I'd missed. "How he didn't hurt himself or someone else, I'll never know."

"It's only a matter of time before he does." Jeffrey's tone was as sharp as his suit, whereas I felt like Monroe's crumpled wreck that had been winched onto the tow truck last night.

I nodded, because he was right. We all knew he was right. Everyone, that was, but Monroe.

"I'll have the insurance forms sent over this afternoon," Jeffrey said. He rarely let his emotions show, but I could tell he was angry and disappointed. He was probably a dozen different emotions right now. What he wasn't was surprised. This was far from the first time.

"Thanks, Jeffrey. He does appreciate it."

He gave a nod and walked toward the grand foyer, but he stopped before he got to the door. "Does he? Does he appreciate all you do for him?"

I didn't answer. Even if I knew what to say, I couldn't get the words out. But Jeffrey didn't wait for a reply. The soft click of the front door was loud in the silence.

My heart was a weighted lump in my chest. My ribs felt too tight like I couldn't breathe properly. Like I hadn't been able to breathe properly in years. The space of Monroe's house was vast—tiled floors, high ceilings, glass walls overlooking the ocean, no expense spared—yet the vast emptiness was overwhelming. A mansion worth several million dollars, on every elite real-estate list in Australia, was a hollow void of loneliness and grief, much like the man who owned it. Who was, at that very moment, passed out drunk in his bed.

The heaviness of the last twelve hours settled over me, and I slumped down on the couch, pulled a cushion under my head, and closed my eyes.

"Hey, sleeping beauty, wake up."

I startled and shot up. Disoriented at first, until I remembered I was on Monroe's couch. He was standing at the end of the sofa with his arms full of brown paper bags, and then I could smell something.

"I was starving," he said. "And Uber Eats is a gift from the gods. Shuffle up."

I slid up the couch a little and he parked himself next to me, shoved the bags and a pizza box onto the coffee table, then pulled it toward us. "I didn't know what you felt like, so I got that wood-fired pizza you like and some curry and—"

"What time is it?" I asked. Usually the view out the window was a good indication of the time, but it had come over cloudy. Summer storms usually rolled in around four.

"Half two."

"Shit. I didn't mean to sleep that long. I was supposed to go into the office today."

Monroe shrugged like he did to most responsibility.

"Here, get this into ya." He opened the pizza box and turned it to face me.

I took a bite and moaned. It was so good. "How long you been up?"

"An hour or so."

His black hair was damp and he smelled of salt water. "I didn't hear you swim." Which was surprising considering the living room opened up into the pool area.

"Stealth mode," he said with a grin, his blue eyes sparkling. "Nah. You were dead to the world."

I didn't bother explaining that I didn't get to sleep till after eight. I studied his face; there was a small scratch on his forehead and marks on his hands, probably from the glass or air bag. "How you feeling?"

"Good."

And that was his problem. He always woke up feeling fine. Maybe if he'd ever suffered just one hangover in his life, he might think twice about drinking so much.

"Your picture's in the paper," I said. "And photos of the car."

He grimaced for half a second before he took another forkful of curry. "You see Jeffrey?"

I nodded. "He was here before eight this morning. He brought the paper with him."

Monroe stirred his curry, frowning. "Was he mad?"

"Yep. Said he'll have the insurance papers sent around for the car." I took a bite of pizza and swallowed it. "Wanna tell me what happened last night?"

He sighed. "Not really. I had one too many. You know how it is."

"One?"

"Okay, a few."

"And you drove."

"I was fine."

"Your blood alcohol level was high range."

He frowned again, this time stabbing a piece of curried beef. "I was fine. I didn't feel drunk at all."

I knew there was no point in arguing with him, so I tried a different approach. "You could have hurt yourself, Monroe," I said gently. "Or someone else. You're lucky it was a pole you hit and not a pedestrian or a car full of kids."

"Yeah, it was stupid, I know. I won't do it again."

"Well, no, you can't. Because now you don't have a car or a licence."

He pointed his fork at me. "That is true. Well, there's the old Discovery in the garage," he said. "Haven't driven that in a while."

"Old? It's two years old," I said. "And you're not driving it anywhere. You get caught driving unlicensed now and the judge will likely throw the book at you to prove a point. Not to mention that unlicensed means uninsured."

"Where's your sense of adventure?" he asked, giving me that sly grin that usually got him out of all kinds of trouble.

"My sense of adventure is keeping you out of jail."

He chuckled and nudged me with his shoulder. "Always looking out for me," he said. "Thanks, by the way, for coming to get me last night."

"I should have left you there," I said, nudging him back. "In a cell with two guys named Warthog and Donk."

He laughed. "Sounds like a dream I had once. It didn't end badly, let's just say that much."

I snorted, unable to stay mad at him. And that was *my* problem. I could never stay mad at him.

He put his curry down and took a slice of pizza, biting into it. "Mmm, this is good too. Hey, we should go out tonight. There's a summer blues night on at the Wharf."

I shook my head, but he was, like always, relentless and charming and so fucking cute, and I could never say no to him. Which was another one of my problems.

"Come on, it'll be fun. It's summer. We'll have a swim, laze about for the afternoon, have a nap, then we can go out later. Who knows, you might even find some random to take home."

I forced a smile, like I always did. "Unlikely."

"Dunno why," he said, oblivious. "You don't look half bad," he said with a smirk and a nudge. "If a young Robert Redford is your thing and you have more money than God. And fuck knows guys throw themselves at you."

"More money than God?"

"Shut up, you know you do." He pushed the pizza box away. "You know what your problem is, Erik?"

Actually, I did. But I played along. "Nope, tell me what my problem is."

"You're too picky."

I snorted. "Is that right?"

"Yep. So tonight, when a guy looks twice at you, take him into the bathrooms."

"Not really my style, but thanks."

He laughed and stood up, then walked toward the pool. The glass doors were all pushed back, transforming the inside living area into a huge outdoor living area. He peeled off his shirt and stopped to face me. He looked even better in the sunlight. "Are you gonna lecture me about swimming after eating?"

"Wouldn't dream of it."

"Then get your arse into the pool with me. It's too nice a day and life is too damn short." He tossed his shirt and dived into the pool.

And there were both our problems laid bare. His was that he shirked off all responsibility, drank far too much, and lived like every day was his last, which in his case, with his drinking problem and reckless nature, it very well could be.

My problem was that I couldn't stay mad at him and I couldn't say no to him.

Oh, that, and I was absolutely head over heels in love with him. Had been since we were eighteen years old. I was so in love with him, I'd let him treat me like a doormat if it just meant he'd keep me around. It was a sickness.

He had his addiction, and he was mine.

His addiction to alcohol was killing him.

And watching him slowly spiral out of control, being so close to him but so far away, was killing me.

Addiction, in all its forms, fucking sucked.

Chapter Two
Monroe Wellman

The club was pumping. The dance floor was packed, the bass of the music thumped in my chest, and the smell made me smile. Under the odour of sweaty bodies, perfume and cologne, was the sweet aroma of alcohol. I didn't even mind the line at the bar because I knew I'd have a drink in my hand soon enough.

I ordered three vodkas. One with lime and soda for Erik, one with a slice of lime for me, and one shot straight for the hell of it. I downed the shot, then took the two glasses back through the crowd to find Erik.

Ah, Erik.

My best mate. The guy had been beside me through everything. See, the thing about having money is not knowing if the people in your life are genuine or not. So many fake people tried to leech on for the benefits, and sometimes it was hard to see who was real or not. There's truth in the saying "Make your friends before you make your money" and I can tell you that for free.

But I didn't have to worry about any of that with Erik because he had more money than me.

Well, his family did. The Keston Real Estate empire was the brainchild of his grandfather. He was a very smart and intuitive man who, in the 1960s, invested in suburbs about to boom, and in a decade he'd turned a few-thousand-dollar investments into a portfolio worth millions. Erik's mother followed in her daddy's footsteps, then Erik followed in hers. Though the Keston name was still synonymous with real estate, the company had branched into all kinds of ventures, so while Erik was taught the fundamentals of real estate like he was taught his ABCs, he was also switched-on in finance, stock markets, and software technology.

So no, I didn't have to worry about Erik only being my friend for money. He was richer than me, and he was smarter than me too. It also didn't hurt that he was sexy as fuck. He had the whole Norse-god look happening, with his floppy blond hair, tanned skin, blue eyes and a straight pointed nose, perfect lips, and square jaw. But he also had that understated class that only *old money* could buy. He never flaunted his wealth. He didn't have to. People *knew* who he was.

And the two of us together? Well, we were Sydney's rich playboys, according to the Sunday newspapers and gossip columns. When we first turned eighteen, they'd labelled us the new Brat Pack and had tried to get photos of us with some lucky girls, making stories out of nothing. Even after we'd only ever been spotted with other guys, even in gay bars, they never clued in; they just wrote us off as sowing our wild and wealthy oats. It took Erik bringing Connor Worthington to the annual Keston gala night as his date for the media to stop asking about his girlfriends. Of course Erik's family were all on board with it—he'd never had to hide anything from them—and he and Connor had gone out a few times so, like most things in the Keston world, it worked out exactly as planned.

But then the media soon turned their attention to me. *Were we still friends? Were we ever lovers? Boyfriends? Did this put a new light on our always being together? Had we broken up?* They hounded us relentlessly looking for some scandalous inside scoop, but the only thing they did was force me to come out to my parents. I wasn't ready, and they weren't exactly pleased.

Not that it mattered in the end.

Not that any of that trivial shit mattered in the end.

Because in the end, I'd still want my parents back even if they didn't love the real me...

"Hey, there you are," Erik said as I finally got through the crowd. "Thought you got lost."

I handed him his drink. "Told you it'd be busy." The crowd was thumping; the music was great; the atmosphere was electric. I had to lean in so he could hear me. "Isn't it awesome?"

He shook his head at me, but his lips tugged with that almost-smile that told me I'd won. His hair and eyes flashed green and pink with the lights above us. He put his hand on my hip and leaned in so he could speak into my ear. "We're not staying long."

I groaned. "Come on, it's the weekend!"

"I need to work tomorrow." He pulled back and gave me his serious face and tapped my chest with his finger. "And so do you."

Yeah, right. I sipped my drink and smiled at him over the glass, and when I could see he wasn't going to just smile and let me win, I played dirty. I downed my drink, left the empty glass on a nearby table, took his hand, and pulled him onto the dance floor.

Because that's how my nights out went.

That's how they always went.

I spent my days avoiding my thoughts, and at night-time, when they all seemed to catch up with me, I'd drink until my thoughts didn't hurt anymore.

And when reality tried to blindside me, like Erik telling me we were leaving early because of work, I played the game of avoid-avoid-avoid, even if that meant dirty dancing with my best friend and pouring vodka down his throat until he agreed with me.

Of course I played dirty.

Because the alternative meant going home to an empty house full of silence and ghosts and memories where my ever-thinking thoughts would mow me down and drag me to that dark place I had to avoid at all costs. Even if that meant I had to be a jerk to Erik. I had to do anything, everything, to protect myself. To not be alone... to not be me.

Avoid-avoid-avoid.

And as the night went on, and as I just started to feel good, they called last drinks. I was on the dance floor with my arms around Erik, and when they turned the lights on, Erik seemed surprised to find it was me he had his hands on. I didn't mind. It felt great. He felt great. But he shook his head and mumbled something that I didn't hear.

"What'd you say?" I asked.

He was pissed for some reason, so he grabbed my arm and pulled me outside and into a waiting cab. "Wassup?" I asked him.

"I have to be at work in five hours," he replied. "And so do you. If you have any intention of showing up."

"Watcha pissed at me for?" I asked, laughing at him. He always got a line between his eyebrows when he was cranky. "I had a great night. You're a really good dancer, by the way. Sexy as fuck, grinding on me."

"Shut up," he mumbled, looking out the window.

When we got to my place, I threw the cabbie some cash and got out. The world spun beautifully, carefree, and that shit felt good. This was what I loved. Being numb and immune to the world, and it was fucking awesome.

"I think my number's changed," I said, trying to punch in the security code to open the front door. "Didju change m'number?"

"No," Erik said, leaning in and entering in his passcode. The door opened immediately.

"Are you the great Ali Baba? Like for real?"

He rolled his eyes and shoved me into the hall. "Get inside."

I made my way to the kitchen and went straight to the cupboard beside the fridge and pulled out a bottle of vodka. I didn't even bother with a glass. I just cracked the lid and took a swig.

"Jesus, Monroe," Erik said. "Haven't you had enough?"

I laughed. "Never."

"Have you had any water? Maybe you could try it?"

I was gonna tell him to fuck off, but... "That's a great idea! We should go for a swim."

"You're not swimming right now," he said, taking the vodka bottle when I was halfway through taking another mouthful.

I wiped my mouth and put my hand on his hip. "We sh'd totally dance more often. You're really fucking sexy. You got them moves like Jagger," I said, pulling our hips together.

He looked into my eyes, then at my mouth, then back to my eyes. He made a pained sound. "I can't do this anymore," he said.

"Can't do what anymore?" I said. "'S just dancing."

He shook his head and took a step back. "I should go."

"No!" I said, far too quickly. "Please don't leave me."

I knew my reaction was too much by the look on his face. He studied me for a long moment, like he could see how much the idea of being alone scared me. Eventually he nodded. "Okay. But you're going to bed. No swimming, and no more drinking."

He put the vodka bottle back and physically led me to my bedroom. "Wow," I said with a laugh as I fell onto my bed. "Didn't know you were such a bossy top."

He didn't laugh, but I did.

"Goodnight, Monroe" was all he said.

"You could stay?" I mumbled. "Immy bed. With me."

He was silent for so long I looked up at him. "I can't. I just... can't."

"Yeah, yeah," I laughed him off. "'I can't do this anymore.' I heard ya say it."

He cringed like it hurt to hear. And he didn't even say goodbye or nothing. He just walked out. So I lay on my bed and let the room spin, relishing the buzz that took away the pain.

***

Erik wasn't there in the morning.

He didn't take my call. He didn't reply to my messages.

And that wasn't like Erik. He always answered. Always. Except for now, when he didn't.

It made me feel weird, like my skin didn't fit me right. Like the world was off its axis, like I couldn't breathe.

I sat in my office, watching everyone around me. I had assistants and managed the payroll of... Well, I didn't know how many people the Wellman Corporation employed. A lot. Even on a Sunday, they were all busy, they all walked with purpose, they had a destination. Whether it was just the office down the hall or photocopy room, the bank, or a meeting with the marketing team. Everybody had a purpose.

Even the people on the street below. Forty levels

down, they scurried around like ants, busy, driven, focused. Every single person had a purpose.

Everyone except me.

It was my business. It was my name on the wall, on the door, on the letterheads, on every-fucking-thing. But I had no clue what was going on. I was the CEO of a company I had no clue how to run.

I felt like a satellite. Out of touch, orbiting, going round and round and never touching the surface.

I had no clue how to be who I was supposed to be. And I needed Erik. I needed to not freak out in the middle of my office. And why wasn't he answering my calls?

All I kept hearing was his voice. *I can't do this anymore.*

What did that mean? What had I done? Had I finally pushed too hard, one time too many? My life was a fucking mess, and everything felt so out of control. I sat at my desk, staring out the glass wall overlooking Sydney harbour, having to remind myself how to breathe. I turned my phone over in my hands, gripping it far too tight, trying not to lose my shit.

I needed Erik. His voice would calm me down. Just knowing there was someone in the world who cared would fix me. But he was avoiding me. And who could really blame him? I certainly couldn't. I mean, it was only a matter of time before he left me too.

I can't do this anymore.

I needed a drink. Just one drink, one sip would fix me. Only one wouldn't be enough. It was never enough.

But I needed it. I could focus better, I could concentrate, and I wouldn't freak the fuck out if I could just have one drink.

I can't do this anymore.

My chest started to hurt, dull and sharp at the same time. And I couldn't seem to breathe right. My ribs felt too small, and my lungs couldn't take in air. The room started to spin, and not in a good way. My head felt fuzzy, and I was dizzy, and I wondered for a second if I was going to black out.

I was freaking the fuck out. I really needed a drink.

And then my phone rang in my hand. It startled the shit out of me, but when I saw it was Erik's name on screen, the relief was overwhelming. Like somehow my lungs could work again. I took a few deep breaths before I answered the call.

"Hey," I said, trying to sound calm.

"What's up?" It sounded wrong. Distant or angry. Both. I didn't know.

"Look, I don't know what I did last night, but if I did something to upset you or to piss you off, I'm really sorry."

"Monroe—"

"You were gone this morning when I woke up, and then you wouldn't take my calls."

There was a long pause. "I'm busy."

"I'm not feeling too good."

"Maybe if you hadn't drunk so much last night—"

"I'm not hung over. This is different. This is my chest, in my head. I don't feel right. I can't breathe." I pushed against my sternum with the heel of my hand. "Erik, I can't breathe. My heart's racing. Like crazy fast. I don't know what this is."

"Monroe," he said. "Just take a breath for me. Do you need me to call you an ambulance?"

"No. I just... I think I'm freaking out."

"Take another breath for me, and stay on the line. Where are you?"

His voice was calming and it sounded like he was walking. "I'm in my office. Where are you? You were gone this morning, and you didn't answer my calls."

"I'm coming to get you."

"I'll meet you downstairs. On the street. I need air." I gulped, trying to catch my breath. But I couldn't. "Fuck. Breathe."

"Okay, just stay on the line. Don't hang up."

It was all a bit of a blur after that. I walked out, no clue if I spoke to anyone or if someone spoke to me. I think I got some strange looks in the elevator, but the sound of Erik's voice in my ear kept me upright at least. I burst out onto Pitt Street like the building was on fire and had to put my hand on my knees so I could breathe. Some random guy put his hand on my shoulder. "Mate, you okay?"

I stood up but got dizzy, still with my phone pressed to my ear. I managed to nod. Then Erik's blue Merc pulled up and he was out of his seat, not giving a shit that he'd just blocked traffic, and he got me into the passenger side door.

Once I was inside, his smell surrounded me,

enveloped me, and my lungs expanded. At least I could breathe. The next thing I knew he was back in the car and we were driving. "Put your seat belt on," he said. He kept glancing at me, to the traffic, back to me, and back to the road. He was concerned, that much was clear, but he still seemed mad at me.

"Thank you," I managed.

"What happened?"

"I don't know. I got to my office, and everything was fine. I mean not fine, because I'd left you messages and I called about a dozen times and you wouldn't answer, and I started to freak out."

He scowled at me, and his knuckles were white on the steering wheel. "You freaked out because I didn't answer your calls?"

"Not only that. I mean there were a bunch of reasons and no reason at all. I was just in my office and all of a sudden the room felt too small and I couldn't breathe, everybody was busy but I... I don't know. I freaked out." I put the heel of my hand to my sternum. "I'm still freaking out. My heart feels like I've run a fucking marathon."

"You're pale," he said, frowning. "And sweating."

I looked out the window. "Where are we going?"

"Prince Alfred."

What? "No! No hospitals. I'm fine. Now. I think I just need to go home. Maybe I just need some sleep, or maybe I'm coming down with something."

Erik scowled again. Not at me this time, just in general. His jaw ticked, like it always did when he was mad.

"Please don't be angry with me. I didn't mean to freak out. I didn't know who else to call."

The truth was I didn't have anyone else to call. We both knew it. He was just too nice a guy to point it out. Instead, he growled in frustration and changed lanes in the direction of home. "I'm not angry at you for freaking out. And I'm glad you called me." He was still frowning, but he sighed and his shoulders relaxed a little. "And I'm sorry I didn't answer your calls or your texts. I was busy. I had to reschedule everything and catch up from what I missed yesterday."

He'd missed work yesterday because of me.

"I'm sorry."

"Hmm" was all he replied with. He never said it was okay, he never said there was nothing to be sorry for, he never said I was forgiven.

Which meant it wasn't, and there was, and I wasn't.

I can't do this anymore.

Those five words would haunt me forever. Not just what he said, but how he'd said it, and the look on his face.

It kind of matched his expression now.

And there was the sinking reality that he was done with me. He was done with my bullshit; he was done with my attitude. And I felt like I was drowning in quicksand. Slowly going under and completely unable to stop it.

And that stabbing pain was back in my chest. I rubbed against it with my palm and I concentrated on my breathing.

When we got to my place, we sat in his car at the front for a while, neither of us speaking until the silence crawled under my skin. The pain partly subsided because I knew my salvation was on the other side of the door. "You don't have to come in," I said quietly. "I'm sorry I called you away from work, again. I'll be fine, I swear. I'm feeling better."

He looked at me like he knew I was lying. He snatched the key from the ignition and got out of the car. He was definitely pissed at me, and I didn't know what was worse: him not taking my calls, or him being mad at me.

I didn't know how to deal with either. I was lost, and I hated feeling so helpless. That sinking feeling was suffocating me, and there was only one way I knew to stop it. I got out of the car and followed him to the front door. He entered in my security code and strode into my house, anger in each of his steps. He stopped in the living room, looking out over the ocean, and ran his hand through his hair.

I was fairly certain I wasn't going to like what he was about to say.

And I knew damn well if he walked out of my life, I wouldn't survive it.

I walked straight into the kitchen, took the bottle of vodka from the cupboard, and grabbed a glass I'd left to drain on the sink.

"What are you doing?" Erik asked disbelievingly.

"What does it look like?" I unscrewed the lid and held the bottle ready to pour.

"Do you really think another drink will fix anything? You just had an anxiety attack."

"I had a what?"

He looked at me like I'd lost my mind. "An anxiety attack, Monroe."

"No I didn't. It wasn't anxiety. I just need to sleep. And this will help me sleep." I poured a healthy dash of vodka into the glass.

He stared at me. "Don't drink it."

Now it was me who stared at him. "What?"

"Don't drink it," he repeated. "For me."

"For you? What do you mean *for you*?"

His chest heaved. "For me. I'm asking you not to drink it. For me, for our friendship. If it means anything to you, you won't drink it." He pointed to the front door. "Because I swear to God, Monroe, if you take one sip of that, I'm gone."

"Gone?"

"Yes. That's where I'm at. I'm done. Your drinking can fuck up your life all you like, but now it's starting to affect mine. Like it didn't already, but now it's getting to the point where I'm not sure it's worth it."

"What are you saying?" I couldn't get his words to compute. "You're seriously giving me an ultimatum?"

He squared his shoulders. "Yes."

"I can't... I don't know..."

"Then that's answer enough." He swallowed hard and his eyes welled with tears, but he shook his head and started to walk to the door.

"No, wait!" I called out, panic rising in my throat. My

heart was squeezing, and I chased after him without even thinking, because somewhere in my brain I knew if he walked out the door, I wouldn't recover. "Erik, stop." I grabbed his arm. "Please don't go. I choose you, of course I choose you. I don't *have* to drink. I promise. I was just going to have something to help me sleep, but I won't."

He was on the verge of tears. He shook his head and whispered, "God, Monroe, you're killing me."

"Please stay. I'll do anything. I can't lose you too."

He groaned up at the ceiling and swiped the tears from his eye. "I'll stay. On one condition. You promise me, you look me right in the eye and promise me, you won't have another drink."

Fuck, he was really making me choose. Yes, drinking was a welcome reprieve, but the idea of not having Erik in my life wasn't fathomable. My mouth was dry and I had to swallow so I could speak, then I looked him right in the eye and lied.

"Yes, of course. I promise."

Chapter Three
Erik

Last night, I'd left Monroe's place as soon as I'd closed his bedroom door. I normally always stayed there. The bedroom next to his had been mine since I was eighteen years old. I spent more time at Monroe's house than I did at my own. But I couldn't stay there. I was supposed to have gone home for an early night; instead he convinced me to go out again and we spent the entire night drinking and dancing. And not just normal dancing, it was slow and grinding, dirty dancing.

I mean, sure, we'd danced like that before, but not for hours on end. I could feel his erection pressed against mine, his hands on my hips over my ass, keeping us locked together. At one point, he'd even had his lips at my neck, and it was everything I'd always wanted. I dreamed of it, fantasised about it, wished for it.

But not like that.

Not when he was too drunk to remember.

My heart just couldn't take it. It was everything I

wanted and had wanted for the better part of a decade. And it was no more than a joke to him.

So I left. I went home, showered, crawled into bed, and just stared at the ceiling until it was time to go to work. By the time I drove myself into the office, I'd convinced myself that I'd had enough.

I deserved better.

I needed to distance myself from him and gain a little perspective. The truth was, I didn't know who I was without him. I'd been Monroe Wellman's best friend for my entire adult life. And after his parents died, I'd also been his crutch, his scapegoat, his alibi for just as long. If I wasn't cleaning up his messes, making sure he got home okay, making sure he ate or didn't drink too much, then who the hell was I?

So I told myself not to take his calls, just for one day. And I knew he would call me first thing; he would have woken up to an empty house and had his phone to his ear before he'd finished looking for me. But what I wasn't expecting was the ten missed calls and half a dozen voicemails, each one sounding more desperate than the last.

And I managed to get a lot of work done for the most part, and it was only when I stopped for lunch that my phone rang and I hit answer without thinking. I could've kicked myself; being at his beck and call was so ingrained...

But then I heard him speak. It was a strangled sound, his breaths were sharp and panting, and I knew immediately something was very wrong. And I was racing toward him before I even knew what I was doing. I needed to get to him, to help him, to save him. I didn't know what was wrong, and it didn't matter. I could tell myself I needed distance, that I could try to stay away, but something was wrong and he needed me.

And I admit when I first saw him and loaded him into my car, I was seriously worried for him. He was pale and sweating, breathing erratically, and I had every intention of taking him to hospital. But within minutes, he relaxed and his breathing was somewhat normal. He said he needed to go home and sleep, and I couldn't deny that was probably very true. But as soon as we walked into his house, he went for a bottle of vodka.

And I drew the line. Right there, right then, I said, *no more*.

Giving him an ultimatum was not my intention, but as soon as the words were out of my mouth, they felt right. He did have to choose: me or booze. He could no longer have both.

As soon as I mentioned leaving, he became panicked. I saw the fear and bewilderment in his eyes, and I hadn't expected that. His fear of losing me pushed him in what I hoped was the right direction.

"I promise," he said shakily. But he looked me right in the eye when he said it, and then maybe I forced his hand, but goddammit, he needed to do something. "Will you stay? Please? I don't want to be alone right now."

"Yeah, okay," I replied. "I will need to go back to work and grab my laptop, and I'll need to make some phone calls, and there are some meetings I'll have to cancel."

He cringed at that, running his hand through his hair. "I'm sorry. I really am."

If he was expecting me to tell him it was okay, he was wrong. "You're always sorry," I replied. I wasn't letting him get out of this. He had to face some hard truths, and the fact of the matter was he was starting to negatively affect my life, and I was done hiding that from him. "I want you to put all of your bottles of liquor on the kitchen counter. We can box them up and put them in the boot of my car."

"What?" he squinted at me, a little panicky. "What for?"

"To remove the temptation. If it's not in the house, you can't have it."

I could tell from the look on his face he didn't want to do it. The panic was back in his eyes. He blinked a few times and glanced around his living room and fidgeted like he was unsure of what to do with his hands. "Um, okay. Yeah. Sure."

"Did you want to come with me to the office? It won't take me long."

"Um, no." He put his hands to his forehead. "I'll take a swim and clear my head and..." He looked around again and frowned. "You know what? Maybe I will. Come with you."

Jesus. He really was a mess. And suddenly I felt bad for being out of patience with him. "Okay. We can pick up some lunch on the way home. How does that sound?"

He nodded quickly. "Good."

"Bottles first though, okay?"

"You can trust me," he said quietly. "If I say I won't drink anything, then I won't. And maybe you're right. Maybe a few days off it will do me good."

I put my hand on his arm. "I hope so. I'm worried about you."

He met my eyes then, and all I saw was honest, guard-down fear. "Me too." Then he licked his lips and looked away. "Thank you. For coming to get me when I called you."

I put my hand to his jaw and waited for him to meet my gaze once more. "We'll get through this, okay?"

He nodded, though he hardly seemed convinced. But I went into the kitchen and opened the cupboard where he kept his alcohol and put the two bottles of vodka onto the kitchen counter. I found beer and wine in the fridge, another bottle of vodka in the freezer, and a bottle of Scotch from under the sink. Then from the pantry I found two bottles of whisky, another vodka, and some gin, Midori, and Bacardi.

He stood there, watching me do it and eyeing the bottles like they were personal canisters of guilt. He swallowed hard and whispered, "There's more. In the pool house."

"Okay. We can get that too."

So we did. Two six-packs of Corona, three bottles of Moët, half a box of pear cider, and half a bottle of schnapps. We'd had some parties here, but Jesus Christ, his kitchen was beginning to look like a Dan Murphy's.

"I think there's some boxes in my dad's office," he said

quietly. "From when I... um, from when I had to box up some stuff."

"Okay," I said gently. Any mention of his parents was hard for him. He still carried their loss with him, so if and when he ever mentioned them, I always trod carefully. It was also a room he didn't go into often. "Want me to grab them?"

"Nah, I can."

I watched him walk out and up the hall toward his parents' end of the house. He very rarely went up there. He had no need. His housekeepers tended to cleaning, given his house was huge; his parents had designed it so they'd have one end and he'd have the other. Mrs Wellman had thought it would give Monroe enough independence to never leave home. Monroe and his mum didn't always see eye to eye, but she adored him and often joked that the house was big enough so he could get married and raise a family all while still living at home. Even after he'd told them he was gay, she still lived in hope of a wife and grandkids one day...

"Erik!" Monroe's voice carried down the hall.

I followed the sound and found him in his dad's old office. The desk sat unused, Mr Wellman's pen still slightly askew on the pad of paper by the phone. The built-in bookcase on the end wall still looked like nothing had changed. The large padded black leather chair at the desk looked far too empty.

Monroe stood, holding an empty cardboard box, staring at the cabinet in the corner. Dark wood panels and glass doors showed off Mr Wellman's treasured things on one side. An ink well and fountain pen that had been his father's, a framed coin, a deck of cards in a wooden box with a small carved duck on top, and his father's war medals. Monroe's grandfather had been in the army...

But on the other side of the cabinet were bottles. Aged whiskies, old liquors that must have meant something to Mr Wellman.

"My dad said he was given that when he closed his first deal," Monroe said, putting his hand to the glass in front of a bottle of port. "And the Chivas Regal was from when he made his first million." Monroe sighed. "He always said he'd open them one day. On a special occasion. He was saving them for a day that would never come."

I put my hand on his shoulder and stood with him as he stared at all the different bottles. Each bottle had a story, a memory.

"Can you lock it?" I whispered.

He nodded. "It's locked. Key's in his top drawer."

"Then we'll leave them." I gave his shoulder a squeeze and rubbed his back. "Come on. Let's do this. I'll get some work done, then we can spend the afternoon in the pool and you can cook me dinner."

He smiled, though it was all too brief. He slid the empty box onto his father's desk and opened the top drawer. He took out the small brass key and felt the weight of it in his hand for a second, then he let out a long and unsteady breath. He handed it to me, his expression one of sadness and grief. "If we're doing this, then we do it right."

I pocketed the key and pulled him in for a hug. And it took me a second to realise what was wrong... He wasn't hugging me back. He was stiff and uncomfortable, which wasn't like him at all. Not with me. He was never like that with me.

But I put it down to the day he'd had. Emotional, stressful, exhausting. I pulled back and gave him a smile I hoped was comforting. I wasn't doing this to hurt him. I was doing this to help him. He took the empty box and walked out of the room.

We packed up all the booze and carried it out to my car, then drove to my work. Monroe came with me into my office. I grabbed my laptop, my pile of messages, and told my PA I was working from location for a day or two. She glanced briefly at Monroe and knew damn well I wasn't with clients, but I didn't care. And we were almost to the elevator when my mother spotted us. She wore a sharp suit, had her phone in one hand, a file in the other, as she powerwalked to her office, no doubt multitasking a dozen things at once, and still managed to smile. "Erik? Have you had a chance to look over that portfolio—" Then she spotted Monroe, who was trying to shrink in behind me. "Monroe, oh my goodness, come here." She handed the file to me and hugged him before pulling back with her hands on his shoulders. "This is a nice surprise! How've you been? I saw the photos of your car. You weren't hurt, were you? I'm sure Erik would have said—"

"No, no. I'm fine," he said, offering a smile that didn't sit well on his face.

I jumped in. "Mum, I'll be working from home today. Maybe tomorrow as well. If you need me for anything, just call."

Her eyes drew to mine and she knew something was wrong. She was a real estate magnate, so she also knew how to read a situation and knew when to speak and when to say nothing. She gave me a serious nod, her gaze intense on mine. "Okay. Don't forget about the Fauchet portfolio."

I lifted up my messenger bag like it was explanation enough. "I'll send the report through this afternoon."

"Okay, boys," she said, still smiling. "Be sure to call if you need anything. And Monroe, you must come over for dinner one night."

"Sure thing, Mrs Keston," he replied quietly.

By the time we were in the elevator, he was starting to sweat, and I was fairly certain this had nothing to do with his earlier anxiety attack or me telling him not to drink. This was about him being confronted by his father's display cabinet, then seeing my mum and being reminded that his own mother was gone, and the realisation that he couldn't drink.

"Hey," I whispered, taking his hand. "You're okay."

He gripped my hand like a vice, and he nodded yes but his eyes were saying no, no, no.

"We'll get you home, and it'll be just us."

He nodded again and let out a breath before the elevator doors opened. He let go of my hand, and we walked out into the basement and got into my car. He was quiet on the drive home, and I gave him the silence he needed to get his thoughts in order. Because knowing Monroe like I did, I knew while he needed me to be with him tonight, that didn't mean he needed me to fill every second with noise. Sometimes just having someone around, someone who didn't ask questions, someone who was just there was what he needed most.

We grabbed some sushi to go, and when we got back to his house, I parked in his empty space in the garage, given his newest car had been towed after the accident, and we ate on the couch. I threw my jacket over the back of the couch and pulled off my tie, and Monroe threw his jacket over mine. He toed out of his shoes and unbuttoned the top two buttons on his shirt. He still didn't say much and I didn't push, but he took our empty bento boxes and came back with bottles of water and gave me a smile. Then he lay down on the couch next to me with his head near my leg while I pulled out my laptop and went through some work, though I kept pausing every other minute to run my hand through his hair until he fell asleep.

He was peaceful when he slept. And beautiful. *God, so beautiful.* His closed eyes hid the heartbreak and loneliness, hid the demons that lurked in the darkness behind those blue eyes and dark lashes. Behind the smile I hadn't seen since his parents died. The smile I missed so much it made my heart ache.

So I tapped away quietly at my keyboard while he slept, and I managed to get more done than I thought I would. But then he woke with a start and bolted upright, breathless.

"Hey," I said, reaching for his hand. I gave it a squeeze and he visibly relaxed.

"Hey," he replied, his voice croaking.

"Bad dream?"

"Mmm," he said, shaking it off. He rolled his shoulders. "I'm gonna hit the pool."

"Okay. I'll join you. I'm done with this for now." I slid my laptop onto the coffee table. "Got some boardies I can borrow?"

He got to the hallway and snorted. "Since when do you ever ask?" His quiet laughter followed him up the hall as he walked to his room. "You can get off your arse and come get them yourself. I ain't your maid."

I smiled, genuinely, for the first time in a long time. That was the Monroe I knew. The joking, funny, smartarse guy who gave as good as he got. I followed him into his room, pretending not to look at his huge California king-size bed, pretending not to imagine what it would be like to be in that bed with him... when a pair of board shorts hit me in the side of the face. I grabbed them and turned toward his walk-in wardrobe just in time to see him pull up the pair of boardies over his naked arse, and he laughed as he stood up to his full height, tying the cord at his waist.

And I was reminded by the rush of blood and the thump of my heart that I wanted more from him than he could possibly give me.

I desired him; I wanted him. I wanted to touch him,

feel him against me. Wanted to kiss him, I wanted to know what he tasted like, and I wanted to know what he sounded like when I pushed inside him. But above all that, I wanted him to love me as much as I loved him. I wanted to wake up next to him, I wanted to go to sleep beside him, make him breakfast, rub his feet after a long day. I wanted to get him his favourite coffee and watch his stupid movies, and I wanted to spend every evening on his couch, raking my fingers through his hair until he fell asleep.

The way I tortured myself was cruel.

He smirked as he walked past, leaving me with my hammering heart and whirlwind thoughts. I stood there trying to catch my breath until I heard him open up the glass doors to the outdoor area and the faint splash of him diving into the pool. It took me a second to put my thoughts in order, but I stripped off and pulled on the swimmers he'd thrown at me and followed him out to the pool.

He was doing laps like he usually did. It explained his physique. I'd been more into rowing, which explained my physique of shoulders and thighs, but he was more streamlined. And he could do laps for hours, just up and down, all day long. He said it cleared his head, and if that were true, after the morning he'd had, he'd probably be doing laps until the sun went down.

I sat on the edge of the pool, leaving him to his mind-clearing laps, and enjoyed the sun on my skin and my feet in the cool water. It had been a crazy few days and it felt good to decompress. It was hard to reconcile the guy swimming effortlessly up and down his pool with the guy who'd crashed his car two nights ago, got rotten drunk again last night, and then freaked out this morning.

From the outside looking in, Monroe seemed to have it all. Million-dollar mansion, successful company, both of which he'd inherited, but he was incredibly smart and he had model-good looks and his sense of style was impeccable. His life appeared to be meticulous from the outside.

On the inside it was a fucking mess.

And it felt like I was spiralling out of control with him. Not that I was just along for the ride, but in over my head, right alongside him.

I didn't know how this would end, but I had a god-awful feeling it wouldn't end well, and the path we were on would end soon, one way or another.

And that scared the ever-loving shit out of me.

I didn't know who I was without him. That was a truth that was following me like a shadow. A truth I didn't want to face, but a truth that was fast gaining ground.

Cold water splashed me and I looked up to see Monroe smiling at me. "You getting in?"

"Didn't want to interrupt your laps."

He rolled his eyes like that was ridiculous. "Shut up and get in here."

I slid in and swam slowly toward him, only when I got close, I palmed the water, splashing his face. He laughed and tackled me and we both went under, both laughing, and for the next hour or so, we played silly-buggers and goofed off. When we were sick of the water, we baked ourselves in the sun for a bit, only to roll back into the water to cool down. Later we played pool and he beat me six balls up; followed by the Xbox where I totally kicked his arse. Then we ordered Korean BBQ to be home-delivered, and I realised my mistake as soon as I'd ordered it.

Because nothing went better with Korean BBQ than a cold beer. And we always had some Coronas when we ordered it. It went together like toast and Vegemite. So I improvised. I opened his fridge and took out a bottle of soda water, diced up some lemon and lime, added some mint leaves and some pineapple juice and a whole bunch of ice cubes.

I poured us a glass each and handed one to him. He smiled at it. "Thanks."

"I'm trying," I said. "And just because it's not alcohol doesn't mean it has to be horrible."

He sipped it and made a face, so I sipped it and made the same face. He laughed. "It's not horrible. It's fucking terrible."

I snorted. "Shut up and drink it."

He grinned, looking cute as hell. We were still only wearing our boardies, shirtless, but long dry. His dark hair was sticking out at all angles, making him more sexy than cute, and I had to make myself look away. He cleared his throat and was about to say something when his intercom buzzed.

He put his drink down and disappeared to the door,

and I stood there trying to get my breathing under control.

He reappeared a few moments later holding a brown Uber Eats bag. "Dinner is served!"

We ended up on the lounge chairs by the pool, with the jug of non-alcoholic punch and some paper towels, and we devoured the lot and I ended up lying back, content to stare at the evening sky.

Monroe, on the other hand, was antsy. He fidgeted and rearranged everything, then tidied up, took all the rubbish out, then sat down again, then stood up and began to tidy up the pool house. He straightened cushions and made sure doors were locked, and it took me a moment to catch on...

He wanted a drink.

"Hey," I said. "Let's go for a run."

He stopped and stared. "A what?"

"A run or a jog. Or we can walk down to the beach if you want."

He scowled, frustrated and twitchy. "No, I don't want to go for a run."

"Okay, so then tell me what you want to do and we'll do it."

"I dunno," he shrugged.

"Can I ask you a question?"

"You're going to ask me it regardless of what I say, so why don't you just ask."

"Do you drink every day?"

His scowl became more of a sneer. "What the hell kind of question is that?"

"Every night, when I'm not here. Do you drink?"

"Oh, fuck off," he said, walking past me. "I don't need judgement from you."

I grabbed his arm. "I'm not judging you."

His eyes flashed with anger. "Oh really? Because it certainly looks like it from where I'm standing."

"I'm just trying to understand," I said gently. The answer to my original question was obviously *yes*. Yes, he drank every single day. "I'm trying to help you."

He shrugged my hand off his arm. "I don't need your help!"

That kind of stung, but I knew he didn't mean it. "Well, you're stuck with me, so deal with it. Go and get your laptop and we'll sit our arses in front of the TV and get through some emails."

His nostrils flared. "I don't need a fucking babysitter."

"Well, I'll tell you what. I'm going to sit there and go through emails and get some shit done because of all the work I've missed this week. You can join me if you want. Or you can go sulk in your room. Whatever."

He stalked up the hall. "Fuck you."

I bit back a growl but didn't yell anything back at him. I knew him. He just needed to blow off steam, and sure enough, ten minutes later he walked back out with his laptop. "You suck arse."

I tried not to smile too much. "Very well, too." I shrugged one shoulder. "Or so I've been told."

He threw himself onto the couch, somewhat petulantly. "What are we watching?"

"Netflix. RuPaul's *Drag Race*."

He actually looked at the TV for a second, then at me. "Season one?"

I chuckled. "All of them. I started at the beginning."

He grumbled next to me, but he opened his laptop and we got through a few episodes and a dozen emails each. His foot tapped and his knee bounced, his agitation still there, until he groaned and shut his laptop. He pulled the glass sliders closed and locked up, then set the alarm, then tidied up again, still needing to keep busy. Distracted. "I'm kinda beat, so I'm gonna go shower and probably just go to bed..." He squinted his eyes shut and raked his hand through his hair. "Thanks. For before, I mean. I didn't mean to be a dick to you."

I closed my laptop and slid it off my thighs. "It's okay." I turned the TV off and stood up. "Any plans for tomorrow? Did you want to go to work for a bit?"

He twitched a little, like he was uneasy in his skin. "I don't know. I'll see how I feel. It's been a crazy couple of days."

I gave him a smile. "It has."

He rolled his shoulders and shook his head, antsy, twitchy, uncomfortable. "God, I feel so..."

"Out of sorts?"

He nodded quickly. "It's fucked up."

I stepped over to him and pulled him into a hug. He was uneasy but I wrapped my arms around him, and after a second, he relaxed, and he slid his arms around my waist and hugged me back.

God, he felt so good against me.

Like he was meant for me. Like my body, heart, and soul *knew* he was meant for me.

Then he whispered, "I don't know if I can get through this."

"Yes you will," I replied. "You've got this, Monroe. And you've got me."

He sighed and held me tighter. "I don't deserve you."

I pulled back so he could see my face. "Yes you do."

And for a long moment we just stared at each other, and for one heart-stopping second, I thought he was going to kiss me. He looked at my lips, and sweet fucking mercy, I wanted him to. With every cell in my body, every minute of the last nine years came down to this one moment. But it wasn't the right time.

It was the worst possible time.

I took a step back and tried to gather my wits. "Good-night, Monroe."

Something flashed across his face that I couldn't quite recognise, and he disappeared down the hall into his room, so, not sure what else to do, I turned off all the lights and went into my room. Well, it was technically one of the guest rooms, but it was the room I always stayed in, and I stayed there so often I even had clothes in the wardrobe and toiletries in the bathroom.

I got ready for bed, but sleep didn't come easy. My head was a mess, and my heart felt like it was getting ready to shatter into a million tiny pieces. I kinda felt like I was at a precipice, wondering what one thing would push me over the edge.

At around half two in the morning, Monroe opened my bedroom door.

Chapter Four
Monroe

I couldn't sleep. My body felt wrong, my mind wouldn't stop spinning in circles, and it was almost like I had an itch I couldn't scratch. Not in one place, but all over, and under my skin and in my bones.

I couldn't sleep.

It was just one day. Erik asked me not to drink for one day, and I literally felt like I was going insane. Just one fucking day.

I didn't want the drink exactly. It wasn't the alcohol I wanted; I wanted the control. I wanted to calm down and be in control of my mind and my body. And I wanted to take the ache in my chest away. I wanted to forget. I wanted nothing to matter.

Just one drink would make it all stop.

But I'd promised him, and I didn't want to let him down. Not one more time. Every time I stumbled, every time I fell apart, Erik put me back together again.

Erik.

He was like a security blanket. He had a soothing effect on me, and I was better, calmer, just being near him. And before I knew it, I was out of my bed and opening his door. It was crazy, and it was reckless. I'd never done anything like this with him before, but then again, I'd never needed to.

And I needed him right now.

"Hey, what's up?" he whispered, sitting up. The room was dark but I could see him well enough. He was only wearing underwear, the sheet pulled up to his hips.

"Can't sleep," I answered.

"Me either."

"Erik, I kinda feel weird, and I don't wanna be alone right now."

"Okay," he replied like it was the most normal thing in the world. He flicked back the sheet as a silent invitation.

And I ran to his bed like I was a little kid who'd had a bad dream. I should've been embarrassed, but I was so fucking grateful. We lay down and faced each other, and he somehow held my hand between us and it felt so good. But it wasn't enough. I needed to be held, needed someone to put their arms around me and to tell me that it was okay. Christ, I was a mess. But I needed... something. So I slid a little bit closer, and a little bit closer still. And when he didn't question or stop me, I shuffled right in to his side and put my head on his chest. Right there in the crook of his arm, his heartbeat pressed to my ear.

He was still for a second, and he slowly put his arm

around me, pulled me in close, and kissed the top of my head.

"Better?"

I nodded. "Yeah. Sorry, I just..."

He gave me a squeeze and rubbed my back. "Don't be sorry. I've got you."

I closed my eyes and sighed, already feeling so much better. And when he rolled onto his side so he could hold me better, I snuggled in, feeling safe and loved for the first time in a long time. Exhaustion crept over me, weighing me down and dragging me under.

I WOKE TO AN EMPTY BED, and it took me a moment to get my bearings. I was in Erik's room, in his bed. It smelled of him and it made me smile.

I don't remember sleeping that well since... Well, probably ever.

But he was gone now, and panic spiked like it had yesterday when I realised he'd left me. Panic burned and seeped into my chest like I'd been shot. It was so blinding, it took my breath away. I tried to sit up, I tried to move, but my body felt crippled. Immobilised with fear and dread...

Until Erik appeared in the doorway with coffee in one hand and a plate in the other. "Morning," he said, oblivious to the war that raged in me. "I made you toast."

I gasped with relief in seeing him, covered it by

sitting up and scratching my head with both hands. "Um, thanks."

He walked in and set the mug and plate on the bedside. "How're you feeling?"

"Um..." I blew out a breath. "I... I don't know yet."

He nodded toward the coffee and toast before turning to walk out. "Well, get some fuel into you, and I'll see you in the pool. It's hot outside already."

I watched him leave and took a second to calm the fuck down. The panic subsided but left a gritty residue in its place. Restless and anxious, I took the coffee first, hoping it would take the edge off.

It didn't.

So I bit into the toast and needed the coffee to wash it down. Everything tasted wrong. Everything felt wrong. So I used the bathroom, brushed my teeth, then splashed some water on my face. The man staring back at me in the mirror was almost unrecognisable. Like a stranger on the street. I didn't know this man. I didn't like how he stared back at me. His eyes... I couldn't bear the truth in his eyes... With both hands on the sink, I let my head drop, trying to get my shit together. I was barely holding on to whatever threads of sanity I had left. This day was going to suck arse. I already knew it. There was no way this was going to end well.

But maybe Erik was right. Maybe a swim would help.

So, in hopes of the cool water washing away my funk, I pulled on some Speedos, dumped the coffee and toast on the kitchen counter, and turned around to face my shitty day.

Erik had the glass doors pulled back, opening the room onto the pool area. It was hot already, the summer sun scorching all it touched. The sky was cloudless; the ocean was a dozen different shades of blue. People walked along the shore, swam in the waves, and boats sailed in the breeze.

It should have been perfect. Glorious, even. But it just seemed to piss me off. I didn't want perfection when I was a fucking mess. I wanted rolling clouds, heavy and dark. I wanted tumultuous storms, driving rain, and thunder and lightning.

And I didn't want Erik with his wet hair slicked back or his playful smile on his perfect face watching me from the edge of the pool. Beads of water glistened on his shoulders, and the sunlight made him look golden. He was everything that was good in my life. A fucking diamond.

And I was a lump of worthless coal that smeared and ruined everything I touched.

"Are you getting in?" he asked, his arms folded on the edge of the pool, grinning at me. "And what the fuck are those?"

I looked down at my Speedos. "Shut the fuck up. I do laps in them."

He laughed. "Well, at least they're not white."

I rolled my eyes and walked toward him. "Don't even act like you wouldn't love it if they were."

He kind of laughed but mumbled something I couldn't quite hear before he pushed off from the edge, going underwater as he did. But the water looked good, so

I dived right in, and when I broke the surface, I gave him a splash.

"What was that for?"

"For hating on the Speedos."

He grinned. "Who said I was hating? I'm all for the bulge."

I splashed him again, and he laughed. He was right though; the water was good. I began swimming laps, finding peace in the measured strokes and regulated breathing. My body felt good sluicing through the water, and there was a purpose to it. Even if it was just doing stupid laps, one after the other, until my lungs burned and my muscles tired. It was the single-mindedness I needed until all the bullshit in my head was replaced with the mechanics of movement and breathing. There was no noise, no swirling thoughts, no spiralling darkness lurking in the periphery. There was nothing but my body and the water.

I wished I could swim forever. I wished I could just do lap after stupid lap until there was nothing left. And I don't know how many laps I did or how long I was in there for, but when I went to touch the wall on a turn, I hit legs instead of wall.

I stopped and looked up, breathless. It was Erik, of course, smiling down at me. He still had his board shorts on, but he was completely dry and now wearing a polo. "You gonna do that forever?"

My eyes hurt. I hadn't realised. I stuck my thumb and forefinger into my squinted eyes. "I should have worn my goggles."

"You could have swum to New Zealand by now." He was still smiling but there was a hint of concern in his eyes. "Come on, get out. We're going out for lunch."

If it was his plan to keep me busy, he succeeded. He grabbed a foam soccer ball from the pool house and we walked down to the beach, grabbed a burger and fries, and it was everything I needed.

Well, not everything. It wasn't a shot of vodka or a Corona, but the salt and grease were a satisfying second best.

Kind of.

Then we kicked the ball around on the sand for a bit, then walked some more. He didn't say a great deal, and neither did I. But just hanging out with him was perfect. His smiling face was a constant reassurance, and when he could see me getting agitated or bored or antsy, he'd distract me.

And that worked really well. Until we went back to my place and he had to check on some work thing on his laptop. I'd turned my emails off, switched my phone to airplane mode, and so I decided to watch some TV.

Except every show on every channel showed someone at a bar or some drink or a bottle. It might have just been some stupid glass prop, but it was a constant freaking reminder. Had I not noticed that before? Was alcohol really so ingrained into our everyday lives that we didn't even notice it? Until I wasn't allowed to have it and I was trying not to think about it and it was everywhere. Christ, it felt like someone tapping me on the shoulder every time I saw it.

Tap. Tap. Nudge. Nudge. Push. Push.

I groaned in frustration and turned the TV off, but it was too late. It may as well have handed me an opened bottle and told me not to sip it. Not to even smell it. And now it was all I wanted. The only thing on the planet I yearned for. And couldn't have.

The itch was back. My bones were wrong, my skin felt too tight. The darkness, the pain was closing in...

"Fuck."

I shot to my feet and paced for a bit, but it was too late.

"You okay?" Erik asked quietly. He cautiously slid his laptop onto the seat beside him.

I stopped in my tracks, ran my hand through my hair, and blew out a breath. "Um. Sure."

"Clearly you're not..."

"It's everywhere. Do you know how much booze is a part of our lives? It's on every show. It's on most ads. An ad for carpet. Here, tip some red wine on it. Need a new BBQ? Sure, here's some beer while you grill your steak. Need home insurance? Of course you fucking do, so let's show a middle-aged couple, and you know what prop makes perfect fucking sense? A glass of wine. No, that's not enough. Give them a whole fucking bottle. Football? Sure, here's an ad for beer. Is it summer? Sure is. Here, have the Bundy fucking Bear on the beach. A music festival on the harbour? Fuck yes, give me all the pre-mixed shit you can dream of. Car racing? Fuck yes, because nothing says don't drink and drive like a bottle of Scotch as the major sponsor."

Erik stood up and put his hand on my arm. "It's everywhere."

"Every-fucking-where I look."

"So we don't turn the TV on."

"Or watch a movie. Or listen to the radio, or even fucking Spotify." I pulled at my hair. "It's bullshit. And it's not fair. Where is the consumer protection advocacy on this? My business is regulated to the fucking hilt and there are rules of what we can and can't show in our advertising. Where are all the do-gooders and the bible brigade that watch every single thing that Wellman Corporation does? Oh, I'll tell you where they are? They're writing gaming legislation with a fucking glass of wine in their hands."

"Tell me what to do," he said. "I'll do anything I can to help."

"You can get me a drink."

His face fell. "No. I can't."

"Your car boot is full of it. In my fucking garage. I could go in there myself and pop your boot and drink whatever the fuck I want."

"But you won't."

My hands were fists and rage bubbled inside me. "Jesus, Erik. Just one fucking drink!"

He shook his head, and I needed to take a step back. I wasn't going to hit him, never, but I sure felt like pummelling the shit out of something. I growled, frustrated and furious, and walked out into the pool house. I needed to not be near anyone right now. I needed some space and distance.

Fuck!

I wanted to pick up a billiard ball and throw it through the plate glass door. I wanted to cause destruction. To break things, smash shit up, until the whole house was a wreck.

I wanted it to match how I felt on the inside.

But I gripped the cushion on the billiards table, my fingers digging into the felt, and bowed my head. I took some deep breaths, trying to contain my anger.

I had some free weights by the treadmill, and all of a sudden, they were a great idea. I needed to expend a shit-load of energy and that was the perfect way. So I lifted dumbbells and did squats and swung kettlebells and pressed weights and did push ups and sit ups and went back to lifting dumbbells over my head until I was a sweating, fucking mess. Then I took off my shirt and started all over again.

I'd tamped the anger a little. Expended the rage as positive energy or some shit like that, but the want to drink was right there. Under my skin, on the tip of my tongue, at the front of my mind.

I hadn't even noticed Erik watching me.

And for a second, he didn't notice me watching him. He was staring at my chest, at my crotch, my arse, and he was looking at me like he wanted me.

What the...?

"See something you like?" I asked.

His eyes shot to mine. "What? No." He shook his head. I'd seen him lie before. He wasn't very good at it.

I smiled and put the dumbbell back on the floor, maybe giving him the full view of my arse.

He looked and he licked his lips, then shook his head and laughed. "You're such a dick."

I chuckled and grabbed my dick. "Yep."

He crossed his arms, then uncrossed them. "Feel better?"

"Kind of. A little."

"Good." He met my eyes. "I'm not saying no to a drink to be deliberately mean to you."

"I know." And that was the truth. I did know that, deep down. I knew he was trying to help me. But that also meant he was first in the firing line. "I didn't mean to get pissy with you."

He smiled and nodded toward the pool. "I'm done with work. Want another swim? You're um..." He looked up and down my torso, his eyes lingering. "You're a little sweaty."

I rubbed my hand over my abs and up over my nipple, and his nostrils flared. He fucking wanted it. Holy shit. Erik was seriously checking me out, and suddenly, I had a much better way to expend energy. "Only if you join me."

His gaze shot to mine, his nostrils flared. It was desire, pure and simple. But he turned away and laughed, resting against the billiard table. "You're an arse."

I walked over to him and stood right in close, the heat of his body against mine. "Make up your mind, Erik. Do you want me to be a dick or an arse? Because you know I do both."

He gasped quietly, his dark eyes going to my mouth, then back to my eyes. "Just get in the pool."

I leaned in a little. This game was so much better than lifting weights. "Only if you join me." I took the hem of his shirt and pulled upwards, ripping it over his head. He came forward an inch, his chest almost touching mine, his cheeks flushed, and his lips parted, his hair mussed up.

I could almost imagine he'd look the same during sex.

I smiled at him, groaning low enough for him to hear. "Join me in the water, Erik."

I turned toward the pool and dropped his shirt near the edge, then slowly pulled my shorts down so I was wearing only briefs, before diving straight in. My God it felt so good. Cool on my warm skin, and it made my briefs pull and tug on my cock in the very best of ways.

I swam real slow to the opposite end and I heard the splash of his entry behind me. I grinned as I turned around, treading water. He splashed me and said, "Shut up."

It made me laugh, and I don't know what possessed me, but I swam over to him and put my arms around his neck. We'd been best friends for years, and of course we'd touched and I'd had my arm around him a thousand times. We'd even slow danced and grinded against each other, on show for the guys in the club who watched us.

And they *did* watch us.

But then I wrapped my legs around his waist and climbed up him a little, rubbing my cock against his lower belly.

It felt so damn good. And I needed to feel good. I needed to be distracted, and maybe a good, hard fucking would do the trick.

Erik held onto me, his eyes were dark, his cheeks flushed, and I could feel his erection. But there was a hint of confusion there too, and his voice sounded almost pained. "What are you doing, Monroe?"

I sucked in my bottom lip and rolled my hips, rubbing my hard-on against him. "It feels good, yeah? I can feel how much you like it."

He reached behind him and unhooked my legs around him, pushing me away. "You don't want to do this."

I pushed him back, up against the side of the pool, holding him there with my body. He could feel my cock, just like I could feel his. "Yes, I do." I took his hand and forced him to palm my erection. "Feel that? I want this."

His eyes fluttered shut and his nostrils flared again. But when he opened his eyes, there was a different kind of darkness. He spun me around, hitched my thigh over his hip, and drove me onto the side of the pool as he crushed his mouth to mine.

And fuck, he kissed me like I've never been kissed before.

He thrust his hips, his hard cock against mine as his tongue invaded my mouth.

And it felt so good. This was what I needed. Everything else disappeared. The bullshit, the white noise. The restlessness, the spiralling out of control, all went away.

This was focus and pure need and pleasure and desire. There was no thinking. Just primal instinct.

And Erik... fucking hell. He was ferocious and demanding and I gave in to him so easily. I melted into him, let him kiss me, let him grind against me, and I loved every second of it. I wanted him to have me, fuck me, use me, and hurt me in ways I never dreamed of.

In all the ways I deserved.

I clung to him with my hands and my legs, I pulled him in closer, but it wasn't enough. I wanted more. I wanted him inside me.

But then he stopped. Like he'd just realised what we'd done... he drew his mouth from mine, his lips red and wet, his eyes downcast. Then he tried to pull back, but I still had my legs and arms around him. "Why did you stop?" I asked, breathless. "Don't stop."

He grimaced, but he was panting and he wouldn't look at me. "I don't think..."

"Then don't think," I said. "Just do it. We could get out of this pool and go to my room, and you can fuck me for hours."

He winced like it hurt to hear, but his cock pulsed against me.

"You know you want to," I whispered, leaning in to suck his ear lobe into my mouth.

He gasped and his hands went to my hips, and I thought he was going to grind me down on his cock, but he didn't. He tried to push me away.

"I don't think this is a line we should cross," he mumbled.

"We already have," I said, letting go with my legs and sliding down his body. I took his hand and led him up the steps of the pool, and I had every intention of taking this into my room, but I only got as far as the deck chairs before he pulled me to a stop. "Where are you going?"

"To my room."

"No."

I stopped and met his eyes. "Why is your mouth saying no when your eyes and your cock are telling me yes? I can see how much you want it." I palmed his dick. "I can feel how much you want it."

He growled, low and from the back of his throat, a sound I'd never heard from him. He pulled me hard against him, kissed me as hard as he had before, then pushed me onto the sunbed. He pressed his weight down on me, holding my face with his left hand, and with his right, he hooked my leg around his hip. He'd given in, and I was getting what I wanted.

It felt so fucking good.

I spread my legs as much as the sunbed allowed and kissed him like my life depended on it. And in that moment, it felt like it did.

I rolled my hips, and he bucked into me. His cock felt so hard, like hot steel through his boardshorts, and I needed to feel it with my hand. I squeezed my fingers between us and pulled at the waist cord until I could slide my hand underneath. As soon as I gripped him, his kiss faltered. He pressed his forehead to mine, his eyes closed, panting.

"You're so fucking gorgeous," I whispered, breathless.

His eyes shot open, dark and stormy. I pumped his cock, sliding it in my fist, and it spurred him into action. He ripped down my briefs and wrapped his fingers around my erection, sliding pre-come from my slit down my shaft.

"Fuck yes, Erik."

"Oh God."

And he took our cocks together, sliding both through his fist. It was hard and hot and he felt like silk, and it was so fucking good, I was close to coming already. But then he slowed his pace, to make it last or to drive me crazy, I wasn't sure. I bucked up into his grip, and I could feel him trembling, like he couldn't hold back any more. And I was so close.

"You're gonna make me come," I whispered.

He jerked, his rhythm faltering with the groan, and a rush of his pre-come slicked our cocks. And I couldn't hold it back any longer. I didn't want to. I wanted to come right the fuck now, and he could make me come all night long. With a final thrust, my orgasm crashed through me, spilling between us, and I cried out with the force of it.

The world spun and my entire body exploded with pleasure, and he kept pumping me, squeezing every ounce of orgasm out of me until my bones were sponge and I was floating in bliss...

"Holy fuck," Erik said above me, his cock still pressed against mine.

I took hold of his erection. "Let me," I said, my voice gruff. I pumped him and twisted my palm over the head of his glorious cock. "I can't wait to have you inside me," I murmured. "I bet you feel like heaven."

He crushed his mouth to mine once more, kissing me hard. His tongue was in my mouth, taking, tasting. But he thrust his hips faster and faster, fucking my fist and then he broke the kiss to rest his forehead on mine once more.

"Look at me," I whispered. "I want to see it in your eyes when you come."

Only when he opened his eyes, what I saw took my breath away.

It wasn't heat or bliss or desire or lust.

It was goodbye.

Then his whole body went rigid and his cock pulsed in my hand. His come coated my belly, and he jerked and spasmed before he collapsed on top of me.

Maybe I'd misread what I saw.

Maybe I'd read it wrong. Lord knows, it wouldn't have been the first time I fucked something up.

I rubbed my hand over his back, down over his arse. "That was fucking hot," I whispered. "I'm up for round two when you are."

I was aiming for a laugh. I didn't want things to be awkward between us. But he didn't laugh. He pulled back and climbed off me, pulling away to sit on the foot of the sunbed. He tucked his dick back in his shorts. "Um..." he started.

And the panic began to ebb at the post coital bliss. "Um, what?"

He kind of looked at me but didn't. He certainly

wouldn't make eye contact. "I don't think there'll be a round two."

"Why not?" I asked. I pulled up my briefs and sat up. The good feeling I'd had just moments ago was dissipating like mist.

He swallowed hard and stood up. "Because I don't want to," he said before walking inside.

I followed him, not giving him a chance to blow this off. "Why not? Wasn't it good for you? Did I do something wrong? Because from my angle, you seemed to like it."

He spun to look at me. "That's not the point."

"Yes it is. This doesn't have to be weird. Don't let this get awkward between us, Erik. Please." Panic started to claw at my insides.

He let out a disbelieving laugh that was so curt it startled me. Then he looked down at my belly, my chest. "God, can you just get cleaned up or something. I can't have this conversation with you when you're covered in..."

"In what? Our come. Yours, mine. Together?" I asked. "Fucking hell, Erik. I never figured you for a prude."

"I'm not a fucking prude. I just... I can't..."

"You can't what?"

"I can't do this!" he cried. He motioned between us. "You and me. You. Like this. This is not what I want."

That stung. "Okay then. So we won't do it again. Whatever. It was just sex. Mutual hand jobs, whatever. No big deal."

His eyes went wide and filled with hurt. "No big deal?" He took a step back. "That... that's why I can't do this. With you." Another step backward, and he put his hand to his forehead, through his hair, and that look of goodbye stared right back at me.

I shook my head and tried to tamp down the panic that was trying to flood its way out of my chest. "It doesn't have to be this way. We can just go back to how it was. I just thought it felt good, you know? I haven't felt good in so long, I kind of forgot what it was like not to feel fucking lost, and I'm sorry if I pushed too hard or made you do something you didn't want, but, Erik, you can't leave me. You can't say goodbye. I don't know how to do this without you. I can't..."

He groaned, frustrated and pained. "And I can't keep doing this either," he said. "It's like I'm watching you kill yourself in slow motion, and I don't know how to stop it."

"I'm sorry," I said, trying to push the words out. "I'll do better. I'll try better and—"

"And what, Monroe?"

I shook my head. "I don't know! Just please don't leave me."

"I can't be here right now," he said, taking another step backward, away from me. "I can't be near you right now."

"It didn't mean anything, Erik," I said, not knowing what to do or what to say. I didn't know what he wanted me to say. Trying to make the last half hour disappear, I said, "We can just pretend it never happened."

He spun to look at me now and his anger surprised

me. "That's what I can't do, Monroe. Because it wasn't just sex. It wasn't nothing. Not to me."

Not to me.

"What? What are you saying?"

He threw out his hand in frustration. "I'm in love with you! I've been in love with you since we were eighteen fucking years old. Every time you took some random home, it fucking killed me. And you never once noticed. How can you not have noticed? How do you not know?" He shook his head, his eyes full of tears. "You are my entire world. Everything revolves around you. You're like the fucking sun, burning so bright, everything that comes too close gets burnt to fucking hell. I can't do it anymore. Being with you and not having you love me the way I need you to. You're killing me, Monroe. You're killing me."

My brain couldn't seem to make sense of his words. "What?"

His chin wobbled and a tear spilled onto his cheek. "You don't see me. And I can't do it anymore."

"I see you," I said. "Of course I see you. I'm seeing you right now."

He put his hand to his chest. "You don't see me!" he yelled. His anger shocked me. "And what we did earlier was all I've ever wanted. For you to want me, to kiss me." He swallowed hard. "And it meant nothing."

"No, Erik," I said, reaching for his arm.

He pulled away from me. "I can't be here right now. I'm sorry. I know you're a fucking mess, but I can't fix you, Monroe. I can't fix you when I can't even fix myself."

"What do you mean?" I asked. It was barely a whisper. A panicked, frantic whisper. "Erik..."

He put his hand up. "I can't. I'm done." He walked to the hall that would lead him to the garage and he stopped to take one last look. "I'm sorry."

I'm sorry.

You're killing me.

I watched him walk out, unable to move. I couldn't follow him. I couldn't tell him to stop. I couldn't beg him to stay.

I heard his car leave, and the silence that followed felt like a vortex in my head.

I needed to make it stop.

I'm sorry.

You're killing me.

I'm done.

Chapter Five
Erik

My mum took one look at me and her smile faded. "Oh, honey."

I don't know what it is about mums, but as soon as she said it and as soon as I saw her, the dam I'd tried to keep contained finally burst. "I can't do it anymore," I sobbed, and she hurried to wrap her arms around me. "I love him so much it hurts, but I had to walk away."

She patted the back of my head and rocked. I didn't even need to explain; she already knew who I was talking about. "I know you do." Then she pulled back and made me look at her. "Sometimes walking away is the right thing to do. I know you love him. But he... well, he's on a different path to you."

"I don't know how to help him," I admitted. "I tried. I took all the booze out of his house and locked it in my car, but it's not enough. He needs more help than I can give him."

She put her hand to my face and thumbed away a

tear. "You did your best, and you tried. For years, you've tried."

"I failed him."

She shook her head, frowning. "No, darling. You didn't." She studied me for a second. "Did something happen between you?"

I nodded. "It was stupid, and I shouldn't have let it happen, but..." I sighed, and more tears came as I admitted my shame and shortcomings. "I just thought it was my one and only chance. You know, to have that with him. It was all I ever wanted, except it wasn't. It didn't mean anything to him."

Mum pulled me in for another hug, and she let me cry on her shoulder. "Oh, sweet child. I'm so sorry."

After a moment, I collected myself and took a few deep breaths. "I feel so stupid," I mumbled. "And I'm supposed to be an adult, but I need help. He needs help, and I need a grown-up to tell me *how*? How do I fix him? Or do I just stay away? I told him I was done, you know, because that's where I'm at. But I love him, Mum, and I don't know what else I can do for him."

Mum frowned again, her eyes teary. "He needs to be the one to ask for help."

"He won't. He could lose his house and his company, and you know, I don't think he'd care. He crashed his car and he just didn't give a shit. There's only one way this ends for him, and that scares the hell out of me." More tears fell. "I don't want him to die, Mum. But I don't know what else I'm supposed to do."

"He needs to book himself into a clinic," she offered.

"He won't." I shook my head vehemently. "He's like an unsupervised kid. He has no accountability, no responsibility. And I get that he has his reasons or whatever, but he's killing himself, and I looked into all those AA programs and they're all about religion, and you know how he feels about that."

Mum nodded. We'd all heard his rants about God and the church that he'd spectacularly let fly at his parents' wake. "Maybe that's what he needs," Mum offered with a shrug.

"He'd refuse, point blank. I know him. There's just no way. He'd go along and fail deliberately just to prove a point."

She almost smiled. "Yeah, he would."

"I kinda hate him right now." And that admission came with a rush of more tears. "I'm so fucking mad at him."

"Love will do that."

"I don't know what else to do." I wiped my face and took a few deep breaths. "I told him that I loved him and he was honestly shocked. He had no clue. How could he not know? After all these years. It just makes me wonder what I ever meant to him."

"Oh, honey. He's so full of anger and resentment right now, he can't see anything else. But he does love you. I know he does. You're the first person he calls, you're the first one he goes to."

"Because I'm the only one who puts up with him. I'm no more to him than a doormat."

Mum's face fell. "Do you think so?"

"Yes." Then I shrugged and groaned. "I honestly don't know what I feel right now. But thanks for listening and letting me rant. And I'm sorry for the f-bomb."

She laughed. "It's fine, darling." She cupped my face and lifted my chin. "Want some dinner? Your dad will be home tonight."

I nodded, feeling all of five years old again. "I'm lucky to have you," I said. "And Dad."

And that just made me feel worse for leaving Monroe, because he didn't have this. He didn't have his parents or any family. He had no one to run to, no one to rant to like I'd just done. He had no one but me, and I'd just walked out on him.

Mum shook her head. "No, Erik. I know what you're thinking. You're not responsible for him. How about we give him some time to sleep on it, then you and I can call around and see him in the morning?"

"He'll already be drunk by now." I looked at the clock. It was half five. "He'll have had a whole case of vodka delivered by now. Or who knows, maybe he caught a cab to some bar and he's drunk and getting handsy with some random guy on the dance floor."

"Do you think he is?"

I shrugged. "Drunk, yes. With someone? I dunno. I just kinda feel that this is it, ya know? Like this is the end of the line for him. Either some miracle will happen and make him stop drinking or we'll find him dead somewhere." My eyes burned with more tears, but I willed them not to fall.

She studied me for a moment, then that little line

appeared between her eyebrows which meant she was strategising, thinking, planning. She spoke in her CEO voice, "I know someone who might know someone that'll be able to help him. I can't make any promises, but I can make some phone calls. How about you go into the kitchen and make yourself busy peeling some potatoes, and I'll call some people." She walked back toward her office. "Enough potatoes for four people. Elektra will be here soon."

I resisted sighing. And yes, my parents had called their kids Erik and Elektra. I loved my sister, I really did. But I didn't feel like being sociable, and I certainly didn't feel like playing twenty-questions with her. My whole family knew what Monroe was like. I didn't have to explain his drinking or his behaviour since his parents died, but I always did feel the need to defend him.

And I didn't know if I could defend him tonight.

By the time I got the potatoes on the stove, Mum came back into the kitchen and slid her mobile onto the bench. "He's going to call me back," she said, just as Elektra walked through the front door. "We'll talk more about it later."

Elektra came in wearing an oversized linen shirt and a pair of tights with ballet flats, looking as glamorous as a runway model. She had a summer bronze glow, her long blonde hair in a high ponytail, and she looked a million without even trying. It was a five-minute look many spent hours trying to pull off, and she was both envied and hated for it in equal measure. The Sunday fashion papers adored her, as did I.

I hadn't realised how much I'd missed her until she walked in, and I had a sneaking suspicion that Mum had sent her a message to pre-warn her about my mood because gone was the usual playful jibe and instead I got a side-on hug and a gentle squeeze. "What's Mum cooking?"

"Meatloaf and mashed potato," I answered, putting the chopping board in the sink.

She groaned. "Mmm, sounds good. I'm starving." She went to the fridge and collected two bottles of Dad's Italian sparkling water, took some strawberries from the fridge, and made short work on two strawberry spritzers. She handed me one and led me to the covered patio. Mum and Dad didn't have ocean views like Monroe, but they did have a huge pool and a tennis court in Rushcutters Bay. We sat facing the pool, and Elektra put her hand on mine. "Tell me what happened?"

"I thought Mum sent you a text."

"She didn't want me to say something stupid. She said you were upset. And I can see that." She nodded. "Is he okay?"

"I don't know." I refused to cry, but I did tell her everything. Starting at the beginning, I told her what happened, and I'd told her what I said, that I'd told him I loved him and that I was done.

"That must have been awful." She frowned. "I'm so sorry, Erik. Do you think that will be his wake-up call?"

I shrugged. "I doubt it."

"Did you mean it when you said you're done?"

"My head says yes. My heart says no." I met her gaze;

her blue eyes sparkled like the pool behind her. "But I just don't know how much more I can take. And I don't know how much more he can take either. I have this sinking feeling that my time with him is over. Whether that's because I've walked away or if it's because he's pushed his luck too far, I just don't know."

We heard Dad's voice and we both turned at the familiar sound. He was talking to Mum in the kitchen, and she was no doubt giving him the rundown. It probably should've pissed me off, but I appreciated it. Whereas Monroe came from a family that kept secrets, my family knew everybody's business. Being witness to Monroe's family dynamics in the years before his parents' death made me appreciate mine a whole lot more.

Dad came out to see us, pulling his tie off as he walked. "Fancy seeing you two here. You'd think your mother was making her famous home-cooked meatloaf or something."

"Hey, Dad," we both replied.

Dad gave my shoulder a squeeze, a silent show of support. "I'm going to get out of this suit, and then I'm on mashed potato duty, or so your mother tells me. And I'm not going to mash potatoes because she told me to; I'm going to do it because of gender equality, and it's not fair that your mother be expected to cook everything just because she's a woman, and it's not the 1950s, Timothy. If I want home-cooked meals I can damn well expect to help cook them," he said, mimicking Mum. He smiled and waited.

"I can hear you," Mum yelled from the kitchen.

Dad laughed as he headed back inside. "Yes, dear. Coming, dear. Be right there, dear."

"Your arse can sleep on the couch," she yelled back. "Dear."

Elektra and I couldn't hear what he mumbled as he kissed her cheek, but she smiled, and soon enough we were sitting at the patio table eating the best comfort food on the planet.

And all I kept thinking was that Monroe didn't have this. He was maybe the one person who needed it the most, and I wondered if I should have invited him instead of walking out.

Hell, maybe he should've had dinner with my parents every night. Maybe he should move in; they had four guest bedrooms... though Monroe would have never agreed. I'd offered for him to stay at my place many times, and he did. It was closer to the city, and sometimes, if we'd been out at a bar or party, we'd crash at my place, which was technically my parents' house. But he always went back to his house. Which was fine. It was his house after all. But it was so big, and his parents' belongings were everywhere. The wooden carved elephant they got from Thailand, the glass bowl they'd got from Venice, the huge floor rug they'd got from Egypt. He'd never changed a thing. It looked now exactly as it had when his parents lived there, and some days I half expected to see his mum walk out and ask what we boys had planned for the weekend.

I wondered if Monroe half expected that too. I assumed he did. And I assumed that was why he never redecorated.

I'd been so lost in my thoughts I hadn't heard Mum's phone ring. We'd been talking about work; not exactly family dinner conversation, but our family was Keston Enterprises. Elektra and I had grown up discussing business at the dinner table. It was what we did, and we could talk about it for hours, so I shouldn't have been shocked to see the sun had gone down. I hadn't realised the time.

While Mum took the call and Dad cleared the table, Elektra used the opportunity to quickly check her phone. "Naughty, naughty," I chided. "You know there's a no-phone-at-the-table rule."

It was my mum's one rule: no checking phones at the dinner table.

But Elektra didn't smile. She shot me a look that was both scared and horrified. "What is it?" I asked.

She handed me her phone so I could read the screen at the same time that Mum called out, "Erik, honey?"

I quickly glanced at the screen. It was on the news headline, and it was Oz-E News, of all sites. I usually rolled my eyes at that sensationalised crap, but Elektra loved the gossip and ridiculous stories. Though this headline was short and as blunt as a blow to the chest.

OZ-E NEWS

Breaking News: Sydney bad boy Monroe Wellman in trouble again. ooo have been called to his Rose Bay mansion. Police and ambulance both on-scene.

Chapter Six
Monroe

I woke up with no clue what time it was, a pounding head, and a sore hand. I was in my bed, which was a blessing. I couldn't remember the night before, only snippets of yelling and bleeding and the police?

I went to scrub my hand over my face and saw that it was bandaged...

More flashes of memories: flashes of Jeffrey yelling at me? What the hell was Jeffrey doing here? What the hell did I do to my hand?

I sat up, only realising now I was still wearing the same clothes I'd had on yesterday. I felt like shit. *What the hell did I drink last night?*

And then I remembered... My dad's liquor cabinet. I remembered fighting with Erik, and I remembered feeling so lost and out of control when he left me. He told me he loved me. He told me he was done. My head, my entire world, went spinning so far out of control I couldn't stop it. But I sure could make myself numb.

Until I remembered he'd taken all the booze with him. I could have had some delivered, but even waiting half an hour for it to arrive at my front door was too long.

I remembered needing to drink. I needed it so bad, I couldn't think straight, I couldn't breathe right, I couldn't function.

I needed to drink.

Then I remembered the locked cabinet in my dad's office. There was alcohol right there, but Erik had taken the key and I tried to pull the door open, to break the latch, but it wouldn't budge.

And everything started to close in round me. The darkness, the pain, memories, regrets, and more pain, and I was sinking deeper. It was dragging me under, trying to drown me... I couldn't breathe...

So I closed my fist and punched the cabinet's glass door. The first bottle I took was Dad's special bottle of Chivas. And without a single thought to what I was doing, I cracked the lid, put the bottle to my lips, and drank.

It burned, and I welcomed it.

I must've drained half the bottle before I even drew a breath. I knew my hand was bleeding, but in that moment, it wasn't important.

Numbing the ache in my chest was the only thing on my mind.

So I grabbed the port and, taking both bottles, went out to the pool, cranked up the music, and then drank until I couldn't feel a thing.

I don't remember what happened after that.

Only snippets that didn't seem to make sense. Pieces of a puzzle I couldn't hope to put together.

I sat on the edge of my bed and undid the bandage around my hand to find plasters on my knuckles. They appeared to have been done by someone with medical training. It hurt like hell and it felt tight and hot. I couldn't be sure, but I had the feeling that under the plasters there were cuts or gashes—that I had no recollection of getting—and I was just about to pull the plasters back when my bedroom door opened.

I wasn't aware anyone else was here, and I certainly was not expecting to see Mrs Keston. "Oh good, you're awake." She didn't give me time to reply. "Get showered and come out to the living room please."

And with that, she closed the door.

What the fuck?

If Mrs Keston was here, maybe Erik was too. Maybe he hadn't left me; maybe he wasn't done with me. I took a quick shower, feeling a little better after I had washed my hair, got rid of the foul taste in my mouth, shaved, threw on some clothes, and went out in search of Panadol and food.

Except I only got as far as the living room.

Because my living room was full of people. Mrs Keston was talking to Jeffrey, both wearing suits and looking very official. Mr Keston was talking to Erik out by the pool, and when Erik looked over at me, Mr Keston moved between us with his back to me like he was shielding Erik, protecting him from me. There was a man I'd never seen before talking to my house cleaners, telling them they weren't required today, but that they would still get paid for their trouble.

What the fuck?

Elektra came out of the kitchen holding a coffee cup, and she stopped when she saw me. She gave me a sad smile but was quick to turn away before I could say anything.

What the hell was Erik's sister doing here? What the hell were his parents doing here, and who was that strange man who was now staring at me?

It was an older guy, maybe in his fifties. He had greying, curly hair, olive skin, and dark-brown eyes. He was wearing grey linen pants and a white shirt with one of those round collars with buttons, and I couldn't tell if he looked more like a hippy or a monk.

He hadn't taken his eyes off me yet, and it was becoming a little unnerving. I looked around to everyone else for some kind of explanation when the hippy monk gestured to the sofa. "Monroe, my name is Saul. Please take a seat."

Everyone watched me sit, and Jeffrey and Mrs Keston came and sat opposite to me. Mr Keston joined them, and Elektra put her arm around Erik. They didn't come any closer, but at least he was now looking at me.

He looked terrible. His eyes were red; it was obvious he'd been crying. And everyone's faces were stoic and grave.

And it dawned on me slowly at first, and then like an avalanche.

This was an intervention.

This was a motherfucking intervention. "Oh, hell no," I said standing up. "I'm not doing this. I'm not."

Mrs Keston answered. "Monroe, we're doing this because we love you."

"No." I shook my head. "No you don't. I don't need a fucking intervention."

"Monroe, son," Mr Keston tried. I really loved Erik's parents, but right then I wanted to scream at the both of them.

"I don't need an intervention," I yelled. "And I am not your son."

Jeffrey stood up. "I made a promise to your parents."

I put my hand out, palm forward. "Stop."

"Do you remember what happened last night?" he asked. "Your neighbours called the police, first because of the noise, and secondly out of concern. They heard yelling and screaming and glass breaking. The police came, and when no one answered the door, they broke in to find you passed out in a puddle of blood and broken glass by the pool."

Flashes of those memories swirled through my mind, but I couldn't seem to grasp them. My mouth was suddenly too dry, and my lungs felt too small.

"They called me," Jeffrey continued, his voice calm, his expression unreadable. "Because I'm down as your legal counsel and point of contact. Or maybe since I'm on a first name basis with them because of your track record, it was a courtesy call."

Hints of anger started to come through, and I'd never seen Jeffrey angry before.

"The Kestons are here because they saw it on the news," Jeffrey added. "The very least you can do, Monroe, is sit down and show some respect. Your problem with alcohol has gone on long enough."

"I don't have a problem." My fists were clenched and the bandages pulled across my knuckles. "I never asked any of you to come here. So don't tell me to sit down and be respectful when you're not being respectful to me."

Mr Keston stood up. "Monroe, all we ask is that you hear us out."

Mrs Keston added, "Last night could have been so much worse. What if you'd fallen in the pool and hit your head?"

There were too many voices and too many faces, too many pairs of judgemental eyes. I didn't need this, I didn't need their help, I didn't need them telling me I was broken. What I needed was some water, some tablets for my pounding headache, and maybe something to eat. I was feeling crowded in, ganged-up on, and powerless.

Out of control.

So, like any animal that'd been cornered, I fought back. "I don't need any of you. I don't need your help. I'm not fucking broken. I can look after myself; I don't need someone else's parents looking after me. So you can all fuck off, get out of my house, get out of my life."

Then Erik walked in closer, touching distance almost, and I can honestly say the look on his face terrified me. "Don't you *dare* speak to my parents like that. You have no right." His jaw clenched, and he spoke through his teeth. "This is it, Monroe. This is your one chance. After this I am done. I am done being treated like shit. I'm done being taken for granted." He groaned out a sob and put his hand to his chest. He could barely speak through his tears. "If you value me in your life, if I mean anything to you at all, you'll sit your arse in that chair and listen. Because this is it, Monroe. This has to be it. I can't take it anymore. Neither can you."

The silence was deafening. Elektra put her hand to her mouth, tears freefalling down her cheeks. Erik was pale and pissed off, and he stared at me, daring me to defy him.

But I couldn't.

Because if I didn't have him, my life was over.

And he'd given me this ultimatum just yesterday, but I hadn't truly believed him. I mean, he said it, and it kind of hurt to hear and I thought he might just need a day or two. Because I'd truly thought Erik would never leave me, not for real. Not forever. He always came back...

Only this time I did believe him.

And I believed the haunted faces that stared back at me.

Erik pointed to the sofa, still barely able to speak. "Sit down and shut up."

So I sat down.

And I shut up.

And I listened. Kind of. It was all a bit of a blur, to be honest. I was still reeling from what Erik had said and how he'd said it. And Elektra took him back out to the seats on the far side of the pool, and as Saul spoke to me, I watched Erik.

At first he cried, and Elektra put her arm around him and they spoke, words I couldn't hear, and I hated that I was the reason for his pain, his anger, his tears.

"Monroe." Saul's voice snapped me back inside the room. His gaze went out to Erik, then back to me. He had one of those annoying calm voices, even tones and modulated. "Have you been listening?"

Mr and Mrs Keston and Jeffrey were all looking at me, waiting...

"Um," I let out a breath. "I kind of zoned out. Sorry. Erik's really upset and I can't seem to focus..."

Saul smiled with all the patience in the world. "My name is Saul Cabello. I'm a qualified psychiatrist and therapist, and I specialise in addictive behaviours. But the clinical side of it was never really my style. I've been a private consultant for twenty-something years, with a whole range of people from all over the world. Celebrities, businesspeople, CEOs, doctors, sports stars, you name it. I've probably seen it. Erik's mother called and asked for a consult."

I looked at Erik's mum and this time tried to give her a small smile.

Saul kept on. "It only took a quick internet search of your name, Monroe, and I could see you have a pattern of destructive behaviour. Alcohol-related incidents have dotted the course of your life in the last three years, increasing in frequency and severity up until this point. And, in my experience, I can tell you that if you stay on that course, you'll be either dead or seriously injured, or you will cause death or serious injury to someone else within the next few months."

Jesus. He just said it so casually. Like he was reading chilling fucking statistics on the weather.

"The toll on your body is another thing, physically," he continued. "And mentally. If I said you were on the verge of a breakdown, do you think that would be fair to surmise?"

A breakdown? It sounded wrong and scary and far-reaching, but the truth was, something in me was broken... "Um, p-possibly."

Saul nodded. "I'm going to ask you some questions and I want you to be brutally honest with me."

I swallowed hard but nodded. "Okay."

"Do you like your life?"

"Um... I don't know. I have... things. Like, material things. I guess. So I'm luckier than most. I guess."

"Let me rephrase," he went on. "Do you like who you are?"

I looked at the three people staring at me, and I felt like a broken plate or a favourite toy that was damaged beyond repair. And that wasn't an unfair assessment, because I agreed with them. Did I like myself? I shook my head. "No."

"Do you wake up every day with a purpose? With goals?"

"No."

"How do you feel when you wake up? Not physically. Not hungover or nauseous. How does it feel in your heart?"

Okay, wow. "I don't know."

"Yes you do," Saul replied. "Out of control. Lost. Like you're being dragged under and you can't breathe, but there's a hand of darkness around your ankle and it's pulling you under and you've often wondered what would happen if you just let it take you."

And with nothing but words, he cracked me right open, splitting my truth apart for everyone to see. Tears sprang from my eyes with the force of it, and I scrubbed at my face, wincing as pain shot through my sore hand.

Saul watched me for a scrutinising moment. "Do you want to change?"

"I don't want to hurt people," I said, crying, my eyes automatically going to Erik.

Saul hummed, and his gaze went to Erik as well. "It's too late for that." I shot Saul a look, and he stared right at me, unflinching. "I'm not here to blow sunshine up your arse, Monroe. You've been on a downward spiral, hurting everyone who loves you, because hurting them, sharing your pain makes it a little bit easier to bear, doesn't it?"

My eyes burned, my head ached, and my hand hurt, and my heart felt like lead. More tears fell and I hated it. I hated this whole thing and I wanted it to be over, and I wanted them to all leave me alone, and I wanted a drink...

"It's a toxic behaviour pattern," Saul said. "You don't mean to hurt them and you wish you could stop, but you can't. Not on your own."

I couldn't even speak. I couldn't form thoughts, let alone words.

"And I can help you, Monroe," Saul went on to say.

"I'm going to be honest with you." He paused. "If you choose to do this—if you agree to partake in this program —it *will* be difficult. There is no easy way to do this, and you will hate it, the program, me, all of it." He met my eyes and something softened in his. "But I can help you."

Fuck. I couldn't think...

"Do you want to take back control of your life?"

I nodded.

"Say it."

"Yes."

"Do you want to be you again?"

"Yes."

"Do you want to feel worthy?"

I sobbed. "Yes."

"Do you want to be loved? Do you want to feel deserving of love?"

I nodded as I cried.

"Say it."

"Yes. I want that." My words were a snotty, sniffled mess.

"Will you give me your word," Saul asked, "that you will do everything I say, you will work with me, and together we'll figure out how to create the life you want?"

I nodded again, wiping my face. "Yes."

Saul finally smiled. "Okay." He gave Jeffrey and Mr and Mrs Keston a nod. "Then let's do this."

I didn't really know what 'this' entailed, but my head was swimming and I wanted to curl up into a ball and fucking cry, but I knew that if I started, I wouldn't be able to stop.

"I'll make you some toast and coffee," Mr Keston said, heading into the kitchen. Mrs Keston, Jeffrey, and Saul spoke around me, but I let my mind wander. I couldn't keep my thoughts straight anyway. I couldn't concentrate.

I just looked around the room, this grand open room in this grand house, a grand space which in that moment felt more like a vacuum than my house.

It'd never really felt like my house. It was my parents' house. Mum had redecorated only a few months before their trip to Macau. The vases on the sideboard, the artwork on the walls, the rug on the floor. Everything had her touch.

Everything except me.

"Monroe?" Mrs Keston said; her voice was gentle, as was her hand on my knee.

I realised then I was crying. Silent tears I couldn't seem to stop. "I'm sorry," I tried to tell her. "For what I said. For swearing. I'm sorry for how I treated Erik. You must hate me..."

She shook her head, her eyes watery. "I could never hate you, darling. And I can't answer on behalf of Erik. He's very hurt right now, but he cares a great deal for you."

I watched him as he sat talking with Elektra. "He deserves someone better than me."

Mrs Keston slid her hand over mine. "You two have a lot to work out."

I nodded and more tears fell. "I know. Do you think he'll forgive me?"

She smiled and squeezed my hand. "I think you need to forgive yourself first."

"I'm scared," I whispered, and a rush of fresh tears fell, hot and burning.

Mrs Keston leaned in then and gave me a hug. "It's okay to be scared," she whispered, pressing a kiss to the top of my head. "But you have all of us, okay? The entire Keston crew. We love you, and we're not going anywhere."

Her words brought on more tears, and her hug... oh my God, I never wanted it to end. I held on a little bit tighter, and it was like she knew—the way mums just knew—that a mother's hug was exactly what I needed. Even when Mr Keston brought me a plate of toast and a cup of coffee, she kept one arm around my shoulder while I tried to eat.

Saul and Jeffrey spoke quietly by the table. There were papers and files and God only knew what else. Jeffrey signed a few pages and Saul went out to speak to Erik. Elektra came inside and plonked herself right beside me; she took my free hand and snuggled in. She didn't say a word, and in a way, I was grateful. I wasn't ready for the conversation we probably needed to have, but she wanted me to know I wasn't alone.

I watched Saul speak to Erik. I couldn't hear a word of it, but Erik nodded a lot, and Saul put his hand to Erik's arm just as often. It was a sign of comfort, and it gnawed at me that Erik needed comforting and I was the reason.

Jeffrey sat beside me and patted my knee. "We'll take

care of everything. The only thing you need to worry about is getting better." I'd known Jeffrey my entire life, and that was the most personal thing he'd ever said to me. Not that he ever had to; he was my lawyer, not my father. Though in the last three years, he'd acted more as a guardian, because I was a fully grown adult who apparently needed supervision. He said he'd be in touch, and he was gone.

Mr and Mrs Keston left soon after, taking Elektra with them. They hugged me, told me they loved me, and said they'd see me again soon.

And then it was just me, Saul, and Erik.

Erik came inside, but he still hadn't spoken to me or even made eye contact. He chewed on his bottom lip, and he shoved his hands in his pockets, clearly nervous or uncomfortable. Maybe both.

There was a distance between us now. A wall, a mountain, an ocean, an impossible void. It was my doing. I put it there, and I wasn't sure what to say to make it right. To make things right between us, the way they'd always been.

And it was then I realised that maybe they never would be. Maybe we were irreparable. But I couldn't seem to find the words to even try. The tears wouldn't stop long enough for me to speak anyway. And sorry was hugely inadequate.

Sorry was so inadequate that for me to say it would be insulting. But it seemed like a good place to start.

"I really am sorry, Erik," I mumbled through fresh tears. "I'm sorry it came to this."

He frowned and it took him a moment to blink. His eyes were still red; he'd obviously not slept. He looked exhausted and utterly wrecked. "So am I."

It wasn't lost on me that for all the times I'd said I was sorry this morning, for all the times I'd apologised, no one told me my apology was not required. No one said apology accepted.

No one told me it was okay.

Because it wasn't okay. No one was letting me off the hook, no one was letting me get away with it. And I guessed that was part of taking responsibility, of owning my mistakes.

Saul appeared beside Erik, but he was looking at me. "Okay, we have a lot of things to cover today, but first things first. I've asked your cleaning staff to leave the mess you made last night. It's very easy to ignore problems when people clean up after you. It's easy to pretend there is no problem when you don't see the ramifications of your actions. Last night, as a result of you drinking alcohol, you smashed bottles and you broke furniture, injuring your hand in the process."

I felt like I was a kid back in primary school being reprimanded by my teacher for breaking a chair. I'd been swinging on it, leaning back, and she told me not to do it. But I did it anyway, the leg snapped, I hit my head and broke Missy Frank's lunchbox in the fall. My parents were called in, which I thought was an overreaction, but my father had agreed with the teacher. I didn't listen. I didn't think the rules applied to me, and he would be happy with whatever punishment she saw fit to impose.

Only this time I was an adult, and yet, like it was a lesson I needed to relearn, I would need to take responsibility. As soon as Saul mentioned my hand, it throbbed.

"Is your hand sore?" Saul asked.

"No. No I'm fine."

"Don't lie to me, Monroe," he said simply. "We must have one hundred per cent honesty. Complete transparency and the complete truth no matter how hard it is, or this will not work." He stared at me. "Now I will ask you again. Is your hand sore?"

I nodded slowly. "Yes."

"Okay, good," he said. "Well, not good that it's sore, but thank you for being honest. I can take a look at it after, if you like."

I half nodded, half shrugged. Erik remained silent.

"So," Saul went on. "Monroe, I want you to stand up and come with me."

I stood slowly. "Where are we going?"

"We're not leaving just yet. But I want to show you what you did last night. The cabinet is still broken, the blood is still on the floor, as is the broken glass. And I want you to clean it up."

I almost laughed despite everything. "Clean it up?"

"Yes." Saul had a way of keeping his voice calm and patient. Like he expected every question and he would happily answer the same question a hundred times, using the same calm and patient tone. "We're going to be talking a lot about responsibility and ownership because it helps to put your actions into perspective with the consequences. I can't make you clean it up, but I would like to think of this as the first step in what will be a long journey."

"Yeah, okay fine," I replied. "But just give me a little heads up, does everything you say sound like an inspirational quote off a calendar?"

Erik shot me a look, but Saul laughed. "Not everything."

I tried to give him a smile; I didn't exactly feel it, but at least I'd stopped crying. "I'll get the dustpan and broom."

I didn't much feel like it, but I swept up the broken glass from beside the pool. Erik and Saul sat at the dining table, talking quietly, and when I was done, Saul suggested I get some rubber gloves, a bucket of water and bleach and a scrubbing brush, to clean the blood off the tiles.

The blood was dried and a dark, dark red. Dots of varying shapes and sizes were splattered along the tiles my mother had specially imported from Italy. I'd spilled my blood in a drunken rage over my mother's floor. The smell of the bleach and dried blood made my stomach roil, and my head pounded. And when I was on the last one, Saul came to stand by me. "How are you going?"

"Almost done. I'm not very useful with my left hand." I held up my injured right hand in explanation.

"Not the most pleasant of jobs."

"No. Though I can understand why you insisted I do it."

"Can you? How does that make you feel?"

"Worse. This sun isn't doing my headache any favours."

He nodded slowly. "I didn't mean physically."

I stood up and threw the scrubbing pad into the bucket. "I didn't think you did."

"And yet, that is how you answered."

"And yet," I copied his ridiculous tone. "Perhaps that is how I answered because your question was ambiguous."

Saul smiled. "True. I shall be mindful of that for future reference."

I began to pull the rubber gloves off my hand, but Saul said, "Leave that on. You're going to need it. Come on, we saved the best for last."

My heart sank. I knew this was coming. Saul had mentioned the broken cabinet and I most definitely didn't want to see it. I considered making some lame-arse justification to get out of it, but then I noticed Erik inside standing by the dining table. I couldn't see his face because the bright sunshine outside made seeing his expression impossible. He had his arms crossed—I could see that much, and I didn't need an explanation for that.

Maybe he knew I would make some excuse, that I would charm or lie my way out of it. Maybe he stuck around to see that I kept my word. Or to see me fail.

So I bit back the desire to lie, to leave, and picked up the bucket. "So, are you leading the way or do I just follow the blood trail?"

Saul smiled again, or maybe it was a smirk. It was kind of hard to tell. But I followed him up the hall to my father's office. I knew it wasn't going to be pretty, and I'd expected it would probably hit me hard, but when I walked in, the coffee and toast I'd had earlier roiled like sour milk in my gut.

I wasn't expecting it to hit me this hard.

The weird part was, I wasn't even drunk when I smashed the glass-panelled doors. I'd done it to *get* drunk. Yet I didn't really remember doing it.

But the mahogany cabinet was ruined. One door of the cabinet, the section that housed my dad's liquor, didn't just have smashed glass panels, but the entire door was also broken. The top hinges were destroyed, pulled from the wood, so the door hung askew. Shattered glass covered the carpet in front of the cabinet, and inside it, glass shards and a fine layer of glistening glass dust covered everything.

There were fat drops of blood on the floor, inside the cabinet, and on the door itself. Dark red splotches of blood—my blood, the same blood as my father's—now covered his most treasured belongings.

"Tell me," Saul said. "What do you feel right now, seeing this?"

"Shame," I said without conscious thought. The word just came out, and once I'd said it, I knew it was the truth. "Shame," I repeated. And my heart threw out some other words that my brain couldn't keep up with, mixed with tears that just kept falling. "Horror. Disbelief. Sorrow. Confusion. And fear, if I'm being completely honest."

I hadn't noticed Erik walk in, but he was standing in

the far corner, his arms crossed in front of him and devastation on his face.

Saul seemed to consider my word choice. "I'd be interested to know why you said confusion and why you said fear with the qualifier of *if* you were being honest."

Jesus Christ. "Are you going to dissect and analyse every single thing I say?"

He looked me right in the eye. "Yes. What is it about seeing this mess that confuses you?"

I tried looking at Erik but couldn't. It just hurt too damn much. Now it was me who couldn't make eye contact. "I'm confused because I don't really remember smashing this cabinet. And the scary part is that I was sober when I did it. I broke into the cabinet to *get* drunk, not because I already was. I don't really remember... I'm not denying I did it because I know I did. But I can't even tell you what I was thinking because I wasn't thinking at all. I just had to get it, like the walls would close in on me if I didn't have a drink in that very moment, and it was like I was in someone else's body."

Saul nodded again, like he had expected me to say as much. "That's not uncommon. Most addicts will get manic before a fix."

I stared at him, and I could literally feel the blood drain from my face and settle into my belly with the spoiled milk. I almost vomited. "I'm not a drug addict," I whispered.

"Alcohol is the most misused drug in the world, and the word *addict* doesn't just apply to people who take narcotics or barbiturates."

I shook my head, my stomach churned, and I swallowed down the bile that threatened to rise. "I'm not an addict," I whispered again, though my breaths were short and sharp, which made it hard to speak. "I'm not..."

Saul studied me for a moment. "Did this cabinet mean a lot to your father?"

The change of direction was sharp and it took my brain a second to catch up. "Yes. Well, not the cabinet, I don't think. More what it held."

"The bottles you drank and smashed?"

"They were gifts," I whispered. "He was saving them for a special occasion. Or maybe they reminded him of the small victories. Each one was from a competitor or an adversary when he beat them, you know. Like a trophy."

"So this was his professional trophy cabinet?"

I nodded and wiped an errant tear from my cheek.

"What do you think he'd say if he saw this right now?" Saul asked.

I glanced at Erik, but he was staring out the window, his arms across his chest like he was cold. "He'd be pissed and disappointed, I guess. But if he was still here, if he was still alive, maybe I..."

"Maybe you what?" Saul asked casually. "Wouldn't drink as much as you do?"

I nodded again and my eyes burned and it was hard to breathe. "I don't feel too good," I said, my hand pressed to my gut.

Erik glanced my way like he was about to speak, but Saul gave a small wave of his hand to stop him. "If you're going to vomit, go to the bathroom. This mess"—Saul gestured to the cabinet—"will be here when you're done."

The broken cabinet, splinters of wood, shards of glass, and drops of blood would be there until I cleaned it up. Until I righted this wrong. But I couldn't fix this because the trophy bottles my dad had kept were gone. I'd drunk them. I hadn't savoured the taste. I hadn't appreciated the expensive liquor or the taste of my dad's success. I'd guzzled it like it was tap water or cheap beer. Like it meant nothing.

I stood in front of the broken cabinet and slowly went to my knees. I was careful of the glass, though I wasn't sure if I'd have felt anything. And piece-by-piece, I set the remnants into a neat pile. "Cleaning this up won't fix it," I mumbled, surprised by how emotional it was. Tears welled in my eyes and a lump formed in my throat. "The damage is done, and I can't bring the trophies back. I wish I could." I wiped my tears with the back of my hand. "I wish I could change a lot of things."

Saul put my dad's empty wastepaper basket beside me, then gave my shoulder a gentle squeeze. "You're taking the first step in changing a lot of things right now," he said.

"I wish I could take everything back," I sobbed. I was sitting on my knees with my feet under my arse, and I began to cry again. I didn't realise I was holding a sliver of glass in my hand until Saul unclenched my fingers and took it from me. I hadn't noticed I was clenching my fists either, and how the glass didn't cut me was pure luck.

"I'll take that," he said.

"I didn't mean…" Christ, the last thing I needed was him thinking I would self-harm. "I didn't know I was holding it…" I was crying again, or still. My head ached and my heart burned and the tears just wouldn't stop.

"I know," Saul said gently. "Come on. You can finish cleaning this up later. Let's take a breather, hmm?"

I nodded again. At that point, I would have agreed to anything.

I was a freaking mess. It truly felt like I'd had everything stuffed into a jar and now the jar was cracked and broken, all the guilt and loss and all my failures just kept pouring out. I couldn't hold it in anymore. I couldn't hide it. And I couldn't stop crying.

Chapter Seven
Erik

Sydney Times

New concerns for the health of Monroe Wellman increased today when Doctor Saul Cabello was seen arriving at Wellman's Mosman Bay home. Doctor Cabello, otherwise known as the Doctor to the Stars, is a psychiatrist who specialises in addiction.

Wellman's latest spate of alcohol-related incidents might have been the final straw for his closest friends, who could have called Dr Cabello on his behalf. Lavinia Keston, mother of Wellman's best friend Erik, was seen arriving and leaving, though Doctor Cabello has remained inside the property.

Police and ambulance were called to Well-

> *man's house late last night after neighbours made*
> *complaints. A court appearance for his recent*
> *drink driving charges is pending.*

I didn't know what to expect, but I was not expecting this. I knew it would be bad, and I knew it would be hard. And I thought I'd prepared myself.

But I was not prepared for this.

I was not prepared for how utterly heartbreaking this was going to be.

Monroe was literally falling apart at the seams. He was unravelling right in front of me. I could barely look at him because it killed me. And once he started to cry, he couldn't seem to stop, and every tear, every sob, just killed me a little bit more.

He was pale; he was dark around the eyes; his hair was a mess. He looked thinner than he had just the day before. He looked older too, like he had aged a decade overnight.

Last night, when Jeffrey had called my parents and asked to meet us at Monroe's house, I knew to expect police and ambulance, flashing lights and media, because I'd seen it on the news. But I didn't expect the house to be trashed, broken glass, broken furniture, and I didn't expect to see Monroe passed out by the pool, being tended to by paramedics.

It scared the hell out of me. Not just me, but my

parents and Elektra as well. And poor Jeffrey; stress and concern didn't begin to cover it. He'd also reached the end of the line.

"No more," he'd said. "He gets help either willingly or unwillingly, but it ends tonight. If he wants to drive himself into the ground, then let him. But he won't drive his father's business into the ground with him. His father worked too damn hard to see it ruined, and I promised him—"

He'd choked up in the end, and I'd never seen Jeffrey get emotional over anything. Even when Monroe's parents had died, Jeffrey had remained stoic, the pillar that held Monroe's world up and business together.

My mum and dad agreed with Jeffrey and it was decided—while Monroe was passed out drunk—that he needed an intervention. Someone had to step in and resume control before Monroe pushed his luck just one step too far.

I'd already reached my breaking point with him, so they found no resistance in me. "It won't be easy," Mum had said gently. "It's going to be hard for Monroe to get through this, and it's going to be hard for you to watch."

"We don't have a choice," I'd answered. And that was the truth. There were no choices. Monroe was out of options. It was only a matter of time before the next phone call came with condolences and funeral arrangements.

The phone call my mother had made earlier, pulling strings and asking for favours, had paid off. Saul Cabello was some kind of private therapist and mentor to the select clientele who could afford him. Apparently my mother knew someone, who knew someone, who knew that Saul was in Melbourne, and after a lengthy phone call, Saul agreed to fly to Sydney first thing in the morning to meet Monroe.

It was two o'clock in the morning when everyone left. I slept on the couch in Monroe's living room, not even opting for the spare room that I'd thought of as mine. I didn't want to risk falling asleep and missing anything, or in case Monroe woke up, or if he started to vomit in his sleep...

Not that I slept much. Hell, I barely even blinked before my parents and Elektra were back, bringing coffee and breakfast, and Jeffery not long after them with contract folders of paperwork.

Saul arrived just after seven. He was probably everything I would have expected a personal therapist to the rich and famous to look like. He looked like he belonged on a beach in the Greek islands. But his smile was wide, and his handshake was warm, and we all sat at Monroe's dining table without Monroe and gave Saul a rundown of Monroe's life. From his childhood, his teen years, the death of his parents, the downward spiral in the events that led up to yesterday's crash and burn. Jeffrey explained the business and legal perspective, and I gave him the personal one.

And it had all seemed like such a good idea until Monroe woke up and realised what was happening.

He fought it at first, which I knew he would. I knew he would dig his heels in and wield his stubborn pride like a shield, and I'd expected him to yell and carry on and deny everything and blame everyone, and the hurt in his eyes was hard to bear. I'd betrayed him, I'd thrown him under a bus, but I hadn't expected him to swear at my mother.

I lost my shit at him then, for the first time ever. I told him to sit down and shut the fuck up. I told him this was it. His last chance. If he refused to even try, I was gone.

And I watched the fight leave him, like a light went out somewhere inside of him. Extinguished, forever dark.

He started to cry, and he didn't seem able to stop.

And it broke my fucking heart.

He'd sobbed and sobbed when he'd tried to clean up the broken cabinet and shattered glass, and then Saul had suggested a break. He led Monroe back out to the living room, sat him down, and inspected his injured hands, pulling the sticky protective plasters off to reveal three cuts, one with two butterfly stitches across the middle knuckle.

"Do you remember the police and ambulance being here last night?" Saul asked.

Monroe swallowed back tears and frowned. "No," he answered as though his voice wouldn't work. "Not really. Bits and pieces, mostly."

Saul nodded. "You were lucky. Lucky Erik and his family came over, lucky the emergency services came, and you're lucky your injuries weren't more severe."

Monroe's face crumpled again. He looked up to where I was, but he still wouldn't make eye contact with me. "I know," he said, beginning to cry again.

"It's always amazing to me," Saul continued, "that we tend to wounds on our outside without question. We seek treatment, doctors, first aid, and no one ever questions it. It's the logical thing to do. There is no shame to have our wounds on our skin tended, cleaned, stitched, and healed. Yet when the wound is internal, when it is in our minds and on our hearts," he said, putting his hand to Monroe's temple, then to his chest, "there is stigma and shame attached to seeking treatment. People think it is a sign of weakness. But I can tell you, Monroe, it takes considerable strength to get through this. There is no shame; there is no stigma. We will treat your mind and heart just like we would treat your hand."

Monroe wiped at his cheeks with the back of his hand. "Will I?" he asked, barely a whisper. "Will I get through this?"

And he sounded so goddamned broken, without hope, that it made my heart ache and my eyes burn.

"I think you're stronger than you know," Saul said. He gave him a soft smile. "Are you tired?"

"I'm so tired," he answered. "I didn't know I could be so tired."

Saul nodded like he expected Monroe to say that. He stood up, pulled a throw cushion down, and patted it. "Take a rest, close your eyes."

And Monroe did exactly that. He curled onto his side, closed his eyes, and cried himself to sleep. It took all of twenty seconds. One second he was sobbing with his eyes closed, then the next he was out.

Saul sighed and looked at me before nodding to the table by the pool. "Can I have a minute of your time?"

"Sure," I mumbled, not trusting my voice.

I followed him into the shade by the pool and he pulled out a seat for me before he sat himself down. "He will likely sleep for a while now," he said.

"Will he be okay?" I asked. "I've never seen him like this."

Saul shot a glance back inside where we could see Monroe still sound asleep on the couch. "He has a long road ahead of him, but I think he'll be okay."

I nodded and fought back my own tears, willing them not to fall.

"It's not easy to watch," he said. It wasn't a question.

I shook my head. "It's awful." My voice cracked and a tear fell down my cheek.

Saul nodded and gave me a sad smile. "He has a troubled relationship with this house."

I took a deep breath in to gather my nerve. "He does. Since his parents... To him, it's still their house."

"Hmm," Saul's brow pinched. "It will make his recovery harder. Right now, we need to work on the alcohol dependence. His drinking is fed by his guilt associated with his parents' death, so I'm not sure if being here is the best thing for him right now."

"I have somewhere," I offered. "It's on the Sunshine Coast. It's a, um, high-end rental. My family uses it as a holiday home."

He raised a brow. "Is it accessible right now? Can we get there tonight?"

"Tonight?" I wasn't expecting the urgency. "Uh..."

"Today he's going through what would be an expected hangover, which won't be too bad. Tonight won't be great, but tomorrow and the next few days are going to be rough. It'd be best if we can get there tonight, or we might have to put off leaving for the first week, which is fine. It just means we hunker down here for the time being."

Fucking hell. This was all sounding far too serious for me. But I knew the beach house was empty, so I nodded. "Whatever you need. For him. Whatever he needs. I can take you both up there and stay—"

"I don't think you being around him right now is a good idea," Saul said. Before I could argue, he held up two fingers. "Two reasons. One, you're not what's best for him right now. He needs someone who won't give in. You want to help him and stop his pain, but giving in to him isn't helping him. It's hurting him."

"Oh."

"And the second reason is that these next few days and weeks will be some of the worst of his life. He will fight me. He will probably have episodes of vomiting, diarrhoea, shaking, sweats. But the worst part is the bouts of jitteriness, anxiety, and anger; he'll be abusive and upset. He'll lash out, and you don't want to be around for that."

"I'll be okay. I can handle that."

Saul shook his head. "No. This will be him at his very worst, and I don't want you to hear him say things he doesn't mean. He will want to misplace blame and pain, and you'll be his first target. If he's going to hate someone, I'd rather it be me." He waited until I met his gaze. "If he was admitted into a clinic, you wouldn't be allowed to stay with him."

When he put it like that, it made sense, even though I didn't like it. "Fair enough."

"Can I ask you something, Erik? And I want you to be completely honest with me."

I frowned. "Sure."

"How long have you been in love with him?"

His question hit me with blunt force. I glanced back to the living room, but Monroe was still sound asleep. He looked so peaceful... Another tear escaped and rolled down my cheek, then another, and another. I swiped them away and cleared my throat. "How long have I been in love with him?" I almost laughed because I'd never really admitted this out loud to anyone, not honestly. Not to anyone who wasn't my family. My first instinct was to deny it, but if Saul needed the truth to help Monroe, then it was the least I could do. "Um, years. Since we first met. We were eighteen and went to the same business college. He walked into my first class, smiled at me, and that was that."

"And he doesn't know?"

I shook my head. "I told him I loved him the other night, but I don't think he got it. Or maybe he just thought I loved him as a friend, I don't know. We had a fight and... I left him and he got plastered and injured himself... I shouldn't have."

"Shouldn't have what?"

"Left him. Told him I loved him. Hurt him. All of it."

"Only he is responsible for his reactions," Saul said gently.

"Except he's not. He's an addict."

Saul made a face. "It's more complicated than that. There are many factors—"

I put my hand up in surrender. "Please don't. I can't get my head around a lecture right now, sorry."

He smiled. "It's okay. I get it."

I let out a long sigh and felt the weight of the world in my bones. I wanted to crawl into a dark room, curl up, and cry myself to sleep. "I'm sorry. Watching him slowly killing himself has been exhausting." I tried not to cry.

"And this is killing you too, isn't it?"

I nodded, and fresh tears sprang to my eyes. I couldn't stop them. "I don't know how to fix him."

Saul patted my arm. "You can't. He's the only one who can do that."

I tilted my head back in a failed attempt to stem the emotions. I tried to speak, to say something, to defend him, but no words would come.

"Erik, this won't be easy."

"I know."

"It will take time."

"How long?"

"Six to eight weeks, maybe longer."

"Two months?" I whispered, disbelieving.

"And that's just with me. Two months' isolation: no phone, no television, no internet. The first month will be detoxing, intense therapy, rehabilitation, and getting him back on track. But this road to recovery he's on will take much longer: months, years. Two months is just the beginning."

"Two months without him..."

Saul gave me a sad nod. "Maybe the time apart will do you good too. It might let you see things a little clearer."

"You mean let me get over him," I bit out. "That's not how love works."

He smiled and took my hand, giving it a squeeze before letting it go. He leaned in, his eyes full of sadness and pity. "You're as addicted to him as he is to alcohol. You need to be you again. Be Erik without Monroe. Because right now, Erik Keston is lost."

His words burned in my ribs, squeezed my heart, and forced more tears to my eyes. It felt like he'd just sledge-hammered me with the truth.

He put his hand to my shoulder. "Your life has become about him. Everything you do is for Monroe. You look after him, you rescue him, you buffer him, and every-thing you do is about him. What about your needs? What about what Erik needs and wants? Who's looking after you?"

I let my head fall forward and sobbed. "He used to. He was never like this before. He was kind and funny and generous and smart. He had such a good heart."

"But he doesn't anymore."

I shook my head. "No."

"Everything is all about him," Saul said, and I nodded

again. "And that's very normal in situations like these. But we also need to help you here too."

Resigned, I nodded again. "I've never spent more than a few days without him," I admitted quietly. "I'm not sure how to be me without him."

Saul smiled sadly. "Let's work on a week-by-week plan. I'm not asking for complete isolation. How about you call him once a week, say six o'clock on Tuesday nights? And maybe after the first month, given how he responds to treatment, we might consider a visit."

I gave a nod. At this point, there was no use in arguing.

"The separation will give you some perspective, that's all. It's not wrong or right, good or bad. You might realise you need more time apart, or you might realise he's not the one for you. Or—" He smiled. "—you might realise that distance makes the heart grow fonder."

I almost smiled.

"I want to have weekly phone calls with you as well," he continued. "Or I can refer you to someone local...?"

"No, no one here," I said. My voice croaked. I couldn't bear explaining all this to someone else. Today had been draining enough. "Phone is fine."

"Okay. And we can talk about how you're feeling and anything you're going through. It won't be easy."

"Yeah, I get that."

"And Erik," he said, waiting for me to meet his gaze before continuing. "Substance addiction is for life. Being an alcoholic is for life. He might seem like he's back to his old self after a week or two, or even a month, but he's always going to be an alcoholic. In six months, in a year, in a decade. He's always going to want a drink, he's always going to think he can handle 'just one,' but he can't. And he's going to have good and bad days. For the rest of his life."

"What are you saying?"

"I'm saying that you need to know what you're getting yourself into."

"I'm not abandoning him."

"I know that. But just know that this will never go away. Twenty years from now, he's still going to be an addict. And that's a lot to take on."

"If he suddenly lost the use of his legs or contracted a disease like diabetes or fucking cancer, I wouldn't turn my back on him because it all became too hard," I replied, maybe a little shorter than I should have. I scrubbed my hand over my face. "For fuck's sake."

Saul smiled like I'd answered correctly. "Addiction is a disease, so that's the right attitude to have."

I was beginning to think outbursts of anger and frustration barely blipped on his radar.

"So this house of yours on the Sunshine Coast," Saul said, redirecting our conversation. "What do we have to do to make that happen?"

I pulled my phone out and dialled Mum's number. "Hello, darling," she answered. "How are you? How's Monroe?"

"Um," I replied. "I don't know yet. I... um." I cleared my throat. "The house at Peregian? It's vacant right now?"

"Yes. Did you want to use it?"

"Saul thinks Monroe would do better in a house that wasn't filled with reminders of his parents. He needs isolation for a bit and a clean slate, you know? Just while he goes through detox, at least. I guess."

Saul nodded, so I must have been right.

"Of course," Mum replied. "Anything for my boys."

Instant tears burned in my eyes and I tried swallowing them back. "Thanks, Mum. I'll be around soon to get the keys. Saul wants to leave today."

"Will you fly?" Mum asked.

"Yep. Can we take the jet? I don't want to go commercial..." There would be witnesses, media, and if Monroe was going to be sick...

"I'll call Peter," Mum said, like it was no problem at all. Peter was the pilot who flew my parents all over for business and holidays. "How long are you going for?"

"I'll fly up with him," I answered, looking Saul right in the eye. "I'll get him to the beach house myself."

Saul looked as though he might object.

"It's not up for discussion," I replied, shaking off more tears. "I need to do this. And I'll be back later tonight. I can't stay with him, but I need to be the one who takes him."

Saul conceded with a nod, and I took it as one of the only wins I might have with him. "Mum, I'll see you soon."

"Okay, love. I'll be here. And I'll call Peter and text the details to your phone."

"Thanks, Mum."

"Of course, love. See you soon."

I disconnected the call and met Saul's inquisitive gaze. "It all should be fine. Mum will send through details once she's spoken to the pilot."

He nodded, like he dealt with clients who had private jets on a daily basis. "I have an exercise I want to do with Monroe, which we could do on the way to the airport, I guess. I have my bags in the car, so I'm ready to go. Perks of being ready to leave at the drop of a hat. I will need to make some calls though, but I'll stay here with him while you leave to get the keys, yes? He shouldn't be alone right now."

I looked back at the living room where Monroe was still sound asleep on the sofa. "I don't want him to hate me," I whispered.

"Go and sit with him a while," he suggested. "He probably shouldn't sleep too long or he'll be awake half the night, and nighttime is usually the worst."

"You want me to wake him?"

Saul nodded with an easy smile. "In a while. I need to make a few calls."

So I did as he suggested. I sat on the floor in front of the sofa, right near where Monroe's injured hand rested on the couch. I studied his palm, his fingers, his breathing, his eyelashes, his beautiful lips.

I knew these parts of him. I knew every line of his face. I knew his hands, his touch.

And it was the weirdest paradox because I didn't really know them at all. I knew them as a best friend would. I knew them because I'd studied them, I'd dreamed of them. I'd longed for them.

But I didn't really know them at all. Not how I wanted to. Not how I wanted him to know me.

It felt like a Ferris wheel. Circuits of highs and lows on repeat, never stopping but never getting anywhere. We'd done it for years; up and down, never gaining any ground.

But we'd reached the point where we couldn't go one more round. I'd had enough, and he'd reached the point of no return with his drinking. We'd come to a point in our journey where something had to change.

And I had to wonder when this was all said and done, if we'd still be on the same path.

I took his hand and put it to my cheek, feeling the gentle warmth and tenderness, wishing it was him who'd initiated the touch. I leaned into it and kissed his palm, sighing and letting my eyes close.

I was so fucking tired.

"Hey," Monroe said, his voice low and croaky.

It took every ounce of strength I had to even open my eyelids, but then when I saw his face, saw the look in his eyes, my heart squeezed to the point of pain. "Hey."

"You okay?" he asked.

I shook my head a little. "No. You okay?"

He shook his head. "No." His expression went from saddened to pained. "I'm sorry."

I almost said it was okay, that it didn't matter, but remembered Saul's advice to acknowledge the apology without saying he was forgiven. He had to prove his remorse before he could earn my forgiveness. I'd absolved him of all wrongdoing for years, and it had to stop. "I know you are."

His bottom lip trembled and he gave a slight nod, but his eyes squinted shut, as though my lack of forgiveness physically hurt him.

I kissed the back of his hand, trying to tell him everything I couldn't with the slight brush of my lips against his skin. Then I held it to my face and a tear slipped from his eyes.

"Want a hug?" I asked.

He nodded and sat up, keeping his head down, and I climbed onto the sofa beside him and pulled him into my arms. He simply melded into me, allowing himself to be held. He was hot and sweaty, but I rubbed his back, ran my fingers through his hair, and I kissed the top of his head. "It'll all be okay," I whispered, kissing his head one more time.

Saul came back out with his phone in his hand and didn't even baulk when he saw us. He simply sat on the coffee table so he could speak to Monroe. "How are you feeling?"

"Okay."

"No, how are you really feeling?" Saul pushed gently.

"Like I'm hungover as fuck."

"Tell me what hurts."

Monroe was quiet a moment. "My head. My hand. My... heart is racing. I feel sick."

Saul gave him a small smile. "That's a better start, for the honesty at least. I can get you some tablets for your head and your hand. Just over the counter stuff to take the edge off, but they won't stress your liver or kidneys. But the pain here—" He put the heel of his hand to his own chest. "—that'll take some time. But we'll work on that. I'll get you the pills and we can talk about our next step."

He disappeared into the kitchen and Monroe gingerly sat up and put his feet on the floor. He ran his hand through his hair and I noticed then how pallid he was. He looked awful. Not just headachy and sore, but he looked sunken in on himself.

Beaten.

Defeated.

I took his not-sore hand and held it, leaning toward him a little so he could rest on me. Saul came back with a blister pack of tablets in hand and a glass of water. "Take two," he said as he handed them to Monroe and sat back on the coffee table. "So here's what we're going to do. We're going to be staying at the Kestons' beach house on the Sunshine Coast. The change of scene and sea air will do you the world of good. We'll all fly up today, as soon as we get clearance. We'll get to the house, get settled in, then Erik will be leaving."

Monroe turned to me then. "Leaving?"

I squeezed his hand and nodded. "Yeah." I swallowed hard. "I'll come back here, to Sydney. I have work and... I have a lot of work to catch up on." It wasn't exactly a lie.

Monroe licked his lips and his breathing quickened. He glanced from me to Saul, almost panicky. "I don't know if I can do that," he whispered in a rush. "I don't know if... without you, Erik. I can't—"

"Yes you can," Saul said. He had a voice that was clearly well practised in his job. Well balanced, authoritative, but somehow kind. "You and I will get through this together. Erik won't be far away, but it's time you both stood on your own two feet for a while."

"No," Monroe shook his head. "I can't."

"Monroe," Saul said. "Erik needs this. He needs time away from you, and you need to give him that, okay?"

Monroe looked at me, his face devoid of colour. He swallowed and I thought for a second he was going to vomit. "You do? Need me to be gone?" he asked.

I squeezed his hand. "Not gone. I just need some time, that's all. I'm not leaving you. I'll call you once a week. You need to concentrate on you, and I need to focus on me for a bit, that's all."

"But you're not staying with me?"

I shook my head and willed myself not to cry. "No. I can't."

He shot Saul a look, his face a dozen emotions. He could barely speak. "If he needs it, then that's okay."

Saul gave a hard nod. "He does. And so do you. You're both going to be fine. I'm not saying it'll be easy. But you will be better for it."

Monroe slumped back and I slid my arm around him and kissed the side of his head. He was clammy and sweaty, pale, but I didn't mind. And Monroe never questioned anything Saul explained after that. The fight in him was gone. He simply let me soothe him and he nodded every now and then, but he didn't say much until it was time for me to leave.

His eyes went wide. "Will you be back?"

"Yep. I just need to grab the keys to the house."

He nodded and took a deep breath. "Okay."

I put my hand to his cheek. "You've got this, Monroe. You can do this." I leaned in and kissed his cheek. "I'll be back later."

"You promise?"

The fear in his eyes was awful. All I could do was nod, and when I got into my car, I cried all the way to my parents' house.

Chapter Eight
Monroe

"Why are we here?" I asked. I felt like utter shit. Like the worst hangover I'd ever had. We were in Saul's car: me in the front passenger side and Erik in the back seat.

"I want you to see something," Saul said, driving through the backstreets of the city, making my stomach churn. My heart was racing and I couldn't seem to concentrate on anything. Did Saul say something else? I couldn't remember...

I didn't like this. I didn't like this at all. "So why are we here? You didn't answer."

"I want you to see something."

Did he repeat that? Or did I imagine he did? He turned onto Hay Street at Belmore Park and pulled to the kerb. It was still daylight, for which I was grateful. Things got scary in the dark. I was getting anxious, which I was pretty sure was the detox, but I couldn't stop. "What is the to see here? That the city has a litter problem?"

"No. That the city has a homeless person problem," he answered.

I wiped my sweaty palms on my thighs and stared out the windscreen. "What does that have to do with me?"

"Can you see those people?" He nodded up the street.

There was a row of small tents and swags, old mattresses, and a mishmash of belongings discarded along the footpath. Three people, two men and one woman, from what I could see, took refuge there. "Yeah."

"I want you to watch them." One of the men held a brown paper bag that obviously concealed a bottle of something. He put it to his mouth, taking a long swig before he handed it to the woman. The other man had his own bottle, which he drank from quickly. They seemed to be disagreeing about something; between frequent mouthfuls of drinking, there was shouting and the shaking of heads, and scowls amongst them.

When the couple finished their bottle, the man produced another and opened it, taking another drink.

It made my mouth water, and my hands itched. I wanted to get out and join them. Just one sip...

"For the purpose of this exercise, we're going to assume those people are addicts. I don't know if they are, and not all homeless people are, but humour me," Saul said. "What's the difference between you and them?"

I turned to face him because *I beg your fucking pardon?* I shot Erik a look in the backseat, but he was staring out the window, frowning. I turned back to Saul. "I'm not like that."

"You're exactly like that."

I blanched. "I am not. I fucking am not. I don't drink out of paper bags in the street."

"Sure, because you've got money," Saul replied. "But you know what you've got that these guys don't?"

That hole inside me that had been a sense of hopelessness all fucking day began to fill with anger. "A house. A job."

Saul shook his head. "Nope. More important than that. You have a support system for every aspect of your life; you have managers who run your business and you have a lawyer who takes care of the details. Housekeepers who sanitise and wipe clean every mess and straighten everything. So you have your business taken care of, your legalities, and your house."

"So I have money. So what?"

"And you have Erik. Someone who will bail you out of trouble, who will pick up your pieces, tell you everything's fine."

I glanced back at Erik and he now had his eyes closed. "He's my best mate. That's what best friends do," I said.

Saul paused, his lips pinched. "He's your enabler, Monroe. He never tells you no."

"He's my friend. We do everything together. We hang out all the time; we have done for years. He doesn't tell me no because he's doing it right along with me. Don't you dare try and put any of this shit on him."

"If you're on equal footing, tell me when was the last time you did something he wanted to do?"

"All the time."

He shook his head. "I don't think that's true."

Fuck. I couldn't actually think of anything. If we did anything, if we went anywhere, it was because I wanted it. But it wasn't like I made him. "He does what he wants. I've never told him what he can and can't do. Like I said, everything I do, he does with me. Willingly. Because he wants to. Erik, tell him it's not like that!"

Erik put his head down and said nothing.

Fuck.

Saul spoke instead. "Does Erik drink every day?"

I frowned. "No, but—"

"Does he drink until he blacks out?"

"Well, no—"

"Does his drinking affect his job?"

God, I'd walked right into this. "No," I whispered.

"What about his relationships? His ability to drive? His ability to function on a daily basis?"

I shook my head. "No."

"So he doesn't do everything you do. He doesn't drink with you. He goes with you to look out for you. To make sure you don't get into trouble, right?"

I looked out the windscreen again. I didn't need to answer that. Because he was fucking right. Erik wasn't just my best friend. He was my babysitter. Because I was incapable of looking after myself.

"You're going to be facing some ugly truths in the next few weeks, Monroe," Saul said after a moment's silence. "And your relationship with Erik will be a part of that."

I chewed the inside of my lip. "He's always been there for me."

"And you take him for granted."

My gaze shot to Saul's. "No I don't. I mean, I don't mean to. I don't... I never..."

Saul nodded. "I know." He looked back out at the homeless people, still chugging away on their bottles. "I just wanted you to see that your privilege, your wealth and safety network are the reasons you are not over there with them. You're one more incident away from possible jail time. You could lose your business, your house. You're one more drink away from rock bottom, Monroe. Do you get that?"

I watched the homeless people, how they bickered and drank, and I knew he was right. "I have a court case pending," I admitted. "For drink driving."

"I know," he replied. "Which is why you need to be able to walk into that courtroom in a few weeks' time, look the judge in the eye, and tell them you're however many days sober."

I wanted to cry again but bit back the tears. "It all seems so uphill right now."

"Because it is. But, Monroe," Saul said with a smile, "you're almost one day sober already."

I met his gaze. "I want a drink."

Saul nodded. "But you haven't had one. So we'll consider that a win, okay?"

I nodded, not feeling at all convinced. I looked back to Erik just as he wiped tears from his cheeks. He wouldn't look at me, so I turned back around and sunk down in my seat.

Saul pulled the car back onto the street and we headed for the airport. I didn't want to do this. It was all going to be too hard and too fucking awful. But to lose Erik would be so much worse, and I was so fucking tired, so I closed my eyes and woke up when Erik gently shook my shoulder. "Hey, Monroe. Wake up. We're here."

The first thing I noticed was that it had grown dark, that we were at the airfield, and then I noticed the pain in my head, the churning in my gut, and I felt hot and cold.

I felt like I was dying.

I couldn't seem to get my body to work, and Erik helped me out of the car and into the hangar where his plane was waiting. I'd been on his plane several times before and I was thankful for the familiarity.

My mind wouldn't get out of first gear.

He helped me onto the plane and into my seat, then went to discuss details with Peter. I was grateful to be left alone for a moment because I needed to breathe through the pain of a vice squeezing my brain. My focus and concentration were shot to hell.

I did notice Saul's expression when he boarded the plane though. He was impressed, no matter how much he tried to hide it. He chose a seat toward the back, but waiting for Erik took forever and my legs became twitchy and restless, and I must have moved around in my seat too much because Saul was soon in the seat next to me. "You feel okay?"

"No," I said, shifting again. "I think I need to stand

up or something. I have leg cramps and stomach cramps, and my head is killing me."

He grimaced and gave a nod. "It's not easy, but you're doing really well, Monroe."

Erik appeared and stopped when he saw Saul sitting next to me. "Everything okay?"

"I was just keeping your seat warm," Saul said as he stood, and he gave Erik's arm a squeeze before he went back to his own.

Erik was quick to take his place. "You okay?"

"Not really," I answered. "To be completely honest, I feel like shit, Erik."

He took my hand and gave it a squeeze. "It will get better, I promise."

I had to peel my tongue from the roof of my mouth, and I dry swallowed. "My mouth…"

"Let me get you a water." He went to the dispenser that held all the bottles. And for a brief second I got excited that there would be bottles of Scotch or gin or vodka, because maybe I could take one without anyone knowing, or even just a sip… but I realised then all the liquor was gone. There were only different types of water or juice, which meant Erik had probably asked ahead of our arrival that all alcohol be removed.

Is this my life now? That I can't even be trusted to be in the same room as it?

And then reality hit me, that only a moment before I'd wished I could steal a bottle, so yeah, maybe this was my life now.

And that thought, that realisation was really fucking exhausting.

Erik came back with a bottle of sparkling water in one hand and an empty ice bucket in his other. "In case it doesn't want to stay down."

I slumped down into my chair. "I'm tired, E."

He took my hand again. "I know."

I closed my eyes, concentrated on my breathing for a while, and tried to quell the urge to vomit. I don't remember the plane taking off.

Erik woke me up as we were about to land, and the jolting of the jet didn't do my stomach any favours. I somehow managed not to vomit, but I knew I couldn't hold it back for long. It was well and truly dark by the time we landed at Maroochydore airport. Erik had a car and driver waiting and he piled me into the back seat, quick to get in beside me. Saul took the front seat and I rested my head on Erik's shoulder wishing none of this was real, wishing it was all over or that it was some fucked-up nightmare I couldn't wake up from.

I felt hot and cold all over, itchy for some stupid reason, and my headache... Fuck. The pain in my head was blinding.

I don't know if I slept or if I passed out or if time had stopped, but I only blinked and we were pulling up at the security gate of Erik's holiday house. I'd been here a few times, before my parents died. It was a ridiculously grand beach house—a lot of white marble, natural wood finishes, on the very white sands of the Pacific Ocean. Beautiful, but it still felt like a home, and nothing short of what you'd expect from Australia's biggest name in real estate.

The Kestons certainly knew what they were doing.

The car pulled up out the front, not into the garage, which struck me as odd. But then Erik spoke to the driver. "I'll be about half an hour."

He really wasn't staying...

Erik went ahead to unlock the house, and Saul helped me out of the car. "Dunno why I can't move," I mumbled.

"Your body is going through a lot right now," he said, helping me walk into the house. "Just take it slow, and tell me if you get dizzy or think you might fall."

Lights came on, making me halt and squint at the glare. "Fuck."

"I'll dim them," Erik said, and the lights dimmed to non-retina-burning levels. But as we came through the hall, the living area opened up to a panoramic view of the deck and pool, and beyond that, the ocean. The windows were black, but we could hear the waves and see the white tips crash against the shore.

"Wow," Saul said.

"Wait till morning," Erik said with a small smile, walking back to us. "The glass is tinted so you don't cook yourselves, but the view is pretty good." He handed an envelope to Saul. "House keys. Your access code is inside. There's a car in the garage, just a small runabout, but it will be all you need. Use whatever you want. Mum organised for some essential supplies to be dropped off this evening, so you'll be right for a day or two. Oh, and she had the pool guys come today as well."

"Pool?" Saul asked.

"Uh, yeah. Monroe likes to swim. It clears his head," Erik said, smiling at me. Then he sighed. "You feel okay?"

I shook my head but couldn't seem to speak.

"How about we get you settled in," Erik said. Then he took my arm. "Which room do you want?"

I swallowed hard. "Yours. The one we stayed in last time we were here."

Erik's smile was more genuine at that, and he took my bag from Saul. "I'll take this, and then I'll have to get going. I can't stay long. Peter's scheduled a return flight tonight."

I nodded sadly, knowing he'd have to leave at some point. God, my head and my gut... "I don't feel too good."

"Come on," Erik said, taking my arm and leading me to the bedroom end of the house. He opened the door and flipped on the lights, the brightness triggered a wave of nausea, and I ran for his bathroom. I made it to the toilet just in time to heave into it.

Fuuuuuuck.

I'd never felt so sick.

A moment or two later, a cool, wet washcloth pressed against my forehead and gentle hands raked my hair, then rubbed my back. I managed to stand upright and meet Erik's gaze. There was only concern and caring in the depths of blue, and maybe that was worse. Maybe pity and anger would have been more fitting.

More deserving.

"You okay?"

I nodded. I did feel a little better, but I knew that was only temporary. I rinsed my mouth out and splashed cold water on my face, ignoring how I'd now gone from feeling too hot to feeling too cold.

Erik handed me a towel and I dried my face. "I'm hoping it doesn't get any worse than this," I managed to say, trying to smile.

"Me too."

"I wish you could stay," I said. "I mean, I know you can't and I get it, but..."

Erik nodded, frowning. "I wish I could stay too."

And the stupid tears were back again. I hadn't cried this much since... ever. "I'm scared."

Erik put his hand to my waist, fisting my shirt. "I know. I'm scared too. But you can do this."

I shook my head. "I don't know if I can. It all changes after this. Nothing will be the same, and that scares the shit out of me, Erik."

"Not everything will change," he whispered. "I'll still be here for you."

Tears spilled down my cheeks. "But I won't be the same. I swear to God, it feels like I'm about to fall apart, and I'm trying not to because I know these pieces won't go back together. I will not be the same after this, and that fucking terrifies me, but I know it needs to happen. Like I'm standing on train tracks watching the train come screaming towards me and I don't want to get hit, but I can't move. And I don't want to move. I need it to hit me, and I want it to hit me, and I want it to hurt, but I don't want the pain. This is fucked up. I am fucked up. I won't be the same. Nothing will be. And all that'll be left of me is pieces that won't go back together."

Erik pulled me against him and wrapped his arms around me, holding me while I sobbed against his chest. "If the pieces of you won't go back together, then we just make a new picture. We'll adapt; we'll be okay. I promise. We'll be even better, just you watch."

I cried some more until I began to sway. Weariness took hold of me, and Erik led me to the bed, where he pulled back the covers and tucked me in. He kissed my forehead, my cheek, then ever so softly he kissed my lips.

"I love you, Monroe Wellman. You just concentrate on getting better, and I'll be back as soon as I can."

I wanted to say something, to thank him, to apologise, but I couldn't even keep my eyes open, let alone speak. I think I nodded. And the next time I opened my eyes, he was gone.

CHAPTER NINE
ERIK

Photos have surfaced tonight of troubled bad-boy Monroe Wellman leaving on a private jet, under the cover of darkness, with Erik Keston and Doctor Saul Cabello. Wellman looked particularly unwell, needing assistance onto the plane. Speculation surrounding Wellman's health arose yesterday when Doctor Cabello arrived at the Wellman mansion. Cabello specialises in addiction treatment, and he's been on the payroll of some celebrity A-listers.

It's believed Wellman was taken to a private clinic for treatment.

. . .

I had no idea that heartbreak could be an actual, physical pain. Sure, I'd had my heart broken before, and I'd been heartsore constantly in the last three years watching Monroe spiral out of control.

But this was actual, physical pain.

I had no clue how I was supposed to get through this month without him.

And yes, what he was going through was so much worse, but I couldn't deny the literal ache in my chest.

I gave Peter a nod as I boarded the jet, letting him know I was good to go. Leaving Monroe behind was the hardest thing I'd ever done. But I needed to be the one to bring him to the beach house. I don't even know why. I just didn't want him to think he'd been abandoned. If I was the one who took him, then he'd know he was okay. And that I'd know where he was. It wasn't like some strange guy had taken him to a foreign place.

That was the only reasoning I could come up with.

Well, that and spending as much time with him as possible.

And at least the house in Peregian would be somewhat familiar to Monroe. We had good memories of that place. Of him learning to surf and late night swims and BBQs on the veranda with the ocean spray and sunshine...

The flight back to Sydney was over in the blink of an eye. And I realised that because we'd taken Saul's car to the airport, I'd have to cab it home, and it was the very last thing in the world I felt like doing. But there was a familiar face waiting for me in the hangar, and I almost cried when I saw her.

Elektra walked straight over and had her arms around me the second my feet were on the tarmac. "Thought you could use a ride home."

I blinked away my tears. "I am so grateful, thank you."

She pulled back and put her hand to my cheek. "Come on. I'm taking you home. Mum said she'll wait up. Dad's on conference calls with Miami, so you know she was going to be up anyway. And she wants to make sure you've eaten."

I nodded, and the whole don't-cry thing wasn't going too well.

Elektra frowned. "How is he?"

I shook my head. "He was vomiting before I left, and he's exhausted, and he looks awful. Saul said this is the beginning, and the next few days will be the worst of it."

"Come on. Let's get you home." Elektra pulled me to her car and pretty soon we were ducking and weaving through darkened streets. Her car was unusually quiet.

"No radio talk-back gossip show tonight?"

She glanced from the road to me and grimaced. She didn't need to tell me... Those trash celeb-radio shows were disgusting. They plastered the private lives of people all over their shows for likes and ratings, and why on earth Elektra followed them, I'd never understand. Maybe she liked to see herself pictured in the top-ten best-dressed lists, and when I was younger I got a kick out of it, but now I couldn't stand it.

I resented it.

"They were talking about Monroe?" I asked, though I already knew the answer.

"And they had photographs online of Saul arriving at his house yesterday, and of you. And Mum and Dad and Jeffrey."

"Is nothing fucking sacred?" I shook my head, too tired to deal with that shit.

"They probably took photos of me picking you up just now," Elektra said. "Noting the fact that Monroe's not with you."

I sighed and closed my eyes, leaning back against the headrest. "Just be careful with them. You know they'll do anything for a photo. Like run-you-off-the-road kind of careful."

She nodded, concentrating on the road for a while before reaching over and taking my hand. "He'll be okay," she said. "He's in the most capable hands."

"He told me he was scared," I whispered. "I've never seen him so scared. Never. Not even when his parents died."

"Do you think that has a lot to do with where he's at right now?"

I nodded. "Yep. I dunno if he ever grieved for them properly. I told Saul that too. So I'd say he's going to have to relive all that." I let out a deep breath. "I hate not being there for him right now."

Elektra nodded. "You need some time for you though, yeah?"

"You sound like Saul..." Oh God. "He told you that, didn't he?"

She grimaced again. "Not me."

"Mum and Dad."

My sister nodded as she drove. "They're worried about you. So am I."

"I'm fine," I said, way, way too tired to be dealing with this shit right now.

"But you're not," she replied quietly.

I stared out at the darkness and blur of lights for a while. "I will be. I'm not allowed to see him for a month, at least. I can call him once a week. Which is a fucking joke."

"Saul knows what he's doing. And believe me, if he can turn Robbie Hunting around, Saul can fix anyone."

"Saul worked with Robbie Hunting?" Robbie Hunting was only one of England's famous bad-boy rockers, teaching generations the true meaning of sex, drugs, and rock 'n' roll.

Elektra nodded. "And a bunch of others. He's good, Erik. And the more you leave Saul to work his magic on Monroe, the quicker he'll be better and back in Sydney."

"Hmm" was all I could say.

"I know you'll miss him, and he'll miss you just as much," Elektra said as she smoothly pulled her car into the drive. The security gate lifted and she eased through. "But let's concentrate on you for a bit."

I turned slowly to face her. I knew that tone. "What have you already planned?"

"Nothing much—"

"I have a lot of work to catch up on."

"But I've made appointments, and Mum's already approved some time off—"

"No, I want to work. I want to bury myself in mountains of paperwork. It's the best distraction for me. Not to mention how I've hardly been a stellar employee these last few months..."

Elektra pulled into the garage, stopped the car, and applied the handbrake. "Erik, you need to de-stress. And I promise you, we're not leaving the country."

"City."

"State, then."

"City. I'm not leaving this city, unless it's to go to Peregian Beach."

"That's in a different state." She did that eyebrow/smirk thing that she did when she knew she'd won an argument. Ever since she was five years old. It never changed.

"Sydney or Peregian Beach. That's it. For the next month. I don't want to think about anything else right now."

She sighed and opened her car door. "Erik, you need to have a little faith in me."

I climbed out of her car just as the entrance door opened. Mum appeared as a silhouette in the doorway. "Oh, thank goodness you're back. How is he, love? How are you?"

"He's awful, never felt worse," I replied, walking toward her. "And I don't think I'm far behind him."

She stepped into the garage to meet me, giving me a quick hug before pulling back to inspect my face. "You need food and a decent night sleep." I nodded and her gaze bore into mine. "And don't even think about coming into work tomorrow."

I groaned. "I have so much to do. I need to feel productive. I've been going in circles for too long and I need to work. Please don't take that away from me too."

Mum frowned. "Okay, honey. Whatever you need."

Elektra whined. "But I already made the appointment!" Mum shot Elektra a pointed look, and Elektra groaned out a sigh. "Okay, we can do a half day."

"An appointment for what?" I asked. "What the hell are you putting me through that needs an appointment?"

Elektra rolled her eyes and gave me a shove into the hallway from the garage to the house. "Get inside. I'm not telling you because it was supposed to be a surprise. And any self-respecting gay man knows you need appointments for everything. Hair, nails, eyebrows, eyelashes. Jesus, Erik. Everything needs an appointment."

We walked into the kitchen, and I sat at the kitchen island and Mum took a plate out of the fridge and popped it into the microwave. "I'm not having any of those things done," I said to Elektra. "I can tell you that for free. You don't need an appointment for that."

"You can tell me that for free? Jeez, you sound like Monroe." She sighed, put her hand on my shoulder, and said, "I'll reschedule first thing in the morning. You and I will be leaving the office tomorrow at one. Be ready. Don't make me drag you out, because you know I will."

She might be sixty kilos wringing wet, but she was almost six-foot tall and she spent years learning taekwondo, so yes, I knew she wouldn't hesitate to put some pain-lock hold on my arm and drag me out of the office.

"Half a day," I conceded. "And that's it."

She smiled. "You'll love it, and you'll be thanking me." She kissed the back of my head before heading off toward her room. "I can tell you that for free."

I almost snorted. "Thanks."

Elektra gave me a parting grin and waved goodbye. "Goodnight, all. I know you all want to chat without me."

Mum put my reheated dinner in front of me: homemade honeyed chicken and mash, and man, it smelt so good. I hadn't realised how hungry I was. I'd scarfed the first few mouthfuls before even looking up. I sat back. "Sorry. I have better manners than that."

She smiled at me. "It's a compliment to my cooking."

"It is."

"And I'm guessing you haven't eaten all day," she said.

I shook my head and took another forkful into my mouth and swallowed it down before I spoke. "Hasn't been the best of days."

"How is he really?"

"Not good. He'd started vomiting before I left. And thanks again for the use of the house."

She smiled sadly at me. "It was only sitting empty. We weren't going to use it until next month anyway, when we have some time off. So now we'll have to go to Tahiti instead. Such a hassle." She winked, and her smile turned sad. "The house up there is perfect for him right now. It's away from the madness, and the sun and surf will do him the world of good."

"Thanks for lining up Saul too," I said, finishing up another mouthful. "Do I even want to know how you have a guy like him on speed dial?"

Mum smirked. "I know a guy who knows a guy."

I rolled my eyes. That was her and Dad's line for all their secret squirrel high-end clientele business. "Well, thank you. If anyone can help Monroe, Saul's the guy."

Mum put her hand on my arm. "You didn't fail, Erik."

"I didn't pass either. I tried to help him and couldn't."

"Monroe's problems are bigger than you and him." She sighed. "And I know you miss him."

I nodded.

"I know you love him," she said. "More than just as a friend. You're in love with him."

I looked at her, and she smiled right back at me. I tried to deny it, but the words wouldn't come. "Honey, you've looked at him like he hung the moon since the day you met."

My eyes burned but I was done with crying. I'd cried enough for one day. "I thought I hid it, but apparently not."

"Maybe from everyone else, but not from me. You wanna know how I knew? Remember when you were, about twelve or thirteen, and you had those posters on your wall of the Backstreet Boys and Savage Garden, and you used to look up at the tall one... What was his name?"

I almost smiled. "Darren Hayes."

"And oh my God, I would catch you looking at him like he was just the cutest thing in all the world," she said with a laugh. "That was also how I knew you fancied boys, by the way. Because you never looked at Kylie Minogue like that. But you looked at that Darren guy with hearts in your eyes."

I snorted. "Um, thanks. I think."

"And you've looked at Monroe the same way, every day since you've known him. When you talk about him, you get the same hearts in your eyes, and I can tell when you're just thinking about him."

I swallowed hard and nodded. My eyes welled with tears, and I couldn't stop them this time.

"So I know how tough this has been on you," she said, getting a little teary herself. "And I promise, we'll do everything we can to help him, okay?"

I nodded again and wiped away a tear. "He was really scared when I left. He said he's worried that when he falls apart, none of the pieces will go back together again."

Mum frowned. "Oh honey. Maybe the pieces aren't supposed to. Maybe he's supposed to be a whole new person. He'll still be the same Monroe, but maybe the way he thinks and lives will be different, and maybe that's a good thing, huh?"

"Maybe," I conceded with half a shrug. "Maybe he won't have room in his life for me anymore."

Mum shook her head, a fierce set to her eyes. "Erik, my love. I can tell you, he looks at you the same way you look at him. His eyes follow you, he smiles different when he's with you—the real Monroe—and I can tell you, I know love when I see it. And that boy loves you so much it scares me."

"It scares you?"

"Because it's a forever kind of love." She smiled sadly. "A love that means you'll start a life with him, and you won't need your poor old mum anymore."

I snorted. "Hardly. But I can't live here forever."

"Why not? Isn't it big enough?"

I laughed at that, because this house was so big that Elektra and I still both lived here, with our parents, in a wing of the house each, living completely separate lives, and basically met in the communal kitchen for dinner once or twice a week. It was massive. "Wherever you are will always be home, Mum."

She melted a little. "Aww, thank you, darling."

I let out a slow breath. "I don't think it will serve me any favours thinking Monroe might feel the same until he's back on his feet. Everything could change for him in these next two months."

"Maybe," Mum said. "Or maybe this will help him see things a bit clearer, yes?" She patted my hand and sighed. "I'm off to bed. I have a breakfast meeting in the morning. Put your plate in the dishwasher and set it going please."

I smiled as she waved me off and disappeared, and my mind began to swim. It had been the day from hell, but somehow my mum had made everything seem like it would be okay. Well, maybe not okay. But the glimmer of hope at least.

And for now, it would have to be enough.

I BARELY SLEPT. Even though exhaustion weighed me down, my mind was in hyperdrive.

My mum's words played over and over in my mind...

"...I know love when I see it. And that boy loves you so much it scares me."

I tried to recall everything from Monroe's and my years as best friends, but nothing stood out for me. Sure, I'd almost hooked up with some random guys and Monroe had drunk too much and fallen over, or he'd intervened on the dance floor or put his arm around me, drunk and handsy. He was always handsy. That was just him.

Wasn't it?

Maybe he was such a good actor, I'd missed it. He'd hid the severity of his drinking until he couldn't hide it any longer. The more I thought back, remembering times when he probably had been drinking and I'd not known. Or was he hiding more than that?

Was he hiding his feelings for me?

Like I'd hidden them from him?

I wouldn't know until I got the chance to speak to him again, but he had more on his plate right now to deal with than stupid romance. And then of course my thoughts went to him, what he was going through.

Was he still vomiting? Did he still look ill and sunken in on himself?

I imagined him in the house at Peregian, so far away. Did he blame me for his intervention?

Was I to blame for his drinking?

I fell asleep sometime after four am.

"WELL, YOU LOOK..." My dad motioned his hand at my face. "Like you didn't sleep a wink."

Suited up and ready for work before seven, I grumbled a noncommittal response. He put his hand to my cheek; his hand was warm and strong, his gaze fierce and blue. "You sure you're up for this?"

"Yeah."

"Your mum said if—"

"I told Mum last night I need to do this. I need to feel productive."

"I get it," Dad said with a nod. "I do. I know that sitting around feeling useless just makes you worse. So here, have this." He shoved his coffee into my hand. "I'll make us some more."

My dad had a quiet way about him that I'd always appreciated. I had many traits of my mother, but I was probably more like my dad. He always stood back, watching, evaluating, assessing. Like Elektra, Mum tended to lead in like a force to be reckoned with, but Dad had unassuming stealth and patience. Just as successful, just a different approach.

"And here, eat this." Dad shoved a bowl of muesli and fruit in front of me, then went back to the coffee machine.

I took a spoonful and grumbled. "Tastes like cardboard."

He chuckled. "Healthy cardboard. Eat up."

The sliced banana and strawberry made it somewhat palatable, but I needed more coffee to wash it down. "So, I take it you're on 'make sure Erik eats breakfast and drive him to work' duty."

Dad grinned over his coffee cup. "You know your mother."

I rolled my eyes, thankful but still a little petulant, and ate as much cardboard and yoghurt as I could stomach. I put my plate in the sink.

"Rinse that," Dad said, picking up his coat. He didn't even turn around, he just had that in-built dad-vision that I assumed was programmed automatically when one became a parent.

I rolled my eyes again—this time without the gratitude—rinsed my plate and grabbed my satchel. "Any clues about what the hell Elektra is putting me through this afternoon?"

Dad turned to face me and with a heavy sigh; he frowned. "Son, I am many things. But brave enough to doublecross a Keston woman is not one of them."

I snorted. "Fair enough. But I'm telling you right now, if it's a colonic cleanse, I'm out."

Dad laughed and clapped me on the shoulder. "Oh hell no. If it was that bad, I'd warn you."

"Thanks."

The ride to work was more or less quiet, which was fine by me. Though, moving through traffic and buildings and madness, while it was quiet inside the car, I felt detached today. And it let my mind wander to Monroe... How was he feeling? What was he going through? How bad was it? Was he okay? Was he mad? Too sick to be mad? How sick was too sick? Would Saul know what to do if things got really bad?

When Dad turned the car off, I realised I'd missed the entire trip and entry into the security car park. I shook my head to clear it and tried to begin my day. I lost a good portion of time to emails, and my poor assistants filled me in on everything they'd done in my absence, which was more than I'd first imagined, and I felt guilty for dumping so much work on them. Janice, my very competent executive PA, assured me otherwise. "Don't feel bad," she sniffed. "They're more than able, and they've enjoyed the challenge. In fact, I'd like to see them this busy more often."

Janice was a tall, thin woman, forty-something years old, who kept her expression and suit starched, her dark hair pulled into a neat scroll, and she ran my life better than I could. I certainly couldn't do half of what I did without her. She kept my schedule, kept everything professional, and kept the other, less experienced staff on their toes.

She came into my office at ten o'clock and wordlessly put a coffee on my desk. I leaned back in my chair and stretched my neck. "Thank you, Janice."

"Of course," she said as she got to the door. But then she paused for a fraction of a second before nodding and stepping out.

"Ah, Janice?" I called out.

She turned and smiled, her spine straight. "Yes."

"Um, was there... was there something you wanted to say?"

A look of surprise crossed her face before she thought to school her expression. "Oh, no... I just..."

"You just what?" I pressed. She clearly looked uncomfortable. "Close the door for a sec, and take a seat. Thank you for the coffee by the way."

"Oh, that's my pleasure," she said, sitting down slowly.

"Is something the matter?"

"No. Well," she swallowed. "Some of the younger girls were talking about some gossip show and what they might or might not have seen in regards to... where you flew to last night. I told them to zip it, and if they took issue with that they could express their outrage in a letter of resignation." She nodded, brows knitting together.

I smiled. "Thank you. It's none of their business." I chewed on my lip. "Was it really on the TV?"

"Or some internet wannabe-talk show," she said, rolling her eyes. "I'm not exactly sure."

I sighed. "Do I even want to know?"

She grimaced. "Probably not. I also believe they aired a segment on the news on The Morning Show this morning."

Fucking hell. "I wish they'd find someone else to harass."

Janice pursed her lips. "I do as well. They have no right to intrude on your lives, and the likes of chattering young girls have no right to demand to see it either. Why they're even interested, I'll never know." Her eyes went wide. "I mean, no offence."

I laughed. "None taken. None taken at all." I sipped my coffee and hummed my appreciation. "Though you'll be pleased to know I'll be more focused on work this next month. I have fewer... distractions." That really wasn't the word I wanted to use. "And at any rate, I'll be available for meetings or consults at any time, whatever you need. Just ask. I'm at your disposal."

Janice blushed. "Don't you mean that the other way? Shouldn't it be me at your disposal?"

"Ah, Janice, flattery is kind. But we both know who runs this office." I smiled at her. "Just don't tell my mother I admitted that."

She smiled. "Wouldn't dream of it." She stood and went to the door, where she stopped again, this time with her hand on the handle. "Is he... is he okay?" she cringed. "I don't mean to pry and I would never repeat a word, but he's a sweet kid who was dealt a bad hand, ya know? And sometimes vices can seem like the only lifeline. Sorry, I don't need to know details or anything, and I would never ask that, I just want to know if he's okay."

"He is, okay," I replied with a smile. "I mean, he will be. Thank you for asking."

She returned the smile, ducked her head, and disappeared out the door.

ELEKTRA WALKED through my door at exactly 12:58pm. I looked up from my desk and resisted groaning. I'd made good headway with listings and clientele markets, and I was just finding my groove. The last thing I wanted to do was stop.

She held up a brown paper bag. "It's katsu chicken salad. I know you love it, and I know you haven't eaten." I was about to object, but she raised her hand. "And I've already changed the booking once. Plus, I'm leaving my desk too. Do you not think I have a thousand other things to do as well?"

"Then why are we doing this?"

"Because you need it." She looked so much like our mother when she used her don't-bother-arguing voice. "So step away from the computer, and come with me."

"Have you ever considered a career change to law enforcement?"

She grinned. "Possibly. But they don't let people enter the ranks as the General." She nodded back out the door. "Come on."

I saved and closed down my files and groaned when I

stood up. This time from a crick in my back, where I'd sat in the wrong position, staring at screens for too long without moving. "Only because you bought me chicken katsu salad."

"You can eat in the car, but if you get any of it on my leather seats, I will have you fed to sharks."

I snorted. "Or I could pay to have them cleaned. You know, like a normal person. Not sure the whole feeding-to-sharks thing was necessary. I mean, your car is nice, but sharks? Really?"

She smiled at me and pressed the elevator button. "Just kidding."

"Any clues as to where you're taking me?"

"Not until we arrive. You still have means of escape until I get you through the doors."

I sighed and considered spilling my salad on her pristine leather seats as payback, but the salad was too damn good to waste. It occurred to me then, that the last three times I'd seen the other three members of my family, they'd fed me. I wondered if they were trying to tell me something... And with the way I mowed through that salad, maybe they didn't have to.

In the last few months, I hadn't been too interested in food. And maybe my clothes felt a little looser, but stress never fared well for my appetite.

And of course, thinking of the reason for my stress brought Monroe back to the front of my mind. Was he eating? Still vomiting? Could he stomach food?

Elektra's voice startled me. "Why are you frowning? I promise it won't be that bad."

I looked out the window then and realised where we were. "Oh, no, I was just thinking…" I looked at her then and sighed. "Really? Those sharks are sounding more fun right now."

She laughed and flicked me with the back of her hand. "Come on. They're expecting us."

Neutral Bay Body Day Spa was an elite version of an ordinary day spa, except their clientele paid a small fortune for every visit. Elektra was a regular and she'd raved about them for years, and now she was subjecting me to them. We were greeted in the reception lounge by the owner, no less, who gave Elektra a kiss on the cheek hello. She was a woman, age indeterminate by the stretch of her skin, with dyed black hair and unnaturally plumped lips. "Hello, beautiful," the woman said.

Elektra was all smiles as she kissed her cheeks in return before turning to me. "Cordelia, this is my brother, Erik."

Cordelia eyed me, up and down. "Well, beauty is a family trait, I see." She held out her hand, which I took, and it was then she inspected my nails. "Oh dear."

Elektra sighed sadly. "He cuts them himself. With nail clippers."

Cordelia looked at me with pity and shame. "Never you mind, we can fix these."

I took my hand back and inspected my nails. They were clean and tidy. "What's wrong with them?"

Elektra laughed and Cordelia led me down a hall. From there, I had my very first manicure, which, I won't lie, felt surprisingly good. I had no idea the muscles in my hands needed to be massaged. Then I had a pedicure, and that too didn't exactly suck. The foot soak was nice. Also something I wouldn't be telling Elektra any time soon.

But the massage...

I had no idea how much I needed that.

Elektra and I both went in wearing our little white robes and lay face down on the tables, side by side. We'd done the whole thing side by side—manicures, pedicures—so this wasn't much different. But then the two massage therapists came in and the guy who worked me over had the hands of a god.

"Holy fuck," I mumbled.

"You're very tight," he said.

And my mind went straight to Monroe because he would have busted something laughing at that.

"You carry your stress here and here." The massagist palmed each shoulder as he said it; then he pushed downward and out, over and over. "Sorry for being rough. You might be sore tomorrow."

Yep. Monroe would have cracked up at that too. I was almost glad he wasn't here.

"Okay, you're done. Roll over, time for your facial."

I shot up and stared at him. "Not that kind of massage, buddy."

He was shocked at first; then he burst out laughing, shaking his head. He looked to Elektra who was now staring at me. "It's his first time, huh?"

"Hmm," Elektra said. "What did you think he meant? You know what a facial is, right?"

"I do. Though clearly you don't," I answered, rolling over and fixing the towel across my waist. Now I was truly glad Monroe wasn't here because he'd have about died laughing by now.

My massage therapist, now sitting down behind my head, was still chuckling. "Close your eyes for me."

I can honestly say I never knew the muscles in my face needed massaging before either, but damn. By the time we shuffled into the sauna, I was just about asleep. We sat in the sauna, our towels around us, heads back, eyes closed.

"Thank you," I mumbled. "For this. I thought this was going to be crap, but I'm wondering why you've kept this place a secret from me and why I've never done this sooner?"

Elektra hummed happily. "You're welcome, though I have been trying to convince you for years. I hardly kept it a secret. Just trying to keep your mind off things and to remind you how long it's been since you did something for yourself."

"Hmm." I wasn't sure what exactly I was supposed to say to that.

"I know you miss him."

"I do."

"But you need to take care of yourself too."

"You sound like Mum."

Elektra laughed. "I'll take that as a compliment."

"I guess I... I guess I didn't realise... a lot of things."

"Can I ask you something?"

"Considering we're enclosed in a sauna, I can't really get away, so..."

She smiled, though her eyes were still closed. "I know you love him. Anyone can see it."

Christ. "Is that a question?"

"Does it need to be?"

"I guess not."

"So?"

"Yes. I do." I cleared my throat. "Love him, that is. I don't know how not to."

She was quiet a moment. "Do you want to not love him?"

I leaned my head back against the wall and stretched out my legs. "No."

"You have a very complex relationship with him."

I snorted at that. "Um, thanks?"

"You're closer than best friends. I can't even imagine how complex it would be if you'd been intimate. I mean it's hard enough being best friends and being in love..."

Well, I couldn't answer that, and my silence gave me away.

Elektra sat forward, her eyes now wide open, aimed right at me. "Noooo."

"It was stupid, and it came from the wrong place."

She tilted her head, confused. "It what? How can it come from the wrong place? Where the hell did you put it?"

I burst out laughing and nudged her shoulder with mine. "Not like that. We... were intimate, and it was good and all, but for the wrong reasons."

She studied me a little while. "What were the wrong reasons?"

"Because I thought it might be the very last time I saw him," I replied. "And he was drunk."

Elektra sat back and sighed before wiping her face down. "He'll be okay, you know. And I might not know much about men, because I'm pretty sure I'll be single forever, but I'd reckon he's in love with you too."

"Mum said something similar."

"And when is she ever wrong?"

I smiled. "I guess time will tell."

"When can you speak to him?"

"Tuesday night, six o'clock." I sighed. "Five days, three hours. Not that I'm counting. I keep thinking of him, what he's going through, how he feels…"

"You'll be okay too," she said, her gaze on me. "You'll get through this. Both of you."

I didn't feel as convinced, but Elektra stood up and tightened her towel. "Okay I think we're done. Time to shower off. Men's showers are to the left."

Fifteen minutes later I met her in the lobby. She was dressed, her skin and hair was fresh and *au naturel,* and *still* looked a million dollars. She smiled brightly at me. "How do you feel?"

"I'm reluctant to admit it," I replied. "But I do feel better."

She grinned, hooked her arm through mine, and led me out to the footpath. "I'm not done yet," she said. Then she stopped at a frozen yoghurt café and ordered two berry specials.

I tasted it with the little spoon. "Oh wow, this is pretty good."

She smiled with the plastic spoon in her mouth. "This is how I end my me-time."

"A full body work over and frozen yoghurt?"

"Yep. We have to take care of ourselves," she said casually. "Mental health, body health." She held up a small dessert. "Soul health."

I laughed, actually feeling pretty good despite myself. We climbed back in Elektra's car, and on the twenty minutes it took us to get home, she answered five business calls, sent three voice-to-text reminders, and scheduled two appointments with clients and photographers for property visuals. She used her no-nonsense business voice that reminded me of Mum so much it was a little scary. She drove into the garage, slid her sunglasses to the top of her head, pulled on the handbrake, and never missed a beat.

"You know what?" I asked. "You're a real-life Elle Woods."

She laughed. "That just might be the nicest thing you've ever said to me."

I was still smiling when we walked inside and even into the next morning. But by the afternoon, my mind kept wandering back to Monroe, taking my heart with it. The day after wasn't much better. I buried myself in work, and when my inbox was finally clear, I began to seek out avenues on investments, returns, growth markets, and economic trends. Then I put proposals together, and even when Janice said goodnight, I didn't stop.

I took my work home in some vain attempt to try not to think of Monroe. But he was always there in the periphery, always on the tip of my tongue, at the front of my mind.

I missed him.

I missed him so fucking much.

And the next day I couldn't concentrate. I went to the office even though it was Sunday, and when security asked if everything was okay, I realised it was dark outside already, I grabbed my laptop and went home.

"Oh, here you are," Dad said when I walked in. "I was wondering when you..." Then he looked at me again and did a double take. "Come in and sit down."

I did, and a moment later Dad slid a cup of hot tea in front of me. "Wanna talk about it?" he asked.

"Talk about what?"

"Why you look so lost." Dad frowned. "You're not doing so good, huh?"

"I miss him. I thought I was okay. I thought..." I ran my hand through my hair. "I think about him all the time. And I've tried to tell myself that he's just away on business or he's on vacation, but a voice in my head keeps telling me he's not coming back."

"The thing is, Erik," Dad said gently, "the Monroe you know isn't coming back. He will be different. A good different. So it's not a bad thing, but there will be changes. It's okay to grieve for what you've lost."

It's okay to grieve for what you've lost...

Maybe he was right. Maybe I did have to let go. Maybe the distancing process was the beginning of the letting go. Maybe I'd already lost him.

And then my phone rang with a number I didn't know. I considered not answering, but what if it was Monroe? "Hello?"

"Erik?" It wasn't Monroe's voice but Saul's.

I was on my feet without realising it. "Oh my God, how is he? Is he okay? Can I speak to him?"

So much for letting go.

Chapter Ten
Monroe

The first three days were hell. I don't remember much except for the pain. There was a piercing, twisting stab in my skull that I couldn't quite seem to pinpoint. I vomited and dry-heaved non-stop, and I was so tired I could hardly lift my head, but I couldn't sleep because my brain was wired and splitting with pain.

My body ached in ways I didn't realise a body could ache. Mostly from vomiting; the muscles in my stomach, my back, my throat all burned, but I also ached from being tensed into a ball and shaking so bad. I shook so much even my fucking teeth hurt. My body twitched, unable to stay still but in dire need of rest. Every single part of me hurt.

But I don't remember what I thought. Apart from wanting to die.

It was all kind of a blur. I had blood tests for all kinds of things, and Saul did give me some medication to help the detox and to ease the symptoms. It helped clear the mind fog a little, but the first three days were an horrendous blur.

I was certain of one thing though. I didn't ever want to go through that again.

Saul said we'd reached the peak by the end of day three. He also said I'd got through the physical trudge, barely, but the mental slog was yet to begin. He'd also said there were pills I could take that'd help, but I didn't see the point taking away one drug only to replace it with another. He'd dropped the subject, thankfully.

I didn't like him a whole bunch. He was too calm, too calculated. Even if I screamed at him to leave me alone or begged him for just one drink, he never flinched. He never batted an eyelid. He knew when to be there and when I needed to be alone. He knew when I needed to eat, even if I wasn't hungry. He never complained if I vomited or had diarrhoea; he never complained if I swore, yelled, cried, begged.

Yeah, okay, so maybe he wasn't so bad.

But I woke up on day four, feeling... weird. Anxious without knowing why. I'd managed a few hours' solid sleep, free from sweats and nightmares and restlessness. I even managed to eat some toast and drink some of Saul's putrid herbal green tea.

"It's not that bad," Saul said, almost smiling as he slid the cup toward me.

"It's not coffee." I sipped it, grimacing. "Or vodka."

Saul's expression didn't change. "A piece of toast is good progress."

I had the last bite and washed it down with the tea.

"How are you feeling?" he pressed. "Headache? Back pain?"

I took stock of my body. "Head feels okay, a little spacey. My lower back hurts the most." I shrugged. "I don't know. Everything hurts, but it doesn't. Does that make sense?"

Saul smiled. "Complete sense, and not at all surprising. I'm still happy with the progress of eating a whole piece of toast."

"Yeah, well, let's not get too excited. It needs to stay down first." I sighed. "I do feel somewhat human, but I don't know how long that will last."

"Like I said last night, the hardest part of the physical detox is over. There are still some residual effects we won't discount just yet."

"But the mental part is coming, right?" I mumbled.

"It's often the hardest part, Monroe."

"You said that last night, too."

"Did you want to go for a walk along the beach? Get some sunshine, fresh air. Stretch your legs for a bit."

"I want to shower first."

"Okay." Nothing fazed him, and every answer was expected. "Then we can go for a walk and begin with some light therapy."

I groaned and pushed my cup of tea away. "I'm not really the let's-talk-about-feelings kinda guy."

Saul smiled at that. "You'll talk. The sooner you want to go back to your life, the sooner you'll talk. I can only help you if you help me. And I can only help you if you talk." He nodded to my plate and cup. "Wash and dry those, get showered, and meet me out the back."

I withheld the sigh until Saul had gone, then sagged. Fucking hell.

I washed my dishes as he'd asked. He'd made me do it yesterday too, as soon as I could stand upright, basically. I wasn't opposed to cleaning up after myself. It had just been a while since I'd had to... well, actually, I'd never really had to.

But I did that, then went back to my room, stripped off, and showered. And there was something comforting about being in Erik's house, his room, his bathroom. Being surrounded by Keston things, Erik things. His room didn't smell like him or anything creepy like that—though I'd be lying if I said I wouldn't mind if it did—but there were reminders of him everywhere.

Photographs placed around the house, erratically and without logic, but apparently Mrs Keston had decided she liked reminders of Erik and Elektra as cute toddlers and gap-toothed primary school kids and as teenagers who didn't need braces or have acne because they were beautiful, while hormones had played hell with my face and my now-perfect teeth had cost a small fortune. But there was also a wooden box that Elektra had made in seventh grade woodwork that now sat on the dining table to hold serviettes, and there was a coffee mug-type thing that was an awful brown, lumpy disaster that had *Erik, Year 8*, scratched into the bottom of it.

A painting Erik had bought his parents five years ago hung on the wall and a stack of well-read books sat in an artful pile on the sideboard. There were old clothes in Erik's drawers that I remembered him wearing when we were here, hats in the laundry, and beach shoes in the garage. A box on the veranda kept a beach cricket set and Frisbees, and they brought back good memories of us laughing on the beach.

I thought the reminders of him might make it harder, but they were a comfort. Like he was with me, when he wasn't. I missed him, so very much. More than I thought possible. The way you miss sunshine when it's been overcast for far too long. You miss the warmth, the life it breathes. The purpose it gives.

But being here, in this house, with him all around me, really helped. I had to wonder if Erik knew that when he suggested we come here.

I was pretty sure he did.

I kept that in mind as I finally met Saul on the beach at the back of the house. It was literally three steps down from the veranda to the sand. He stood in the water, the tide at his ankles and his hemp pants rolled to his calves. He held his arms out, gesturing to the blue sky and warm breeze, and he grinned at me. "How beautiful is this?"

I matched his rhetorical question with my own. "Not a bad spot, huh? The sun's a bit bright though." It had been a few days since I'd seen it.

"Feel better after your shower?"

I nodded and we began to walk up the beach. "Showers are like magic."

"They are indeed."

Saul had a quiet patience to him and was never in any hurry to fill the silence. I liked that about him.

"I'm about ready for a nap though," I admitted. "Not a fan of the tiredness, I must say."

"It will pass, and it will soon be replaced with energy. Just give your body time."

"I don't know how far I can walk today," I said. I hated admitting weakness but we'd only walked a short way and I was already tiring.

"We don't have to go far." He stopped and walked back into the water. "Come put your feet in. It's invigorating."

It was cool and crystal blue. Seagulls flew overhead, boats sailed in the distance, and there looked to be some people further up the beach, but it was literally nothing but hundreds of metres of white sand and aqua ocean. The closest neighbours were a few hundred metres in either direction, but they were mostly holiday homes, so Saul and I were basically alone.

And I was grateful.

I missed Erik though.

"What are you thinking about right now?" Saul prompted.

"Nothing."

"Hmm, you're not a very good liar."

I snorted. Jesus, I almost smiled. "You're not the first person to tell me that."

Saul studied me for a moment. "Erik?"

My heart clenched at his name. I looked out at the horizon. "And yet, I lied to him for years."

"About?"

"Drinking."

"How so?"

"The extent of it. That I drank every day. For breakfast, some days. I would put vodka in my water bottle..." I kept my gaze locked on the horizon until the line blurred and I couldn't discern where the ocean met the sky. "That way I could drink whenever I wanted and no one would question it."

He nodded, again, like he expected me to say what I'd said.

"Does anything surprise you?"

Saul sighed. "Yes, and no. I knew from your level of detox that you drank more than they knew. And it's pretty safe to take whatever amount of drinking an addict will admit to and triple it, at least."

I closed my eyes and let the sun warm my face. "Do you think Erik knew?"

"Yes."

And that answer, that simple three-letter word sent a pang of guilt through my heart. I almost swayed with the weariness of it.

Saul didn't speak for a bit, like he knew I needed a moment to process. The sun and the ebb and flow of the water, hurting Erik, made me tired.

"Ready to head back?"

I nodded. "Yep."

I made it as far as the egg-shaped sun lounge on the veranda. I lay down, put my feet up, and closed my eyes...

And woke up with a start. I couldn't recall the dream

that startled me, but I shot awake just as Saul came over carrying a tray. "Oh good, you're awake." He slid the tray onto the edge of the sun lounge and pulled over another chair before going back inside. He'd cut up apple and strawberries, cheese, and added grapes and crackers. Small, bite-sized food to pick at was kind of perfect. He came back out with a cup in each hand. "More tea."

"More?" I grumbled at him. "Thanks."

He looked far too pleased. "Oh, cheer up. It's good for you."

I grimaced. "Still not coffee."

Saul laughed and sat on his seat, then picked a slice of apple from the plate. I tried a cracker and some grapes, then cheese with another cracker, and I even managed to drink some of the tea. He seemed happy that I was eating.

"You know," he started, "when Erik said he had a holiday home, I wasn't quite expecting this." He waved his hand to the living room, to the view.

"Yeah. If you thought I had money," I said, shaking my head, "it's pennies compared to the Kestons. Private jet, multimillion-dollar houses all over the world. Erik has his own portfolio."

Saul nodded. "The Keston name didn't need any introduction," he said. "And I assumed there was some merit to the net worth listed on Forbes."

I shouldn't have been surprised Saul had done his homework. "But you'd never guess it by talking to him. Erik, that is. He never flaunts it; he never tells people. Not that he has to, I guess. But he wears old, worn clothes, much to Elektra's disgust." I kinda smiled at that. "It's reassuring."

"Reassuring?"

"Well, yeah. I mean, I've got money and assets, you know. And growing up in elite schools—" I rolled my eyes. "—everyone knew who was the richest in school, because that's what shitty rich kids do. And all the way through school, I never really knew who was a true friend or who was just in it for the perks, ya know? But that's not something I ever had to worry about with Erik."

"You met him in college?"

I nodded. "At Hartington's."

"I know of it."

Hartington was Australia's version of an Ivy League college, so I assumed he'd heard of it. "And most of the guys from school went through and I was thinking it was just gonna be a continuation of high school. But in walked this tall blond guy, and I had no clue who he was, but other people whispered like it was a big deal and I figured he must have been someone famous. But he couldn't have given a shit. He looked at me and rolled his eyes, and it made me smile. I still didn't even know who he was, even after he'd introduced himself. I think he liked that." I shrugged. "But anyway, I didn't have to worry about Erik only liking me for my money because compared to him..."

"He is very grounded. As are his whole family." Saul looked back into the house. "I probably would have expected a Keston beach house to be redecorated every season by interior designers, with the latest soft furnishings that can sometimes make a house feel like a museum, but it's very much a home."

"Elektra made the fruit bowl and serviette holder," I said. "Erik's attempt at high school ceramics is the brown thing in the coffee cup cupboard."

Saul's eyes went wide. "That lopsided abomination? He made that? I was afraid to touch it in case it fell apart. Or if it was used in demon summoning rituals."

I laughed for the first time in days. "Yep. Don't worry. There's jokes about it every time they come here. But it's still his dad's favourite cup to drink from."

Saul smiled and ate some more fruit. "I'll tell you something. When I first met them, the Kestons, the psychiatrist in me wanted to know what their dark secret was. Cheating, addiction, fraud, political bribes to secure land deals. You know, what you might expect from successful, wealthy families." He gave me a wry smirk. "But they're really just decent, decidedly normal people. Parents who love their kids, who want the best for them. Siblings who genuinely love and protect each other and their parents."

I tried to smile but couldn't quite manage it. "They are."

"It's rare."

I nodded.

"Were you close to your parents?"

I flinched. "I um... really? We're just gonna do this now?"

Saul shook his head. "Not if you don't want to."

"I don't."

"Okay," he said like he couldn't have cared less. "But if you want to help—"

"Yeah, I know. I need to help myself." I sighed. "I will talk. I want to. I just... I never was much good at it."

Saul smiled again, like that small admission made him happy. "I'll tell you what. We'll trade. You ask me one question, I will answer with complete transparency and honesty. Then we trade places."

"One question?"

He nodded. "You go first."

God, what the hell did I want to ask him? "Um, why psychiatry? Why work with... people like me?"

"I wanted to help people," he answered. "I know that sounds like a cliché, but it's the truth. I grew up with an abusive father. He was what we would now call bipolar. Back then it was labelled manic depression. He was violent, an alcoholic, and he made our lives a living hell. He drank the hate that consumed him. And through it all, I could never understand why. I wanted to know why he behaved the way he did. *What* made him behave that way? And not in the naïve way a small boy might want to know why his father hurt his family. I wanted to break it down and analyse it. I wanted to take apart the cause and effect and study it. I wanted to know *why*."

Well, shit.

He drank the hate that consumed him.

That kind of made me feel a little ill, and I almost wished he'd stopped at the wanting-to-help-people cliché comment. "I'm sorry you went through that."

"Me too. But thank you."

I tried to eat another cracker but my mouth had gone dry. I took a mouthful of tea but it had gone cold. I swallowed it anyway.

"My turn," he said. "Were you close to your parents?"

Jesus. I knew he was gonna ask me that again, but it still didn't prepare me. I suddenly couldn't speak, nor could I swallow. My eyes burned and as much as I tried to speak, I just couldn't. So I shook my head.

But that was enough for Saul. Because he patted my knee. "That's a start, Monroe." He stood up, taking the plate and tea with him. "I have an activity for you to try."

He came back a short while later carrying a laundry basket full of... sticks? His smile should have told me something was up. He sat it on the floor in front of the sofa. "Come inside. The sun will cook you. Are you crafty at all?"

"Crafty?" I walked inside, and yes, he had a basket full of sticks. "If by crafty you mean a paper aeroplane, then yeah, sure."

"Did you build with LEGO as a child?" he asked, as he picked up a stick.

"I uh, don't know what they taught in psych school, but I can tell you one thing for free." I nodded to the basket. "That's not LEGO."

Saul chuckled. "No, it's driftwood. I saw some on the beach on our first day here, so I tracked down some legal, ethically sourced pieces and had them delivered."

"What for?"

"To make things. Craft, art. Whatever you want."

"A raft so I can sail for Sydney?"

Saul snorted. "Uh, not quite."

I sat opposite him, the basket of sticks between us. I didn't feel like doing this. Or anything, if I was being honest. My head was starting to pulse again, and my legs were aching and restless. But I picked up one stick. It was a foot long, lighter than it should have been, and smooth to the touch. I ran my fingers along it.

"They have a pleasing texture, don't they?" Saul said, marvelling at the piece he held.

"Pleasing texture? Who the hell says pleasing texture?" I didn't mean for that to sound so rude, so I added, "We mere heathen folk would just say that it feels good."

Saul seemed to appreciate my effort. He smiled. "Sorry. I'll try to remember that next time I address the mere heathen folk."

"What do people do with this... stuff?" I asked. Then I shook my head. "Sorry. I can't seem to think real well."

"Still a bit foggy?"

I nodded. "And tired. But I can't think of things. Like my brain is stuck in first gear."

Saul nodded. "I'll be right back," he said as he walked out. He came back out with his stethoscope, fixing the earpieces into place, and without a word, he shoved the cold metal part onto my back. He moved it around, listening each time, and I tried to concentrate on breathing. Then he made me look at him, turn my head one way, turn it back, move my eyes this way, look over there, look back here. Then I had to squeeze his fingers, which I could barely even summon the strength to do. When he was satisfied, he sat down across from me again. "Your heart rate is a little high, but that's to be expected, but everything else is okay. Why don't you lie down and watch a movie or something? We can do the driftwood thing another time."

I nodded, because suggesting I lie down was the best thing he'd said all day. I picked up the remote, turned the TV on, but don't even remember trying to decide what to watch.

I woke up an hour or so later, feeling marginally better. "It's weird that I can be this tired but unable to sleep properly," I grumbled.

"Disrupted sleep is the worst," Saul agreed. "But you *are* getting better."

While I still felt like shit, I was a helluva lot better than I had been on day one or two. But I'd woken up from my nap with a new and improved craving for a drink. I didn't just want a drink. I *needed* a drink. I needed it like I needed air.

I stood up and walked to the veranda and walked back again, beginning to pace. It didn't take Saul long to stop me. He put his hand on my arm and I stopped pacing. "Craving?"

I nodded and tried to breathe.

"Come on then," he said. "Let's go for another walk up the beach. Or just down to the water."

"Can I call Erik?" I asked. "That would help, I'm sure."

Saul stopped and was quiet a moment, clearly weighing up his options and how he should approach saying no. "Maybe later. I want to speak to him first, but we can try calling him later. A walk down to the water first, yes?"

If he'd let me speak to Erik, I'd agree to anything.

The sun was hot on my skin. I don't know if my skin was oversensitive, but the water was cool and I walked in up to my thighs. Saul didn't come out as far as me, and I wondered what he'd do if I just kept walking out...

"Erik said you like to swim," Saul said.

I glanced back at him. "Yeah. Pool, though. Not ocean. Not a fan of the things that bite." I waited for a wave to roll in, and when the foam had dissipated, I splashed the salt water on my face. A breeze picked up at that moment and felt so good against my skin.

And a thought struck me, simple and complex, both dark and enlightening at the same time.

If I weren't here, I wouldn't feel this.

The breeze, the water lapping at my thighs, the sun on my skin.

Such a simple joy that I would have missed if I hadn't taken these steps to change my life. Or if I'd just kept walking into the ocean until the waves took me under. Or if I'd drunk myself into oblivion.

I didn't want to miss the good things.

I didn't want to not be here, in this world, in this life.

Saul was beside me then, like he somehow knew I needed him, and together we faced the horizon. "Makes you realise how small we are," he said. "When you see the vastness of the ocean."

I took a deep breath, the salt cloying at the back of my

throat. "Makes you realise how lucky we are," I replied. Then I looked at him. "I don't want to *not* be here."

It clearly didn't make a lot of sense to him, but was cryptic enough for worry to cross his face. "What do you mean?"

"I was just thinking," I said, smiling back out to the horizon, "that if I wasn't here—not here on the beach with you, but here as in *alive*—like if I'd drowned myself in a bottle somewhere and didn't wake up or if I just kept walking out into the ocean, that I'd miss the little things. Like the breeze or the waves. Or that bird," I said, looking up as a gull cried overhead. We both watched as it soared on the wind and swooped. I turned to him, a little teary again. "I don't want to miss the little things."

Saul smiled, though he still seemed a little perplexed. "Well, that's good. For what it's worth, I'm glad you're still here." He stared out at the horizon for a moment. "It's the little things that make life worthwhile. If we could just get life to slow down sometimes, we'd all be better off. Don't you think?"

"Deadlines and investors and shareholders don't seem to think so."

He frowned and looked at me. "I guess not. It can't be easy."

"It's not. And I failed."

"You didn't fail," he said. "You—"

"Failed," I corrected him. "If I'm going to be owning up to my shortcomings, my faults, and my misgivings, then I think it's safe to say I failed. I failed Jeffrey. I failed Erik. I failed Mr and Mrs Keston. And I failed my parents." I stared at the ocean, not game enough to make eye contact with him. "I didn't handle the pressure or the responsibility."

"No, Monroe, you didn't handle the grief," Saul said gently.

His words hit their intended mark. My heart physically ached. "I didn't handle any of it. Everything was too fucking hard and it hurt so much. So I drank because it numbed me, but then I had to keep drinking more every time."

"When did you start?" he asked. "When did it become a coping mechanism?"

"At my parents' funeral. Someone handed me a drink and told me it would help."

"Who?"

"Why does it matter?"

"It helps me see a bigger picture."

"It's not anyone's fault but mine. It wasn't like they were getting me illegal drugs. I had cabinets full of it."

"Who was it?"

I realised then he wasn't asking to find out who. He was asking to see how willing I was to open up.

"Mr Keston," I whispered. "Erik's dad. He thought he was helping. And he was. It did help, in the beginning."

Saul gave a small smile and looked back out at the horizon. "It's common to offer a drink to someone to help take the edge off. It's not his fault. It's not your fault either. Some people are prone toward addictive behaviours, and some are not. There's no rhyme or reason.

Addictions take away your control. They're inhibitors; it's what they do. What we're going to do is take back that control."

"You make it sound easy."

"It's not. It's actually really fucking hard." Saul smiled at me. "But you've taken a huge step forward today, Monroe. I'm very proud of you. You faced a craving, and you sought a positive counteraction, and you beat it. Erik said you were stubborn, so it's good to see you use some of that stubbornness in a positive way."

"Erik said that, did he?"

Saul smiled. "He said you were a lot of things."

"I bet he did."

"Come on, let's get out of this water. My toes are starting to prune." He clapped me on the shoulder. "I'm going to run through some coping mechanisms while you prepare dinner."

"You want me to cook? Christ, Erik told you that I can't cook, right?"

Saul laughed. "Yes, he did. He said you were terrible."

I smiled. Hell, I even laughed a little, and it felt really good. "He did not say that."

"He absolutely said exactly that." Saul grinned as he walked up on the veranda. "And you can ask him all about it when you talk to him tonight."

Chapter Eleven
Erik

"You can speak to him in a moment," Saul said. "I just wanted to check in with you first."

I ran my hand through my hair and swallowed. "Uh, sure. Is he... is he okay?"

"He is. He's over the worst of the physical detox."

"Was it awful? I mean, I know it was awful. But did he get through it okay?"

"It wasn't pleasant, but it wasn't the worst I've seen. He's experiencing some residual cravings, but we're working on that."

"Where is he?"

"Right now, he's sitting on the sand at the water's edge. I'm inside. I can keep an eye on him but he can't hear me."

I nodded and all but collapsed onto the sofa. "Well, that's good. I mean, I'm glad to hear he's okay."

"And you? How are you going?"

"Um, I'm okay. Putting a dent in my workload and keeping myself busy. It helps." I swallowed hard.

"Helps to keep your mind off him? Or helps to distance yourself?"

I wasn't sure there was a difference. "Uh, both?"

"Distracting yourself until you speak to him again isn't the same as distancing yourself to establish boundaries."

"Is that what I'm supposed to be doing? Establishing boundaries?"

"Boundaries are a good thing. I thought we'd agreed you would work on keeping some distance."

"I have. A thousand kilometres, to be exact."

The sharpness of my reply had no effect on his. "And how has your week been in his absence?"

"Long. My family are taking it in turns to ensure I'm busy and not alone. And well-fed."

"That's a good thing, yes?"

"Yeah, I guess." I sighed. Being pissy with Saul would get me nowhere. "I miss him though. Today especially. I don't know why. I just missed him today. I thought about him every minute. I haven't not seen or spoken to him for this long. It's weird."

Saul spoke for a while about distance and boundaries and how best to address anxiety over the absence of someone, and for the most part, I listened. Knowing Monroe was so close but still so far—he was right there!— but Saul kept talking as a way to torture me, I'm sure.

"Erik? Did you hear what I just said?" Saul asked.

"Um, sorry. I uh, yeah, no. You lost me and I keep

thinking he's just right there and if you could put him on the phone, that'd be great. Please. I can listen all you like afterwards, but can I just say hi? I just want to hear his voice. That's all."

Saul made a sound that could have almost been a laugh. "Okay, okay. I know when to tap out. I'll put him on." It sounded like Saul was walking and the wind picked up in the phone, and I pictured him crossing the veranda and taking the steps to the beach. "I'll be in touch. Here he is."

The next voice I heard changed something inside me. "Hello?"

The knots of anxiety in my belly unravelled, the hold around my heart loosened, and I could finally breathe. "Hey. It's me."

"Oh my God, Erik. It's so good to hear your voice."

"And yours." I swallowed back my emotions. "How are you holding up?"

"I'm... I'm okay. I'm supposed to be doing this whole honesty thing and not telling people I'm fine when I'm not. So I'm doing okay."

"Honesty is good, right?"

"Apparently." He sighed in my ear. "And what about you? How's life in old Sydney town?"

"Busy. Hectic. I miss you." I hadn't meant to say it like that, but if we were doing the honesty thing. "I thought about you a lot today."

"Just today?"

It sounded like he was smiling, though it was hard to tell. "Every day, but today, a lot, yeah. I've been worried, and not speaking to you for so long is weird." I shook my head at myself. "How's it been? Are you holding up okay?"

"It's been... rough. The first three days were... well, I don't remember a lot, to be honest. My body hates me right now. Headaches are constant. Cravings are too. Saul said it should get better every day."

I stuck my finger and thumb into my eyes to stop the tears. "I'm really proud of you," I whispered. "For making it this far."

"It's not easy," he murmured in return.

"I know it's not, but thank you for being honest with me. I want you to tell me if you're having a shit day."

"Well, I'm having a shit day. Not the shittiest since I've been here, but still pretty shitty. I'm sorry if that's not what you want to hear."

"I want to hear everything. The good, the bad. Every-thing. And to hear that it's not easy but you're still trying, that just makes me prouder of you."

He was quiet a moment. "Are you just gonna keep saying that? That you're proud of me."

"Only until you believe me."

There was silence for a bit, then he laughed. I could just picture him shaking his head. "Saul said I had a bit of a breakthrough today. I dunno what exactly, but he liked something I said."

"I have to talk to him every week too."

"What for?"

"Just to check where I'm up to."

"With what?"

"Do you remember the day I flew with you up to Peregian?" I asked. "He told you I needed to stand on my own two feet for a bit."

"I don't remember much of the last few days in Sydney. It's all kind of a blur, sorry. I remember some stuff... I was a bit of a mess. I still am, I guess." Then he sighed. "And you've always stood on your own two feet. What the hell is he talking about?"

I smiled. "I'm supposed to use the time you're away to be productive and positive. Or some kind of shrink talk. You know how he is."

"Oh yeah. I do. How's that working out for you?"

"Well, Elektra took me to a day spa and we had massages and pedicures."

"Jesus."

I snorted. "Yeah, it was terrible. And by terrible, I mean actually not that bad, and I wouldn't mind doing it again. I carry stress in my shoulders, apparently."

It sounded like he was smiling. "I can't believe you agreed to go."

"It was under duress, and I only went to shut her up."

"What did Saul mean by you standing on your own two feet?" he asked. "Sorry, my brain is like sludge. It's supposed to get better, but man, I can't even seem to think..."

"It's okay. Take your time. Don't rush it, just let it take however long it takes," I murmured. "And Saul said I need to learn how to be me without you. That's all. That I need to spend some time on me."

"Did he?"

"Yeah. Don't be mad. He was probably right. A little bit. So I get to order pizza with olives instead of without. Big deal."

"I fucking hate olives."

I laughed. "I know."

"But if you want pizza with olives, you should have just told me."

"I should have ordered half and half. I think that's the point Saul's trying to make. That we need to be equal, ya know? Fifty, fifty."

"I took more than my half for a long time," he whispered. "And I'm sorry about that."

"It's okay," I said. "Sometimes we need more than half. And you did need more than half, Monroe."

"But I never gave you back your half," he mumbled again. "When I didn't need it anymore, I kept taking."

"I think that's what we're working on now," I said gently.

"Did you say for me not to rush, just let it take however long it takes?"

"I did, yes."

"Don't you want me back sooner?"

"I want you back today. But more than that, I want you back when you're ready and when you're better. I don't want you to rush it and not be ready, know what I mean?"

His words were slow and distant. "I think so."

"You sound tired."

"I am. So tired, E. I've never been this tired. I tried to walk up the beach today, didn't get far."

"Where are you now?"

"Sitting on the beach, watching the waves and the horizon and the birds."

"Sounds nice."

"I wish you were here," he mumbled.

"Me too." God, if only he knew how much. "Me too."

"Saul's coming back now. The fun police have arrived."

"I'll let you go."

"Hey, just one thing," he said. "Did you tell Saul I suck at cooking?"

I snorted. "Yes. Because it's the truth."

"Thanks."

"You're welcome."

"He wants his phone back."

"I'll talk to you again real soon, okay?"

"Yeah."

"You got this, Monroe. You're stronger than you think."

He didn't say anything.

"I love you," I said, my heart thumping. He didn't say anything to that either. The phone clicked off in my ear and it took a second for my heart to calm down. I told myself he didn't need to say it back to me. He didn't need to reply at all if he wasn't comfortable. He just needed to hear it. He needed to know he was loved, nothing more, nothing less.

I made a promise with myself, right then and there, that I'd keep telling him until he believed me.

SYDNEY SUNDAY, PAGE 2

Erik Keston has been seen around Sydney without his usual best friend and sidekick, Monroe Wellman. Last week, Erik was spotted escorting Monroe Wellman to an undisclosed location with private clinician to the stars, Saul Cabello. After recent alcohol-related incidents, it is believed Wellman is undergoing rehab. Erik Keston, seen here with his sister, Elektra, leaving Tetsuya's exclusive restaurant. Erik was wearing a blue Armani suit from their newest summer collection.

Elektra slid her iPad across my desk and raised her eyebrow at me. "I barely get a mention."

I rolled my eyes. "I wish they'd leave me the fuck alone."

"I'm just an accessory of yours, apparently."

I snorted at that. "Who cares what they think? It's a trash tabloid. That's two days old."

She slumped into a chair across from me. "And it was a business lunch. They make it sound like we were out having a good time because Monroe's not here." She sighed. "I know, I know, it's just trash and I shouldn't let it bother me."

I pushed her iPad back to her. "You really shouldn't. It'll give you wrinkles and grey hair."

She feigned a gasp. "I'm going to pretend you didn't say that." She studied me for a moment. "Did you speak to Monroe last night?"

"No, why?"

"You're smiling."

My smile widened. "I'll speak to him tonight."

Elektra smiled back at me. "You were happier after you spoke to him last week. You're almost buzzing from just the idea of speaking to him today."

"I know. And I shouldn't be. I mean," I said, running my hand through my hair. "Of course I should be happy that he's okay, but my happiness shouldn't be hinged on whether I speak to him or not."

"Is that what Saul said?"

"No, but I know he will."

"You know what I think? And I'm not a shrink like Saul, so maybe I don't know what the hell I'm talking about, but I think you need to take happiness wherever you can find it."

I gave a nod. "You'd think so."

The truth was I was happier just thinking about speaking to him. Talking to Monroe on the phone last week had given me a boost. Maybe Saul would call that a fix. But either way, I felt better knowing he was okay and that he was through the worst of it. He'd gotten through the physical detox. I had to believe he was going to be okay.

He sounded okay last week. And he sounded happy to speak to me. Quieter and more subdued than normal, but that was to be expected. I mean, I could hardly blame him. He'd just been through hell and that was bound to have taken its toll. I wasn't downplaying or cheapening how hard it must have been for him. I'd read all sorts of things online about what he would have been going through this week, and if the steps program was on track, he'd have been working on building and maintaining motivation and coping with urges.

It didn't sound like fun, but maybe the idea of speaking to me was a bright spot in what might have been a dark week.

Only it wasn't.

Saul phoned at the same time he did last week, and I was so anxious to speak to Monroe, I almost dropped my phone. Thankfully, I managed to press Answer instead of Decline. "Hello?"

"Erik," Saul said calmly. "How's your week been?"

"Okay. Pretty good. Busy. How's Monroe?"

"He's fine," he answered, his voice annoyingly monotone. "I want to talk about you first."

Again, I was so close to Monroe yet impossibly far.

"I've been good," I prompted. "Productive. I've been working on a pretty big contract that I'm excited about. I've been eating, thanks to my parents who haven't stopped trying to feed me."

"That's good, Erik," Saul said, but then he paused,

like it wasn't good at all. "I'd like to ask you some questions though, if that's all right with you."

I was pretty sure I didn't have much choice. "Uh, sure."

And then he wanted to know all sorts of things like what techniques I was using to combat any urges I had to call Monroe, speak to Monroe, think of Monroe. To which my answer was that I didn't have much choice. I was going cold turkey, like Monroe was.

Which I think was Saul's point, but whatever. I just wanted to speak to Monroe.

But then he began talking about shifting focus and opening new circles and trying new things like hobbies. "A hobby?" I asked, incredulously. "Like what? Knitting? Ice skating?"

"If they are what takes your interest, then yes. Something you've always wanted to do. A cooking class, painting, an art class."

"Why would I want to do those things?"

"To spark other interests. To occupy your time. To widen your social circles."

"My social circles are just fine, thanks."

"I've never heard you mention any other friends..."

"I've never heard you mention any friends at all, but that doesn't mean I assume you don't have any." I didn't have time for this psyched-up bullshit. "Are we done? I'd like to speak to Monroe now, thanks."

Silence.

"Saul?"

"Yes, look, Erik, Monroe hasn't had a good week."

Monroe hasn't had a good week. I repeated that over in my head. "What... what does that mean?"

"It means he's not in a good place right now."

I couldn't get the dots to connect in my head. "Wh-what does that mean?"

"He's struggled with his addiction this week. The first week went rather well, and I'd hoped we'd make some strides this week, but he's had a difficult few days."

My stomach twisted. "Is he... is he okay?"

"He still isn't sleeping very well, and although his energy is increasing, his appetite is almost nil. Those are all to be expected, to some degree. He's tried swimming laps but he doesn't have the energy. He's... distant and angry. I've been getting him to talk about his parents and he's very closed off."

Oh God. Just hearing this made my heart ache. And I went from pissy to begging. "Can I speak to him? Please?"

"I would very much like you to," Saul replied. "But he's refusing."

Refusing... "He doesn't want to speak to me?"

"No, I'm afraid not. He doesn't want to speak to anyone."

"Where is he?"

"Sitting out on the beach, watching the horizon. It's where he goes to get away from me."

My chest felt far too tight. "Can you just try? Please? Just tell him it's me. Please."

"I'll try, but his language was fairly colourful when I told him I was calling you."

I slumped back in my chair with my hand to my heart. I felt so helpless, being so far away. And he didn't want to speak to me. I hadn't expected that, and it made me feel sick. Heartsick.

Through the phone, I could hear the wind as though Saul had just stepped out onto the veranda and then as he walked through sand. I could picture the scene in my head: Monroe sitting there, looking out to sea, and Saul approaching him.

"Monroe," Saul said. "Erik wishes to speak to you."

There was mumbling, then I heard Monroe shout, very clearly. "I told you before, I don't want to speak to him! I wouldn't be in this fucking hell-hole if it weren't for him. If he'd just left me the fuck alone. Tell him to leave me the fucking hell alone! I won't speak to him, not now, not ever!"

Saul mumbled something, then there was silence. But all I could hear on repeat in my mind.

I wouldn't be in this fucking hell-hole if it weren't for him. If he'd just left me the fuck alone. Tell him to leave me the fucking hell alone! I won't speak to him.

Not now.

Not ever...

"I'm sorry, Erik," Saul said.

I nodded, which was useless because he couldn't see. But I couldn't speak.

"Tomorrow will be a better day," Saul said. "And I'll have him call you. He can apologise."

I nodded again.

"He doesn't mean what he says. He's angry at the world, not at you."

My eyes burned and my heart hurt. I still couldn't get words out. My lungs, my voice wouldn't work.

"Erik..."

"I have to go," I pushed out, just a broken whisper. I clicked off the call and tried to breathe.

Then Elektra was there, sitting in front of me. I hadn't heard her come home. "E, what's wrong?"

"Monroe doesn't want to speak to me," I answered. Saying it out loud made it sound so stupid, like I was a teenager with a crush. "He shut me out."

"Oh no, that's not true," she replied. "He's just going through something right now, that's all."

I laughed at myself, despite my tears, for being so stupid and childish and selfish. "I was so excited to talk to him. All I wanted this week was to speak to him. But he... said it was my fault he's in hell right now."

Elektra reached over and put her hand on my knee. "It's not your fault."

"Well, it kind of is," I said, with a rush of more tears. "I told him if he didn't go with Saul, I wouldn't be around to watch."

Elektra shook her head. "What did Saul say?"

"That he'd call me tomorrow."

She nodded. "He'll come around. Just you watch."

EXCEPT HE DIDN'T. Not the next day, or the day after that. And my days seemed to pass in a blur of work, meetings, emails, and phone calls, while dragging on and on, each minute an hour, each hour a day.

And by the end of the third day, it dawned on me.

Saul was right.

What he'd said made sense, because he knew. He knew Monroe was severing ties and Saul was trying to let me down gently. Take up a hobby. Meet new people. Widen your social circle.

He knew...

He'd said it from the very beginning. I needed to separate myself from Monroe. I had no identity without him. Everything I did revolved around him.

Because that's what happens when you're hopelessly in love with someone.

And now that I no longer had Monroe, I was left with nothing but a void. A negative space.

A negative space where my heart used to be.

Where Monroe used to be.

And now I needed to reshape my life and try to move forward.

Move on.

Without him.

And I didn't know how to do that. Because Saul was right all along. I had no clue who Erik Keston was without Monroe Wellman. And I wasn't the one moving on. I was being left behind.

And that was so much worse.

Chapter Twelve
Monroe

"Elektra Keston calling for Saul Cabello, please."

I blinked.

Saul had left the phone on the kitchen bench for a second while he went to the bathroom. But it rang and the number was private, and I wasn't going to answer it. But I did.

"Elektra?"

"Monroe? Is that you?" she said.

I smiled at the sound of her voice. It sounded like she was in her car. "Yeah. It's me."

"Well, you can suck a bag of dicks, Monroe. Put Saul on the phone."

I blinked again, this time in shock.

"What?"

"You heard. Until you can pull your head out of your arse and until you start treating my brother with the respect he deserves, you can suck a bag of dicks. All of them. Every single last one." She paused. "Please put Saul on the phone, or I'll hang up."

I was stunned into silence. I'd known Elektra for years and I'd heard her business tone before. But she'd never used it at me before. "Is Erik—"

"Who is it?" Saul asked. He didn't look too pleased that I'd answered his phone.

"Um, it rang and I answered it without thinking..." I held the phone out for him. "It's Elektra. Erik's sister. She won't speak to me."

Saul took the phone. "Hello, Elektra. ... Yes, of course, it's fine. ... Oh, I see." There was a longer pause. I couldn't hear what she was saying, but Saul nodded a few times, then he made eye contact with me and I had a sinking feeling in my gut.

Something was wrong.

"Yes, I will," Saul said. "I'll call him. Thank you for letting me know." Elektra said something else and Saul almost smiled. "I will. Bye for now." Saul disconnected the call and put the phone back on the kitchen bench.

"What's wrong? Is Erik okay?" My anxiety was rising way too fast. "Elektra wouldn't have called if something wasn't wrong. She wouldn't speak to me. She told me to go suck a bag of dicks and that she wouldn't speak to me until I treated Erik with the respect he deserves. But she wouldn't tell me what was wrong. Saul, please—"

Saul put his hand on my arm. "Monroe, breathe. In." He waited for me to inhale. "And out. Nice and slow."

I tried the breathing techniques we'd been working

on. Which were all fucking stupid. "What's wrong with Erik?"

"I'll tell you when you've calmed down," he said. "Breathe in."

I hated that my body did what he said.

"That's it. Nice and slow."

My heart rate had eased back a notch or two. "Is he okay?"

Saul nodded. "Elektra is concerned, that's all. Erik's fine," he added, giving me a serious look. "Physically, he's fine."

"Physically? What happened?" I asked, then from Saul's narrowed eyes, I remembered my breathing. He gave a nod, happy that I'd caught and corrected myself. "Was he in an accident or something? Is his family okay?"

Saul gave me a genuine smile. "No, there was no accident. Erik hasn't had a great week and Elektra thought perhaps I should call him."

I was about to ask why, what happened, but then I remembered.

Me. I happened. "Oh."

Saul sighed. "Can we sit and chat for a moment. I said I'd call Erik, so it won't be a long session or anything."

Thank God. Saul's idea of a long, intense session was more exhausting than a cardio workout at the gym.

We sat on the sofa, and Saul did that thing where he made full eye contact. I was used to it now, but it was still a little weird. And it also meant there was a hard truth coming my way. "In the last three years, even longer, but in particular since the death of your parents, Erik has been focused on you. Every spare ounce of his time, energy, and focus has been solely on you."

"He's been there for me," I said weakly.

"He's been there too much for you," Saul said simply. "It's human nature to want to help those we care for, and Erik is no exception. Though perhaps he cared for you too much, meaning he fixed your mistakes, he cleaned up after you, he made excuses for you."

"He was just trying to help."

Saul nodded. "He was, yes. And after three years of holding you together, now that he no longer has you, he's struggling. And, in the name of transparency and taking responsibility for your own behaviour, I would think you telling him the other day that it was his fault you were here and you never wanted to see him again hurt him, very much."

Frowning, I nodded. "I didn't mean that."

"I told him you didn't."

"And?"

"He was too upset to answer."

My frown deepened, as did my anxiety and the strange pain in my heart. "I need to apologise."

Saul smiled. "Yes, you do. I'll speak to him first. Though he may decide not to speak to either of us."

Jesus. "What if he...? What if he doesn't...? What if he says...?"

"Monroe, breathe." Saul's firm tone snapped at me and I let out a gasp. I took a deep breath in, and once Saul was happy, he continued. "If he chooses a different path, then we'll accept his decision and we'll move on."

I shook my head. "I can't... I need him. I know that sounds weird, and I don't even get it. But no one gets me like he does. No one understands like he does."

Saul patted my knee. "We'll talk more on this, but I should call him now."

"Can I speak to him after?"

Saul stood and gave me a nod. "If he agrees."

Saul took his phone and disappeared down the hall, and I sat there in the fading sunlight, the far cry of seagulls over the ocean and the crash of the waves, with my darkening thoughts and pounding heart.

What if Erik never wanted to speak to me again, if he said we were through and that I was no good for him? I had taken him for granted, I knew that. And I had abused his kindness because I'd known he'd take whatever I could throw at him.

But not anymore.

He must have been bad if Elektra needed to call... Christ. What had I done?

I'd told him I never wanted to speak to him again. But if he'd said that to me...?

I concentrated on my breathing. Deep inhale, slow exhale. I made fists. I let them out. I rolled my neck, letting the tension go. "I can do this," I whispered. "I am stronger; I am better. I am in control."

Stupid techniques that Saul had made me do every day. Stupid breathing and stupid mantras. Stupid every-fucking-thing.

Just one drink would fix it.

Just one drink would fix everything.

I'd be better if I had just one drink...

And that hit me like a bucket of ice water.

The reality was that the urges would never go away. The craving for a drink would never be far away, always at the back of my mind, on the tip of my tongue.

And in my mind, I was already mentally rummaging through the house for a hidden stash. But there wasn't any. Saul had made sure of that. Though there might have been some rubbing alcohol swabs under the sink. Mrs Keston had a box of them... I remembered when we'd come here and Erik had sliced his finger on a rusty fishing hook and he'd cried out when she'd swabbed it because it had alcohol in it and it had stung, and she'd told him to stop being a baby...

I was looking under the kitchen sink before I even realised I'd gotten off the couch. Christ. I couldn't even remember moving. I had no recollection of the conscious thought to make myself get up and look. Somewhere in my brain thought there was a chance at getting alcohol and my body moved without my permission...

And that was fucking scary as hell.

I closed the kitchen cupboards slowly and dropped my head.

"Everything okay?" Saul asked from across the room.

I nodded, then shook my head. "No."

Saul looked to the phone in his hand and then to me. "Erik wants to speak to you. Are you up for it?"

Again, my body moved without me thinking about it,

and I was halfway across the room before I nodded. "Yes."

Saul looked doubtful and concerned, and I knew I'd have to own up to what I'd just done. But first, Erik. I went to the couch and put the phone to my ear. "Erik?"

"Hey," he replied.

The sound of his voice, the sound of his wariness, of his pain, brought instant tears to my eyes. "I'm really sorry," I said, trying not to cry. "About the other day. I had a really bad day and I know that's no excuse. I shouldn't have taken it out on you. I don't blame you, for anything. Everything that's led me to this point is my doing, no one else's. And of course I want to speak to you. All the time. Every day. I'm sorry I said what I said. I hate myself for hurting you. I'm sorry, E. I really am."

He breathed like it could've been a laugh or a sob. "I miss you."

More tears burned my eyes and spilled down my cheeks. "Oh, fucking hell, I really miss you too."

"I've been miserable," he said.

"Me too."

"It's so good to hear your voice," he whispered. "I thought I was going to kill Elektra for calling Saul, but now I'm not so sure."

"She told me to eat a bag of dicks."

He let out a teary laugh. "Did she?"

"I deserved it. She told me I need to treat you with more respect and she's right. I'm so sorry I hurt you, Erik. I really am."

"I know. And I accept your apology."

The weight that his acceptance lifted from me was enormous. "Thank you." I had no idea how much I needed to hear that. "Hug her for me, please."

"I will." We both took a moment to breathe. "How's life without a phone?"

"Awful. Well, not being able to call when I want sucks, but being disconnected from the world isn't so bad."

"I bet."

But it wasn't just my phone, and being cut off from everything... And fresh tears welled in my eyes. "It's not easy, E." I scrubbed at my face. "This whole thing, everything is so fucking hard. I thought I was doing okay, but I still think about it. Drinking. I still think about it. I still want it, and if I was at home, I would've found something to drink by now. So as much as I don't want to be here, away from you, I know I need to be. I need to get better."

He let out a shaky breath. "I know."

"Can you talk to me?"

"About what?"

"Everything. Anything. What you've been doing. Work, home. It doesn't matter." I wiped my face and curled up on the couch with the phone still pressed to my ear. I knew that Saul could and more than likely was listening to every word, but I didn't care. This right here, Erik, was more important. "I just want to hear your voice."

"Well, I thought I was doing okay too. I mean, work's been busy and keeping me distracted. Been working a lot, actually. It helps to keep my mind ticking over, ya know?

Because when I stop, that's when my mind takes me to you. And I get wondering how you're going, what you're up to, how much I miss seeing your stupid face."

That made me laugh despite the tears. "Thanks."

"You're welcome. I started some new projects at work, so they are taking up most of my time. Which is a good thing, I guess. I'm not sure Mum's convinced, but I'm crunching some numbers and statistics. You know how she is. A full analysis report or nothing."

"Yeah."

"And Elektra's been great. She's been helping me with some market research. I think Mum might have paired her with me to keep an eye on me, but now Elektra is helping me, so Mum's plan might have backfired because she knows once we get set on something, we very rarely let it go."

"Yeah, I know."

He kind of laughed. "Elektra took me out to the summer regatta at Botany, and there was a bunch of guys from college."

Oh.

"You remember Sterling and Busby?"

I remembered Sterling. He rowed with Erik, and I never much cared for how he watched Erik, how he laughed a little too loud at his jokes, or how he tried too hard to get close to him. "Yeah. I remember."

Erik snorted. "Well, they're even bigger wankers now than when they were in school. Fucking tossers, the both of them. And if Saul suggests I broaden my social circles with them, he can think again. I'd really rather not."

I couldn't help but laugh. So very relieved as well. "Not a fan, I take it."

"No. I'll stick with work. It's what I know, and it's not fake. The regatta was good though. Probably not enough to make me miss rowing enough to start again. Saul wanted me to take up a hobby in case I got bored or lonely, and just between you and me, I considered it. I weighed up my options on which I would hate the least. So out of rowing, which was a nope, cooking, knitting, and the model train making club that meets every second Thursday, I can state with unequivocal certainty that I would hate them all equally. So if I have to either sit at home and wallow in my misery or bury myself in work, I'll take work."

I barked out I laugh. "Model train making. I didn't even know that was a thing."

"Neither did I. There is one for boats as well. It was all quite depressing, actually. And that was as far as the getting-a-hobby idea went. Don't tell Saul. I'd rather sit at home wallowing in my misery than take up cross-stitching. And anyway, I'm a Keston. We don't do hobbies. We work. Working is my hobby. Well, spending time with you was my main hobby, but now that's on hold for a bit, so I'll just work some more."

"I was your hobby?"

"In a good way. And I have to be honest, when you said you didn't want to speak to me ever again, I did wonder what I'd do with my life. Isn't that weird? I couldn't picture my life without you in it. I mean, if you truly do never want to speak to me again, I'd cope, I guess. But it was strange. When I picture myself, my life, and my future, you're a part of it. As much as I am. I really couldn't separate us in my head... And maybe that's what Saul means. Maybe that is a problem, I don't know. And I get that what you're going through right now is infinitely more horrible than I could even imagine, but I'm supposed to be trying to figure out how to stand on my own two feet. And you're supposed to be trying to figure out how to stand on your own two feet. I can probably see why Saul is insisting we do this. We would both be stronger; I get that. But I don't want to not have you in my life, so I guess what I'm saying is that I'll take any part of you I can get. And maybe that's not a healthy attitude to have, but when I was faced with not having any part of you at all, I told myself it was what you wanted and therefore must have been better for you. And I only want what's best for you, but at some point I also need what's best for me..."

"What are you saying?"

"That I can have both. Or more to the point, that it's the same thing. Right now, what's best for you is what's best for me, and vice versa. You want what's best for me, I know you do."

"Of course I do. I just..."

"You just what?"

"I'm just not sure what that is."

"The best thing for me right now is you getting better. Right now, I want you to be healthy and happy. That's it. Nothing else." He swallowed hard. "Then maybe later we can re-evaluate. Or *I* can, re-evaluate, that is. It's going to depend on what your goals are, where you want to be, and how you want to live. Then I will know where I'm at. But don't go getting a fat head. My entire happiness and existence doesn't revolve around you; it just includes you. When I said I wasn't going anywhere, I meant it."

I nodded, a little teary again. "Thank you."

"Unless you decide you want to live out your days in a Tibetan monastery without coffee or Wi-Fi. Then you're on your own. I'm not that invested."

I snorted out a laugh and wiped my face with the back of my hand. "I'll keep that in mind."

"I just need you to concentrate on getting better."

"Okay."

"So stop being stubborn. And stop fighting Saul."

"I will."

"And one more thing."

"What's that?"

"Please don't decide you want to live out your days in a Tibetan monastery without coffee and Wi-Fi."

I laughed again. "Thank you. For talking to me. I feel better."

"Thank you for deciding to talk to me again. I almost took up model train making because of you."

I found myself smiling. "I really am sorry I acted like such a prat. I was horrible."

"You were. But you're forgiven. Just don't do it again."

"I won't. Well, I'll no doubt have bad days again, but I'll aim my pissy attitude somewhere else."

"I hear train modelling is relaxing. I'll send Saul a link."

"Don't you dare. He already makes me cook."

"Oh Christ."

"Shut up. I'm not that bad."

"I'll believe that when I see it."

"And he's making me do woodwork."

"Woodwork? That's not a euphemism, is it?"

I snorted. "No. Actual wood. Driftwood, to be exact." I looked up and found Saul in the kitchen, smiling at me.

"And he's enjoying it," Saul said loud enough for Erik to hear.

I rolled my eyes. "Well, it was either that or yoga."

"Driftwood?"

"Yeah, um... it sounds kinda lame."

"No it doesn't. It sounds great. You'll have to show me what you're doing. Tell Saul to take a photo and send it to me."

His immediate acceptance of anything I did felt like a comforting hug. He'd never take the piss out of me... well, apart from the cooking thing. "It's not so bad. It feels good to be doing something with my hands, anyway. Everything else is..." I groaned. "Mental. Emotional. It's... exhausting."

"You're doing great."

"I wish you were here."

"Me too." He was quiet for a while. We both were. "It's been so good to talk to you. You have no idea."

I almost laughed at that. "Uh, yes I do. Talking to you today..." And then there were tears. I shook my head and wiped my face. "Jesus. I'm a freaking basket case."

"Oh, Monroe."

"I just miss you. And I'm sorry I hurt you."

"Just think, every day you get through is a day closer to me visiting, okay?"

"Keep my eye on the prize."

"Exactly."

"Tell Elektra I'm sorry, and I'm working on treating you better."

"You have to treat yourself better first."

"I'm working on that too."

"I know you are."

Saul came and sat on the couch beside me, and I assumed my time on his phone was up. "Hey, I gotta go."

"Okay. I'm proud of you, Monroe," Erik said softly. "I love you."

I shook my head, blinking away more tears. "I'm not sure I deserve that."

"Yes, you do. We'll talk again soon, okay?"

"'Kay."

Erik hung up and I handed Saul back his phone. Then I shook my head again and tried to get a handle on my emotions. Stupid fucking tears.

"You okay?" Saul asked.

I nodded but then shook my head. "Not really. I just need a minute, okay?"

Saul nodded, and I walked out the back to the beach and sat my arse in the sand. I concentrated on my breathing, and I thought all the positive thoughts that

Saul had taught me while the pulse of the ocean soothed my mind.

Erik was right; I needed to get myself better first. Erik was right about everything. I should have never tried to do this without him. And I could tell myself that maybe he would be better off without me, but the truth was he was miserable. And I was miserable. I didn't know how to begin to describe what we had. It was more than a friendship; it was more than brothers. We were closer. Inexplicably entwined. And I knew I had to get better for myself —I knew that, Saul had told me that a hundred times— but I had to do it for Erik too.

He was in this with me, so I needed to be the best version of myself I could be.

For him. For me. For us.

I must have sat out there long enough, because Saul sat down beside me. "How are you feeling?"

"To be honest, I'm not sure."

"List all the words for me. A jumble of everything you're feeling right now."

"Scared. Lonely. Sad." I took a breath. In and out. "Determined."

"Determined for what?"

"To get better."

"For who?"

"For me." We both knew that was the answer he wanted to hear.

"And for Erik," Saul added.

I nodded, quickly sparing Saul a glance before looking back out to sea. "For Erik. And I know what you're going to say. You're going to tell me I can't do this for him. I can't hinge my happiness on someone else. But it's different with him."

"How?"

I shrugged because I didn't know. "I can't explain it. He's my best friend; he's my family. But he's more than that. And you'll probably say this is bullshit, but Erik and I are... We're like one unit. I don't know how else to describe it. He's miserable without me. I'm miserable without him. When we're in the same room, we don't even have to speak. Just having him around is like being able to breathe."

Saul nodded slowly. "I wouldn't say that's bullshit."

I looked at him then. "You wouldn't?"

Saul gave me a smile. "No, Monroe. I wouldn't. Because I know exactly how you feel."

"You do?"

He laughed quietly. "Everything you just described is how I feel about my wife."

I wasn't sure I understood. I mean, I knew he was married. He'd told me about his wife a few times... but that made no sense in comparison to Erik. "What?"

Saul turned his smile to the water and took a deep breath of ocean air. "Monroe, do you believe in soulmates?"

Soulmates? "Um, I'm not sure. I haven't really thought about it... What's that got to do with me?"

Saul gave me a thoughtful look, then shook his head like he couldn't believe it. "It seems we have a lot of work to do."

"I know. And I'm ready. I'm done fighting it. I need to get better."

"Good. I'm glad to hear that."

"I wanted a drink before," I blurted out. "When you were talking to Erik. I kinda freaked out because you said he might not want to speak to me ever again, after the way I treated him. And I wouldn't blame him, just so you know. But the idea of not having him in my life freaked me the fuck out, and I went looking for something to drink without even thinking about it. I didn't even realise I'd moved until I was looking under the kitchen sink. Is that normal? Not even knowing I'd got up and was searching for alcohol? Because if I'd found some, I would have drunk it before I knew what I was doing."

Saul's expression was a little concerned but also a little happy?

"What are you smiling for?" I asked. "I just told you I wanted to drink. I had every intention of ripping into alcohol swabs, of all the fucking things, without making a conscious decision to do it. That's hardly funny."

"No, it's not. But you admitted it. You owned it, and your reaction tells me that you've come further than you think. That's progress, Monroe."

"It certainly doesn't feel like it."

"The urges will get easier," he said casually. "You can't ignore them and you can't pretend they don't happen. You need to own them, admit and talk about them. It will help you get through them. The urge to drink will lessen, but it's not likely to ever go away, but you'll learn how to recognise the impulse and how to cope."

I nodded, more determined now. "Okay."

He studied me for a bit. "Can I ask you something?"

Shit. This never ended well. "Yeah?"

"What does love mean to you?"

"Love?" I frowned and watched a wave crash against the shore. "I'm not sure I know."

"Your parents loved you."

I shot him a look. "Sure. Until they didn't."

"Until you came out as gay."

"Until I showed them the real me."

"Do you think perhaps they would have come around? That if they'd had more time, they would have accepted your sexuality?"

"We'll never know," I answered. "Anything I say is conjecture. Or wishful thinking. And completely pointless."

"Perhaps," he mused. "But they didn't ask you to move out or to choose a different path, did they?"

I shook my head. "No."

"So perhaps they never stopped loving you. Perhaps the wall between you was your own doing?"

I clenched my jaw and stared at the horizon.

Saul kept pushing. "If they were here right now and you could tell them one thing, what would it be?"

"I don't know."

"Just give me a jumble of words."

Christ. Him and his jumble of words...

"Sorry," I whispered. "I'd tell them I'm sorry."

"And? What other words do you feel?"

"Regret. Sorry. Guilt. Longing. Want. Need." I shrugged. "Wishful."

Saul nodded slowly, but then he frowned. "Not love? You wouldn't tell them you loved them?"

"We... we didn't talk about that. We weren't like Erik's family. They tell each other all the time, like they're the freaking Brady Bunch or something."

He almost smiled. "You said the first thing you'd tell them was that you were sorry. What are you sorry for?"

"That they're gone. That I never got to say goodbye. That I couldn't be what they wanted. That I fucked up. I'm supposed to be running the business and I'm not. That they left it all to me and I failed. That I'm not the son they wanted. I can't be the son they wanted."

"If they were still alive would you be any different? Would you hide your sexuality?"

I looked at him and met his gaze. "No."

That made him smile. "Good. Reconciling with deceased loved ones is never easy. The only way for you to get closure is from acceptance, in here"—he put his hand to his chest— "and letting go of what we can't change."

"Easier said than done."

"Very much so." He looked out over the ocean for a while. "Tell me, if Erik was here right now, what would you tell him?"

"That I'm sorry for being an arse the other day. I'm sorry for hurting him. And I'm sorry for the last three years. He's pretty much been my babysitter, and that wasn't fair."

"And you can't change those three years, can you?"

"No."

"So how do you fix it?"

"By getting better. By being better."

"And what words would you use to describe your relationship with him?"

"Solid."

"How do you feel about him?"

"What do you mean?"

"What do you feel for Erik, in here?" He put his hand to his heart again. "One word."

I looked from him to the ocean again and shook my head. "I... I don't know."

Saul was quiet for a moment. "Okay. Just think about it for me. I think you've had enough questions for now. You did really well, and thank you for being honest with me."

I nodded without looking at him.

"I just want to leave one more thing with you before I go and make us a quick dinner," he said. "I don't want you to answer me right now. I want you to think about it."

I nodded, waiting... dreading...

"Why do you think you don't deserve love?"

Chapter Thirteen
Erik

"Excellent. I'll hand-deliver the contract myself if I have to," I said. The call wrapped up, I hung up the receiver, and I gave my mother a smile across the desk. She'd listened to the conversation but had let me lead. "That's a helluva coincidence."

"Erik," she replied tentatively. "We can have it couriered."

"Where's the Keston personal touch in sending a courier? You know this client. Hand delivering the paperwork with a bottle of '64 vintage Penfolds and a Montblanc pen will ensure he thinks of us the next time he wants to buy a ten-million-dollar house or two."

She gave me a look I knew well. I played the right hand, but she saw straight through me regardless. "Just curious. If the house he'd just bought was in, say Melbourne, instead of the Sunshine Coast, would you still be so eager to hand deliver the paperwork?"

I tried not to smile. "Of course I would. But it's a crazy coincidence that Monroe's just down the road…"

Mum sighed. "Erik, you know you're not supposed to visit."

"I'll be in the area. For work."

"I could send Elektra instead of you."

"You wouldn't dare!"

"He was better this week, yes?"

I nodded. "Yep. He's had a much better week." It'd been a week since his meltdown over the phone and refusal to speak to me, and I'd spoken to him twice since then. First time when I called Saul and Monroe apologised, and then again just last night. He'd had some breakthroughs with Saul during the week, and together they thought it would be a great idea for him to share his milestones. It wasn't our agreed day for calls, so when Saul's number flashed on my screen, I immediately thought something was wrong, but to hear Monroe's voice was so unexpected and such a relief. He sounded happier, and if anything, it had left me more determined to see him.

The corner of Mum's lips twitched. "There are conditions. If I say yes," she stated. "Elektra will be going with you. And you'll be speaking to Saul first. If he vetoes you, the answer is no."

"Deal," I said, clearing the first hurdle. Now I just needed to clear the hurdle that was Saul.

"Honey, I don't want you to get your hopes up."

I sighed. "I know, I know."

She out-sighed me. "But it's too late for that, isn't it?"

"Yeah."

My mother studied me for a long moment. "If Saul says yes," she began.

"Yes?"

"I take it you'll be leaving first thing?"

"Yep."

Her eyes softened. "Then give him our love."

I grinned. "I will."

As soon as she left my office, I pulled my phone out and sent a text to Saul first. *Do you have a moment? Can I call?*

His reply came through a moment later. *Sure.*

I realised then he might have thought I needed to speak to him as a therapist, but it was too late now. I hit Call. "Saul?"

"Erik, is everything okay?"

"Yeah, yeah. I should have said that in my text, sorry. It's not an emergency or anything. Well, it kind of is."

"Okay," he answered cautiously. "You sound happy. Should I be worried?"

I laughed. "Um, that depends. I have the opportunity to fly into Maroochydore tomorrow morning. I have a business meeting first thing in Noosa. I was hoping I could see him."

Silence.

I swear to God, if he says no, I'm going to lose my shit. "Saul? Did you hear what I said?"

"Yes, yes, I heard."

"I know it's not what we discussed. And it's like a week or so earlier than you first suggested. But I'll be up there, just twenty minutes up the road. And he's had such a good week, right? And I haven't seen him in almost a month... I won't stay the night, if you don't think I should. I just thought a visit would be nice, ya know?"

More silence.

"Saul?"

"You know, Erik. I think that sounds like a great idea."

Now the silence was mine. "You what?"

He laughed. "I said I think that's a great idea. He could do with the boost, and I was going to talk about possible visits next week anyway."

"You said yes..."

He laughed again. "I did. This is tomorrow, right? Is that what you said?"

"Yes! I have a meeting in Noosa at nine. It won't take long. I should be at the beach house around ten-ish? Does that sound okay?"

"It does, though I won't tell him until tomorrow, after breakfast."

I was grinning. "I'll bring us some coffees."

"I'm not opposed to you staying overnight," Saul said. "Though I think separate rooms would be best. Monroe doesn't need any... thing complicating his recovery."

I snorted. "Um, what?"

"Separate rooms," he began.

"Yeah, I got that part."

"Emotional complications could be a setback, Erik—"

"Uh, I'm not, we're not... we don't... Separate rooms is

fine." I let out a bit of a laugh. "Elektra will be with me. My mother insists I bring supervision."

Saul laughed. "Great minds, I see. Then I shall plan a dinner for the four of us."

It seriously felt like I was about to burst. "Perfect. That's perfect. I can't wait."

He gave me a few details, and no sooner had I ended the call, my mother appeared in my doorway. She took one look at me and smiled. "I take it his answer was a yes."

"He thought it was a great idea. I just need to confirm with him when my plane arrives. He won't tell Monroe I'm coming until he knows for sure. In case he tells him and he'd be all excited, and then if something came up and I couldn't go, he'd be devastated and that'd be a bit of a setback. Apparently." I was still grinning. "I can't believe he agreed."

"He must be pleased with Monroe's progress."

I nodded quickly. "Yeah, I think so. Maybe he can come home sooner than we first thought."

Mum put her hand up. "Slow down, Erik. One step at a time. You can't rush him."

"I know," I replied. And I *did* know. In my head, I knew that all too well. But there was no telling that to my heart.

I was pretty much useless for the rest of the day.

And Mum was still trying to caution me over an early breakfast the next day. She asked me if I had the paperwork I was supposed to deliver, and short of actually nailing it to my hand, I told her for the fiftieth time, yes, of course I did. And waiting for Elektra took forever. "We're going to be late!"

She came out wheeling her small carry-on. "I'm ten minutes early!"

"Yeah, but still," I said, taking her bag for her and shoving it in the car.

She looked at me. Like, really looked at me. "God, Erik. Did you sleep at all? The bags under your eyes..."

"Not really."

"I can tell. And if you get arrested for impersonating a panda bear, I'll disown you."

"Thanks."

"And there'd better be coffee in my future."

"Promise."

She opened the passenger door to my car. "Erik?"

"Yeah?"

"Get in the car."

"Oh!" I dashed to the driver's side and got in. I managed not to speed too much on the way to the airport, spoke briefly to Peter before boarding, and tried to do some calm breathing for the hour we were in the air. Elektra managed to close off two portfolios in her hour of uninterrupted flying-office time while I managed to chew all ten nails down to the quick.

We landed, and after an eternity, we got the keys to the rental car. Elektra was faster than me and snatched them. "I don't think so, Erik. You're not driving in the state you're in. I'm not interested in breaking the land-speed record today, thanks."

She was probably right, but I grumped at her anyway.

I sent a quick message to Saul. *Arrived. We'll see you around ten.*

The drive to Noosa took forever. And the meeting with our client did too. We gave him the gifts and he signed the contracts happily, and then he decided he wanted to chat about the weather and tide charts and buying boats, and before I could start foaming at the mouth, Elektra politely made our excuses to leave.

She shoved me in the direction of a café and told me she'd bring the car around, and after waiting for all eternity for the barista to make four coffees—did it really have to take that long to steam the milk?—I was finally, finally in the car and on our way to Peregian Beach.

"I know Mum hasn't stopped lecturing you," Elektra said as she drove. "But I just want to add something."

"I know what you're about to say," I grumbled. "Don't rush him, don't pressure him, don't expect anything, don't be upset if he's out of sorts, different, stand-offish. It's nothing personal, it's part of the process. Mum hasn't stopped."

Elektra smiled. "I was just going to say I know this is important to you. I know you miss him. I just don't want to see you get hurt."

"I know. And thank you."

"Just... when you walk in, see how he reacts first. If he's stand-offish, then read that as his need for space."

As much as what she said annoyed me, I knew she was right. I had to read his cues and let him set the rules.

We pulled up at the house and Elektra put her hands

out. "Give those to me," she said, taking the coffees. "God forbid they get dropped."

That was probably a good idea. My hands were a little shaky. I made fists and released them, took in a deep breath, and let it out slowly.

"Erik?" Elektra asked.

"Yeah?"

She grinned. "What are you waiting for?"

Spurred into action, I shot out of the car and made my way to the front door.

Chapter Fourteen
Monroe

When Saul told me we were having visitors, I almost didn't believe him. At first I wondered if it was some other group of recovering alcoholics or therapists, and I'd already decided just how much it was going to suck.

But then he told me who it was. And I honestly did not believe him. But he'd nodded and promised it was true.

"You're not kidding?"

"I'm not kidding."

"He's really going to be here?"

"He really is."

"Holy shit."

Saul had laughed and told me to breathe. They'd be here around ten o'clock, he'd said. That gave me about an hour not to freak the complete fuck out. I swam a few laps of the pool to expend some of the energy that threatened to bubble out of me. I showered to get the saltwater off my skin, and then Saul made me prepare some morning tea. It was just fruit, crackers and cheese, and that's where I was when Saul went to the door. "Welcome," I heard him say. "Come in, come in!"

I froze. I'm pretty sure my heart stopped, and my nerves ratcheted up a notch or five. I couldn't get my body to move. My head was saying *go to him*, but my feet were glued to the floor...

And there he was.

He walked out into the living room, wearing blue suit pants, a light blue business shirt, top button undone, sleeves rolled to his elbows. His blond hair was kind of floppy. His blue eyes searched the room, then landed on me. And he smiled...

And everything Saul and I had worked on this week came crashing down around me, taking hold and making perfect sense.

Then I was moving, like my body overruled my brain. And I walked to him without stopping, without thinking, and I collected him in a crushing hug. He was really here. My God, he was here and I knew in my heart that it was right.

He slowly slid his arms around me, his hands at my back, pressing me close and holding me as tight as I held him. Neither of us pulled away, neither of us dared move. I buried my face in his neck and he smelled so good, and he sighed and he was everything good in my life, and he was here.

"You're really here," I whispered.

"I am." He pulled back and put his hand to my face.

"You look great." His eyes went to my mouth and he licked his lips, and I thought for a second he was going to kiss me. And I wanted him to. Which was new, because I'd never thought of him like that, but now... now everything Saul had said made sense. Now it was all I wanted. I licked my lips and leaned in a little and—

Someone cleared their throat.

We both turned to the sound, not really letting go of each other, to find Elektra and Saul at the kitchen counter, both smiling at us. "I brought coffee," Elektra said, smirking now. "Hi, by the way."

"Hi," I replied, a little breathier than normal.

Erik laughed, and when I turned to face him, he pulled me in for another hug. I fit against him so perfectly. My head fit in that nook at the side of his neck, under his chin, and I never wanted to leave.

God, I had so much I needed to say, which warred with my need to stay pressed against him.

A little reluctantly, I pulled away so I could look up at him. "I can't believe you're here."

Erik put his hand to my face and traced his fingers through my hair at my temple. "You look... really good. Life here agrees with you."

"You too," I replied. "I mean, you always look good. Maybe I forgot just how much..."

Erik smiled and drew his bottom lip between his teeth.

"Coffee?" Elektra asked. When I could drag my gaze away from Erik, I saw she was holding out a coffee for me.

"Thank you," I said, embarrassed at my reaction to seeing Erik. "And you look amazing too, as always." It was true. She always looked gorgeous.

She rolled her eyes and smiled. "But Erik's right. You do look good, Monroe. Your skin's got some colour, and your eyes are brighter. Whatever Saul's doing, he's doing right."

"I'm actually not doing much," Saul said.

"That's such bullshit," I corrected.

"No, you might be surprised to learn, but you're not my most high-maintenance client." He smiled as he sipped his coffee. "You stopped fighting me, and while I might have course-corrected you a few times, you're definitely the one leading the way here."

I rolled my eyes and Saul clapped me on the shoulder. "Ah, the eye-roll. I've lost count at how many I've been given. He's still not very good at taking praise."

I sighed, and Erik chuckled. "He's never been very good at taking compliments."

"I'm working on it. One thing at a time," I replied. "The list of my faults is pretty long, so it might take a while."

"I don't think the issue is how long the list is. There's really only a few faults," Erik said. Then he grinned, and his blue eyes sparkled with humour. "They are fucking doozies, though."

"Shut up," I said with a laugh. "Or I'll start on yours." It felt so good to laugh with him. It felt good to be with him, to see him, to be able to touch him.

I put my hand on his waist, and he moved in closer so

he could wrap his arm around my shoulder. I sipped the coffee, which was divine. "Thank you for the coffee. Saul's been subjecting me to tea, so this is very much appreciated."

"It was actually Erik who bought them," Elektra said.

"She threatened bodily harm," Erik added.

Elektra nodded, then looked right at me. "And don't get too comfortable being all cute wrapped against my brother. There's an ocean out there that I intend to immerse myself in shortly, and you can join me. It will let these two discuss you while you're out of earshot." She motioned to Saul and Erik. "And as a trade-off, I'll take Saul into Noosa after lunch so you two have a few minutes alone—to talk." Then she raised her eyebrow at Erik. "I promised Mum I'd keep an eye on you at all times, so us leaving you two alone doesn't get back to her. Are we clear?"

"Crystal," Erik said.

I laughed and gave Saul a shrug. "You learn at an early age not to argue with the Keston women."

He smiled. "So it would seem. But yes," he added, motioning toward me and Erik, "you two have a lot to talk about. And I do mean talk."

I looked up at Erik. He was so close I could see every pore on his beautiful face. "Sure, I mean, what else would we do?"

Erik's eyes went to my lips, then to my eyes, darkening with desire. His voice was low and rough. "I um... I can't..."

"Christ almighty, the UST is suffocating," Elektra

said, flustered, grabbing me by the arm and pulling me to the hall. "How cold is the sea water?"

"What is UST?" Saul asked. "Do I even want to know?"

"Um." Erik cleared his throat. "Unresolved sexual tension. I think that's what the kids are calling it."

I didn't hear anything after that, as Elektra shoved me into Erik's room. "The sooner Saul and Erik have a chat, the sooner you and Erik will be alone."

To be completely honest, my head was still spinning. "What?"

"What do you think I'm doing here? Someone has to keep Saul distracted so you and Erik can sort your shit out. So"—she waved her hand at me—"hurry up and get changed into some boardies or budgie smugglers, whatever you wear to go swimming."

She closed the door, leaving me a little bewildered yet unable to stop the smile from spreading on my face. I still couldn't quite believe they were here, and I couldn't quite get my head around my reaction to seeing Erik and his reaction to seeing me. Everything Saul and I had talked about during the week now made sense. Well it made sense to me. I guess I wouldn't find out what Erik thought until we talked about it.

Face-to-face. Just the two of us.

Butterflies flooded my stomach, and it wasn't until I was changed, walking across the sand to the water with Elektra, that I realised I hadn't thought about drinking, hadn't craved it all morning.

Elektra grabbed my hand and laughed as we walked

into the water, the first wave hitting up our legs. Elektra squealed, making me laugh, and I turned to see Saul and Erik sitting on the deck chairs watching us as they spoke.

"I'm sorry about the bag-of-dicks comment," Elektra said.

"I'm not," I replied. "I needed to hear it. And what you said was true."

She smiled. "Glad to hear that. I probably could have worked on my tact though."

Another wave crashed into us, but I held Elektra's hand firmly in mine. "I still can't believe you're both here."

"He was almost beside himself once he knew he was coming to see you. It was ridiculous how happy he was."

I laughed at that. "I want you to know that I've been working really hard to get better. I have a lot of shit to sort out, but I've had some pretty big revelations this week."

Another wave barrelled into us, and when it had passed, Elektra said, "That's a good thing, isn't it?"

"I think so. I mean, I hope so. I'm still trying to get my head around it, and it's hard to recognise something that you've never really had, but Saul seems to think that Erik will understand."

"Understand what?"

I let out a breath and tried, for the first time, to own my truth. If anyone would understand, it would be Elektra. And if it was the worst revelation in the history of the world and it was doomed to crash and burn, she would know that too. And although Saul would probably think I should tell Erik first, it wasn't technically cheating on this test; it was more like testing the waters, so to speak.

After another wave had rolled through, Elektra stood in front of me. "Monroe, what is it? You're starting to worry me."

I put my hand to my forehead and let out a laugh that sounded a little crazy. "I can't be absolutely sure, and I have some issues that Saul is trying to help me with, but I think there is a very good chance and a very real possibility that I could be a little bit or even a whole lot in love with your brother."

Chapter Fifteen
Erik

Saul and I sat on the veranda and watched Monroe and Elektra walk out into the ocean. I pulled off my shoes and socks and got comfortable on the deck chair. The sun was glorious, the smell of the ocean air, seeing Monroe...

My God, it was so good to see him.

"I must say," Saul began, "his reaction to seeing you was remarkable. I don't know whether to be surprised or not."

I snorted out a laugh. "You and me both. I was surprised, in a good way." And that was the understatement of the century. It was so much more than remarkable.

"He's had a good week. It's been hard, but he pushed through. He's committed to getting better, and I'm very proud of him."

"Me too."

"I won't go into detail, but I can say we've been

working on relationships this week. That's why I'm glad you're here. You two do have much to talk about. Well, he has a lot to talk about, and I would ask that you listen. It's not going to be easy for him, so I would caution you to perhaps hear what he doesn't say."

"Okay."

"He's going to need support."

"I know."

Saul's eyebrow pinched. "I'm not going to give anything away. What he needs to tell you has to come from him, and I would never take that away from him."

"But?"

"I have concerns. Professional concerns." He watched as Monroe and Elektra laughed as they broke through waves. "You play a very important role in his life. And it worries me, frightens me, what it would do to him if your role in his life became conflicted or compromised."

"I wouldn't hurt him."

"Not intentionally, I know. And I'm conflicted within myself," he furthered, almost smiling, "as to what advice to give, from his therapist or from an older, fatherly type who wants his son to be happy."

The fact he cared for Monroe like that warmed my heart. "Is it not the same advice?"

Saul laughed. "Not always. The therapist in me would suggest caution and calculated steps. Action, reaction, evaluate, assess, implement." He sighed. "Which is always sound advice, especially for a recovering addict. But the artist, free-spirited side of me wants to tell him to take this chance with both hands and run with it."

I wasn't sure which part of that to unpack first. "You're an artist?"

Saul laughed. "I paint when I can and sketch when I can't. I can't always paint when I'm with clients, but I can take a sketchbook and some graphites. It's my own form of therapy. My wife paints and does some sculpting as well."

This surprised me. "A therapist and an artist. Two very different sides to the one coin."

Saul smiled. "Not really. Holistic perception and spatial reasoning are all connected. Like with Monroe. Unlocking his creative side allows me access to things I might not always see."

"The woodwork?"

Saul nodded. "He's really very good at it."

"I'll have to ask him to show me."

Saul was quiet for a moment. "I can see you've had a better week as well."

"Yeah. Much better." I had a feeling he wasn't going to like this, but I had to tell him. "And you'll probably give me a dozen reasons why this is a bad idea, but I realised something this week. My happiness involves him. I don't know how else to explain it without you pulling it apart, but it's like he's meant to be a part of my life. In whatever capacity."

I was expecting Saul to frown or to give me some Freudian analysis why my reasoning was a disaster. I was certain he was going to rebuke me in some way.

But he didn't.

He just nodded as though he expected me to say all that. His expression warred between smiling and frowning. "I want to sit down with both of you together. Tomorrow before you leave."

"Um... okay?"

Just then, Elektra's high-pitched squeal carried up to the house, and Saul and I both glanced up in time to see her launch herself at Monroe. She hugged him, both of them laughing, until Monroe dumped them both underwater. Elektra came up spluttering, Monroe was still laughing, and they began to wrestle in the water like they always did.

It made me laugh, and it made my heart very happy and full. I could feel Saul's eyes on me, studying me, and when I looked at him, he nodded. And without a word but with the small smile playing at his lips, he stood up, clapped me gently on the shoulder, and went inside.

Monroe and Elektra soon walked out of the water, collected their towels from the sand, and walked onto the deck. "The water's beautiful," she said. "You should get in."

"Maybe later," I replied. I couldn't seem to take my eyes off Monroe. His swimmer's physique, his all-over tan, the way his wet board shorts clung to his hips... He towelled off his face and grinned at me. I knew what he was going to do before he did it, and I made no move to stop him.

He leaned in close, closed his eyes, then shook his

dripping-wet hair like a dog, spraying me with water. "Ugh, thanks!" I said, laughing.

He collapsed onto the deck chair next to me, still grinning. "You're welcome. That's what you get for wearing suit pants and a long-sleeve shirt at the beach."

"Yeah, I should change," I agreed. "But then I'd have missed the free swimsuit model show."

He laughed and patted the towel down his abs. Totally on purpose. Then he did his crotch.

"You're such a jerk," I mumbled.

He laughed and threw his towel at me, and his smile slowly faded. "I can't believe you're here," he whispered.

"Me either. It's so good to see you. I've missed you," I murmured.

He turned on his side to face me and held out his hand. I took it without question, and he quickly threaded our fingers. "I've missed you too." He licked his lips. "I have so much I need to tell you. Things I need to say."

"Okay."

He looked back inside the house, where I could hear Elektra and Saul talking. "Later. When it's just us."

"Okay." I gave his fingers a bit of a squeeze. "Whatever you need."

Something flashed in his eyes, and his cheeks flushed a little. But he never said anything else. He just stared at me, like he couldn't make himself look away. Like if he did, I might vanish.

"Want to show me your woodwork? I hear you're rather good with your hands," I said.

He smiled, maybe even blushed a little. He took the

towel back and wrapped it around his waist, pulled on an old shirt, then taking a deep breath, he walked over to the end of the patio and tapped the pendulum on a windchime that hung from the rafter. "Well, there's this one."

I stood up and stared at him disbelievingly. "You made that?"

It was kind of like an inverted triangle made from different lengths of driftwood. They were strung together with twine and they spun and clanged gently in the breeze. "I thought Mum must have bought it at the markets!"

He smiled, all shy-like. "It wasn't hard. Just different knots for different lengths and sounds."

"Wow."

He grinned and said, "And there's another one." He went inside and headed toward the front door. Only he stopped at the hallstand. I hadn't even noticed it when I'd come in. I'd been too eager to find Monroe, but next to the bowl where everyone threw their keys was a xylophone. It was about forty centimetres long, different sized pieces of smooth driftwood tapering in size, tied tight with twine.

"Monroe," I whispered. "You made this?"

He nodded, a little embarrassed.

"It's..." I touched the smooth wood, some light, some dark. "It's beautiful."

His gaze shot to mine. "You like it?"

I nodded. "I really do."

"It feels good to take something useless and give it a

purpose," he said. "Pretty sure that's the lesson Saul's trying to teach me."

I put my hand to his face, so very tempted to kiss him. My heart was hammering and I wanted to lean in and just—

"You boys hungry?" Elektra called out. "Lunch is served!"

Monroe blinked like he was in a trance, then smiled. "Food sounds good." We went back out to find Elektra, and Saul had put the fruit and cheese platter on the table with some deli meats and some slices of crusty bread. It looked great. There was a bottle of cold water and one of juice and four small plates at the table. We took a seat and began to eat, and to my surprise, it was Monroe who led the conversation.

"Saul only told me this morning you guys were coming. He said he knew last night it was a possibility but didn't want to tell me in case it didn't happen." He shoved a grape in his mouth and chewed it. "Probably just as well, because I would have been too wired to sleep."

"Like Erik," Elektra said, throwing me under the bus. "He was completely useless at work yesterday, he was insufferable at dinner, and he barely slept a wink all night. And this morning he was a jittery mess. I wouldn't let him drive."

"I wasn't that bad," I said, ignoring the heat of embarrassment on my cheeks.

Monroe laughed. "Like a kid on Christmas morning."

Elektra leaned in. "Exactly."

Monroe smiled happily and ate some rockmelon and prosciutto. "Well, your being here is a very welcome distraction at any rate. I haven't wanted a drink or even thought about it all day. Well, so far."

I could tell Monroe was a little embarrassed, but the fact he was open about this and willing to discuss it at the table was huge for him. I reached over and took his hand. "That's good. That's really good. You've come a long way, Monroe. You should be really proud."

He blushed a little. "I've done okay. Saul might not agree."

"You've done better than okay," Saul replied with a fond smile.

"It hasn't been easy," Monroe said. I got the feeling that he needed to say this. He needed to be upfront and honest about his experiences. If that was part of his therapy or of his own volition, I wasn't sure. But I would listen either way. "Some days, like in the very beginning, those first few days, I didn't think I was gonna make it. But then I got through the physical stuff and I began to feel better. Actually, I hadn't felt that good in a long time. But that didn't last long. Then it became mental. Physical demons you can fight. It's like a sprint. You know there's an end point. But the mental fight... Saul described it more like a marathon, and well, he wasn't wrong."

He took a deep breath in and let it out slowly, a sure sign that this was not easy for him to discuss. But he looked at Saul and forged on. "The mental fight is the cravings, the habit of drinking, and being drunk. I never used to drink just to drink. I drank to get drunk. To blur the lines and to make me numb to things I didn't want to feel." Monroe squeezed my hand. "So now I have to deal with a whole bunch of emotional issues I never wanted to deal with, and I am. One by one, I'm getting through them. It's not easy. But part of the mental therapy involves emotional therapy, and it's exhausting. Not gonna lie. The hardest thing I've ever gone through. On some days, it felt like I had lost my parents all over again."

He let out a shaky breath.

"And I've been very closed off to a lot of things, but I'm trying to fix that." Finally he looked at me and smiled. "One day at a time."

"One day at a time," I repeated.

Elektra held up her glass of water. "One day at a time."

Saul smiled like a proud dad, and Monroe let out a sigh of relief, followed by a bit of a laugh. "That wasn't so bad."

I squeezed his hand again. "You did real good. Talking about some things isn't easy. But if you need to talk, I've got nothing but time to listen, okay?"

He nodded quickly, then swallowed hard. He opened his mouth, then shut it, then tried again but looked to Saul for help.

"Perhaps you and Erik could take a walk along the beach?" Saul suggested.

"Great idea," I replied. "Just give me a second to change."

I went to my room and stripped out of my suit, opting for shorts and an old T-shirt that I wasn't sure whether it was mine or Monroe's. We'd both worn it over the years so I had no idea... I smiled as I pulled it on, and when I walked out, Monroe stood up. He wiped his hands on his thighs and swallowed.

He was nervous and I wasn't sure if that was a good thing or a bad thing. I was suddenly thinking it was a bad thing...

"We'll be here when you get back," Saul said, giving Monroe a nod. A silent reassurance of support.

Okay, so perhaps it really was a bad thing.

Fuck.

"You ready?" he asked. His smile was back, but there was a hint of something behind it.

I aimed for bright and cheery. No clue if I pulled it off. "Sure."

"Nice shirt," Monroe deadpanned.

I chuckled, knowing now it must have been his. "Thanks."

We crossed the deck and went down the few steps to the beach, and we began to walk north, right where the water crept up to the sand. It was easier to walk on. He tried to shove his hands in non-existent pockets, then tried crossing his arms, but that didn't work either. I held out my hand, and he snatched it up eagerly. "Thanks."

"You're nervous," I said. "I would say you don't have to be, but I don't know what you're going to tell me..."

"It's nothing bad," he said. "Well. I hope it's not."

"It won't be. No matter what it is. Unless you've decided you really do want to live in a Tibetan monastery that has no Wi-Fi or coffee."

Monroe laughed and leaned into me a little. "Not quite."

We walked a little further up and he stopped. He dropped my hand and ran his through his hair. "I need to say this, so if you could not interrupt me until I'm done, that'd be great. I'm supposed to speak my truths, lay it all bare. It's supposed to help me heal and grow. You know, transparency and all that. But I'm not good at it so I'll probably fuck it up, so bear with me?"

I nodded. "Okay I'm listening."

He took a deep breath and looked me right in the eye. "I treated you like shit. I never meant to. I just never realised. And that probably makes it worse, but I can see now what a jerk I was to you. And you deserve so much better than that. You deserve someone who treats you like the kind and incredible guy you are. And these last few weeks have been hard. I looked for you at every turn, every hurdle. I expected to see you there because you've always been there. And I realise now that wasn't fair on you. I mean it wasn't fair on me either, but man, it was *so* unfair to you. I want you to know you were never a back-up plan, I just didn't know how else to cope. I drank to forget, and I drank to take away the pain, and it made me feel better for half a second but it made you feel terrible and I am profoundly sorry for that. I never meant to hurt you."

I did as he asked and didn't interrupt, even though I wanted to.

"Erik, you never, not once, did anything wrong by

me. Honestly, if it weren't for you, I'd have more than likely ended up right alongside my parents."

That hurt to hear but still, I said nothing.

He took a deep breath and narrowed his eyes, like he was fortifying himself. "Erik, I'm an alcoholic. It's not something that will go away. It will always be there, and it will always be something I need to work on. Some days are going to be good and some are going to be downright fucking awful. But I'm ready for that. These last few weeks have been rough, but I'm in a better place now, mentally, that is. And with hindsight and clarity, I've learned more about myself these last three or so weeks than I ever did. Not all of it good, but there is one constant thing I keep coming back to."

"What's that?"

"You."

"Me?"

"I can also now see how much you mean to me and how much I've missed you. Not just having you around to pick me up, and not just to go out to the clubs with me and not just to make sure I woke up in the mornings. You were the only one who checked up on me."

"Because I love you."

He sucked back a breath and his eyes became glassy. But he shook it off.

Fuck. And that voice in my head said, *he needs a friend right now, he needs support. He doesn't need complications.* "I'm sorry if that's not what you want to hear," I whispered.

He shook his head quickly and his eyes welled with

tears. "You told me you loved me every time we spoke on the phone."

"Because I thought you needed to hear it."

Now he nodded, and a tear slipped down his cheek. "I've been going over this all week with Saul. He asked me what it meant to me, and I said I don't know. Because I don't think I know what love even is. Because I don't think I deserve it..." He could barely speak, and more tears spilled down his face, but he pushed on.

"And Saul asked me what I felt for you, and I couldn't describe it. Not at first. And I said, when I'm with you I can breathe." He put his hand to his sternum. "You get me. And I can't picture what life without you would be like. That when I'm with you, everything feels right, and I'm safe with you, and you're more than a best mate, and you're more than family."

He scrubbed at his face, wiping away the tears, and he let out an incredulous laugh. "He said it sounded a lot like love, but how can I know what that really is? And he's been helping me with that, with trying to under-stand my relationships with my parents and you, and trying to get me to see that I do deserve to be loved. That I'm worthy of love..." He sobbed and tears escaped my eyes.

"Monroe. You do deserve it. You are worthy of it. You are loved."

He nodded and sobbed again. "I think I'm beginning to get it. It's not easy. And you'd think every person knows they're deserving of such a thing, but... I told you I have issues."

I laughed through my tears. "And I still love you, issues and all."

He looked at me then, with tears and snot and wobbling chin. "Thank you. Thank you for being patient and for loving me. It's taken me a while to realise that maybe I do deserve it. So I'm saying thank you. For loving me and for giving me the space and time to learn how to be loved and what it means. It's been a long road, but I can say it now, because love is not just words. And it's not just something you repeat because you feel you have to. I want to tell you that I love you too. I'm still learning what it means, but I know now that what I feel here"—he put his hand to his heart—"is love, and I feel stupid for being so blind and such a fucking mess." He wiped his face and took a fortifying breath and gave a nod. "I deserve to be loved and I also am worthy of giving love. Or that the love I have to give is worth something. I know it comes from a good place now. It's organic and it beats inside my chest, and when I think of you, it beats double time, and when I see you, it becomes something else. I'm in love with you, Erik. I think I always have been. But I was messed-up before, and I hope you can see that I'm trying to be honest and real. From here on out, I need you to know what I feel for you is real and good. I don't know what it means for us and Saul is kind of freaking out, but he said he knows love when he sees it and he wants me to be happy, but he wants me to be healthy as well."

"Hang on, back up." I blinked a few times. "What did you say?"

"Saul, he's kind of freaking out—"

"No, not that part," I said with a laugh. "The 'I'm in love with you' part."

"Oh." He blanched. "I'm not very good at this emotional dialogue part..."

"I don't know; I think it was perfect."

His eyes went wide. "It was?"

I nodded. "It was about how the love you have to give is worth something. How it comes from a good place now, and that it's organic and it beats inside your chest, and how it beats double time when you think of me, and when you see me it becomes something else." I cupped his face in my hands. "And you said you're in love with me and you think you might have always been."

He nodded and leaned into my palm, closing his eyes. "I have fucked everything up and I'm trying to right everything I did wrong."

"I forgive you," I whispered. He opened his eyes and looked at me. "I love you. I know I always have. Since I first saw you in class on that first day of college."

He barked out a teary laugh. "You remember that?"

I nodded and whispered, "I'd really like to kiss you right now."

He gasped and licked his lips. "I want that. Very much."

Still holding his face, I tipped his chin a little and watched as his eyes fluttered closed and his lips softly parted. And I kissed him. As gentle as a butterfly wing, as devastating as a nuclear bomb.

Nothing else existed.

Every moment, everything I'd ever wanted, longed for, and dreamed of came down to this.

Just him, his soft lips, his body against mine, and his surrender to that kiss. He let me deepen it, and when our tongues met, he groaned low in the back of his throat. He slid his arms around me, holding me to him, his fingers digging into my back, and I kept my hands at his jaw and kept his mouth to mine.

I was kissing Monroe. My Monroe, my best friend, my entire world, and he was kissing me back.

He loved me. Like I loved him. This beautiful man.

And he wanted me. I could feel his desire pressing against me, and mine was rock hard against him. But it was my heart that wanted him more.

He pulled away and gasped, his eyes locked on mine, and then he kissed me again. This time he had one hand to my jaw, pulling me in, kissing me so impossibly deep.

So impossibly perfect.

This time he pulled back, he kept his forehead pressed to mine, his eyes closed. "Oh wow," he panted.

"Maybe we should cool it a little," I whispered. "Before I pull you down into the sand and we get arrested for indecent exposure."

He laughed breathily, but then he fisted my shirt, kept his forehead to mine, and closed his eyes. "I'm a mess, and I have no idea what I'm doing, and I don't really even know what love is."

I pulled back and cupped his face and waited for him to look at me. "I'll show you. I'll show you what it means to love, and I'll show you how much you deserve to be loved."

"I have more baggage than a Louis Vuitton catalogue."

I snorted.

"And I'm a mess, E. It's not going to be easy."

"Hey," I said, holding his gaze. "You're worth it. And give yourself some credit."

He nodded but hardly looked convinced. "Is this what love is? This feeling right here?" he pulled my hand to his chest, over his heart. "I don't know if it's the best feeling in the world or if I'm going to be sick."

That made me laugh. "Sounds about right."

He eventually smiled. "I do love you. And I'm sorry I fucked everything up."

"I forgive you. And for what it's worth, I'm sorry I walked out on you. I gave you an ultimatum because I didn't know what else to do."

He shook his head. "It was the only thing that made me stop. The idea of not having you in my life almost crippled me, and it made me have to choose in that split second—you or drinking—and it was no contest. I chose you. So don't apologise for that. I needed the ultimatum, and I needed the push. I realised what was more important. It was you. And it will always be you. Every time."

I traced my thumb over his cheek. "And I choose you too."

He smiled and pressed himself against me, his face in my neck and his arms around my waist. "And seeing you today, when you first walked in... Saul's been trying to get me to process what you mean to me, and as soon as I saw you... Fuck, it just made everything so clear."

"That hug was kind of incredible." I kissed the side of his head. "I was going to take whatever distance you put between us as my cue, but you surprised the hell out of me."

"Surprised the hell out of myself," he mumbled. His arms tightened around me. "Remember back in Sydney when we made out and got each other off on the sun chair by the pool?"

I froze. "Yes...?"

"I'm sorry about that. I was drunk, obviously, and—"

"No." I pulled back so he could see my face. "It's me who should apologise for that. I wanted it because I thought it was a goodbye, and I was willing to take whatever I could get."

Monroe frowned. "I'm sorry."

"Me too." I gave him a soft kiss. "Maybe we could pretend that never happened and try again? A new first time?"

He locked one leg behind mine and threw me into the sand, landing on top of me with a grin. "Like now?"

I rolled us over and drove myself between his thighs, making him groan and roll his hips. I took both his hands and pinned them into the sand above his head. "Not here. I want to take my time with you and worship every inch of your body. I want to show you what you mean to me."

I ghosted my lips over his and he strained underneath me for more. And he was so hot, and so turned on, and he was driving me crazy. And my orgasm started to curl in my belly and... And he was worth more than just a romp in the sand.

I lifted myself off him and collapsed at his side, drawing his lips in for another quick kiss. "You're going to make me come in broad daylight," I whispered.

He groaned out a laugh, then writhed a little. Then he put his hand to his forehead and I was quickly reminded that he was in a different headspace than me. "Wanna go for a swim?" I asked, not really giving him time to answer. I sat up, pulled my shirt off, and ran across the beach into the surf.

He was two seconds behind me, grinning as he dove under a wave that I was too slow to miss. Well, too busy watching him to see it coming was more the truth...

He broke the surface, hair slicked back, water streaming down his skin, and he smiled. He made my heart skip a beat when he looked at me, knowing now how he felt about me. He launched himself at me, his arms around my neck and his legs wrapped around my hips. He gave me smiley-kisses. "I can't believe you're here," he said again. "And I can't believe I actually said everything I wanted to say." Another kiss. "And I can't believe you didn't turn me down or run away screaming."

I pecked his lips with mine. "Never."

He clung tighter to me and kissed me deeper: lips, teeth, tongue... He ground his hard cock against me. "I want you inside me," he whispered. But then he stopped and pulled back, his eyes closed. "When I'm ready, for that. When we're ready. For that kind of sex. I don't even know what I'm saying."

"Hey, look at me," I pleaded.

I waited until his eyes met mine.

"I'll wait. Until you're sure. We don't have to do anything at all if you don't want."

"I want," he said quickly. "Fuck. I want it so bad, but it terrifies me..."

I set him down so his feet were on the ocean floor, and I put my hands to his jaw. "What scares you?"

"I've never... I mean, I have. I've bottomed before, of course I have. But never with anyone I cared about." He frowned. "It's only ever been a quick and dirty fuck that left me feeling worse..."

I kissed him gently. "It won't be like that with us, I promise. I'll make love to you," I whispered, kissing him again. "Slow and beautiful. I'll prove to you how much I love you, how much you deserve to be loved. Whenever you're ready."

He nodded. "Thank you." Then he sighed. "I feel stupid and broken. Like there won't be one thing we can do without me having an issue or a meltdown. Or a relapse..."

I gave him an incredulous look. "Are you fucking kidding me? I can still kick your arse at Xbox. That won't ever change."

He eventually smiled. "Thanks."

"But, Monroe?" I said seriously. "You were embarrassed and scared to talk about sex and what you're ready for, but you did it. You just came right out and said it. That's pretty brave. And you've been upfront with your progress and your therapy, and that's amazing."

He gave me a half smile. "Saul's good at his job, apparently."

"Give yourself some credit in that equation."

He smirked. "Yeah, I know."

I carded my fingers through his wet hair, marvelling at how I could now touch him. I let my hand fall to his shoulder and pressed a kiss to his forehead. But then a loud whistle carried on the wind. It was how my dad always got our attention... I turned to find Elektra on the deck, waving. "Uh, boys?" she yelled out. "Saul and I are leaving for half an hour. You're welcome."

Saul appeared beside her and said something to her, but Elektra repeated it for us. "And that conversation Saul wanted to have with you tomorrow? You're now having that tonight." She laughed, then tapped her watch. "Half an hour. No more."

They waved us off and disappeared inside, and Monroe sighed. "Can't imagine what they needed to leave for."

"Or why we'd need thirty minutes uninterrupted time," I added.

"You know how you wanted to take your time with me?" Monroe asked, biting his bottom lip. "Thirty minutes in the shower long enough?"

I grabbed his hand and dragged him out of the sea. He laughed and ran ahead, picking up our shirts and shaking them out; then he ran for the house and was up the deck stairs before I'd made it to dry sand.

I followed him inside and could hear the shower turn on in my en suite. He was undoing his board shorts, peeling them down over his arse as I walked in. "Let me," I murmured. I pulled at the waist cord, enjoying how it brought his hips forward. Then I slid my fingers under the waistband and slowly pushed them down. His cock sprung forward, hard and heavy, nestled in a dark thatch of pubic hair. I fisted him and he shuddered at the contact, then fumbled with my shorts until we were both naked.

I walked him backwards into the shower. His eyes were dark, his lips full and parted. His cock looked painfully hard. But he couldn't take his eyes off me. "You're so hot," he breathed. He palmed me, wrapping his fingers around my shaft. "And your cock... It's fucking gorgeous."

I crushed my mouth to his, pushing him against the tiled wall. The spray of water was warm but felt cool against his flushed skin. Soon we were grinding against each other, hands and fingers, bruising kisses; loud gasps filled the room.

He gave into it, letting me lead, letting me take charge. His hands fell to his sides and he offered me his body. I poured shower gel into my palm and fisted both our cocks, and he groaned into my mouth. I sucked on his bottom lip and pumped him, me, us.

It was more than physical. It was emotional and with my entire body, my every cell, my everything.

Monroe shuddered and gasped for air. "Erik... Erik. I... I'm..."

"Come, Monroe," I rasped, so close. So close. "I want to see you come."

He thrust up into my fist and shuddered, convulsed, and he cried out. His cock swelled against mine, spilling his seed, coaxing my own orgasm.

We slumped against each other, holding each other up. He chuckled against my collarbone. "Holy shit."

I laughed, a little light-headed. Then I caught his chin and drew him in for another kiss. We stood under the water and added some more shower gel and soaped each other up, laughing, with slippery hands and mouths as we explored each other's bodies.

When I opened my eyes after rinsing my hair, I found him staring at me, smiling. "What? Did I miss some suds?" I stuck my head under the water again.

"No," he said, running his hand over my chest, thumbing my nipple. When he met my eyes, he shook his head as if in wonder. "I just... I'm naked in the shower with you."

"Like you can't believe it's real?" I asked. He nodded, and I put my hand to his chest. "I know. I feel the same. I guess it'll take some getting used to. I'll just have to pinch myself every so often."

"Me too." He shut the water off and handed me a towel. "But if we're still in this shower when Saul gets back, we won't need pinching."

I chuckled, and we dried off and got dressed, and Monroe led the way to the kitchen. He filled the kettle and switched it on. "I don't profess to love this tea shit that Saul makes me drink, and I'd never tell him this, but it's actually not that bad."

He set about making a pot and moved around the

kitchen with a deft familiarity. "Saul really did make you cook?"

He laughed. "Yep. He made me do everything. Cleaning, laundry, meditation or reflection or whatever you want to call it." He leaned against the counter and sighed. "Taking responsibility isn't all fun and games."

"Well, the change in you is a good one," I said. "Remember when I brought you here, you were worried about not being the same person?"

"I remember," he answered quietly.

"But you are the same person. You're just a better version of you. And when I say better, I mean a healthier you. A you that's—"

"Spent three weeks in detox and intense therapy?"

"A man who changed his ways to be a better version of himself." I stood between his feet and leaned against him, slotting together perfectly. "You didn't change that much. I still recognise the man I've known for years. The man I fell in love with years ago. It's still you." I cringed. "Did I say that right?"

He put his hands on my hips and almost smiled. "Perfect."

He kissed me and I reciprocated in kind, and it began to get deeper, hotter, when the kettle whistled its interruption. He groaned and I stood back. "Probably just as well. Elektra's kept Saul out for long enough, and I have a feeling he won't be too happy about this," I said, motioning between us. "I think he's concerned about us being together."

Monroe filled the teapot and left it to brew. "No. It's

quite the opposite," Monroe said. "It was Saul who pushed me to open up about you."

"It was?"

He smiled. "Yeah. He kept going on about soulmates or something."

"Soulmates?"

He laughed. "Yeah. Crazy, huh?"

My heart started to do all kinds of crazy things. "Yeah, crazy... Tell me, do you believe that? In soulmates?"

"I'm not sure. Last week I wasn't even sure I knew what love was." He poured two cups of tea and handed me one. "But after I'd told him how I felt about you, how it was like finding a missing piece of me, a piece I didn't even know was missing, he just smiled and nodded. He said sometimes soulmates come into our lives in unexpected places, at times we didn't know we needed them. He said some people have more than one soulmate, which I didn't really understand, but I think Saul is the type of guy to live with his wife in a free-love commune where they grow veggies in the mountains and have naked meditation sessions and mass orgies." That made me laugh, and Monroe sipped his tea, hiding his smile behind his cup. "But he asked if we could strip away our minds and our bodies and all the physical, material bullshit, if all that was left was the light of our souls in some vastness of space, if my light could recognise your light, and I said yes. Without a doubt."

I wasn't expecting to be so affected by his words but that hit me really hard. My heart was about to burst and my eyes watered. "I'd recognise your light too." I put down my tea and took his cup from him and set it on the counter so I could wrap my arms around him in a fierce, soul-binding hug. "I love you, Monroe."

He held me just as tight. "And I'll never take you for granted again. I promise." He pulled back and touched my eyebrow, my cheek. "Saul said I need to take each day at a time, and if I have to treat every day with you like it's my first and my last, then I'm okay with that."

I kissed him again, hard and deep, pressing him against the kitchen counter, my desire and need to have him, taste him; my one and only focus was him.

I didn't hear Saul come in. "Well, at least you've brought it inside," he said, startling me. "I held great concern for the wildlife, not to mention humans who might have happened past."

I ducked my head, embarrassed, but Monroe burst out laughing. Whereas I was tempted, for Saul's sake, to put some distance between us, Monroe pulled me in close and chuckled.

"We didn't hear you come in," Monroe murmured, his cheek against my shoulder.

"Is Elektra not with you?" I asked.

"No, she thought it best to give us some privacy. She said as a trade-off for couple's therapy," Saul said, smirking to himself, "she'll bring back pizza for dinner."

Monroe perked up, eyes wide. "Real pizza?"

Saul laughed before walking through to the hall. "Therapy room. Five minutes."

Chapter Sixteen
Monroe

Saul's *therapy room* was Mr and Mrs Keston's private lounge room. It was a smaller room off the master bedroom where they could read and enjoy peace and quiet away from teenaged Erik and Elektra's music and movies or their squabbling over Scrabble or Monopoly. Saul had pushed the coffee table out of the way, and we usually sat on the rug. Cross-legged, like kindergarteners.

It was weird at first, but he said it helped with breathing techniques, and he was right.

We sat on the floor, Erik and I closer together, facing Saul. "First off, I just want to say I'm glad things between you worked out. And the embrace when Erik walked in this morning reaffirmed my decision to involve him with your progress, Monroe.

"I have concerns, and we'll get to those," he furthered, "but I want you both to know that I do believe that Monroe, working on his own strengths and weaknesses and being self-sufficient is a good thing, but having the support from Erik could be beneficial."

"I agree," I said.

"You've come a long way, Monroe," Saul replied. "And it's important not to lose focus. I know having Erik here and establishing a relationship with him is exciting and important, but your recovery must remain your top priority. And likewise, Erik, Monroe's recovery must be our main focus. For now."

"Of course," Erik answered.

"Erik, what are your wants and needs, and what are your expectations in moving forward in your relationship with Monroe?"

He blanched and shot me a look. "You get used to it," I said with a laugh.

Erik let out a breath. "Well, I want him to be happy." He gave me a small smile. "I mean, I want to be happy too. But I want him to be happy... and sober. I want the best for him. I want him to be well and healthy."

"You said sober," Saul said.

"Yeah, I mean, being sober is part of his well-being, so then, yes, that's what I want."

Saul nodded slowly. "And what are your fears?"

He blinked, surprised. "Oh, um. I'm guessing you don't mean heights or spiders."

I snorted, and Saul smiled too. "No. Your fears surrounding your relationship with Monroe."

Erik frowned. "I worry... I worry that I won't be enough. Or that I'll say the wrong thing and upset him enough to relapse. Or that—"

"No you won't," I interjected.

"Let him speak," Saul replied gently.

"I worry about it, nonetheless," Erik said with an apologetic shrug.

I frowned at him. "I'm sorry."

"You don't need to apologise," he said, taking my hand.

"Monroe," Saul prompted. "What do you want from your relationship with Erik?"

"I want him to be happy. With me. I don't want to be a burden or for him to walk on eggshells around me. I want to get past this. I know I'll always be an alcoholic. It's something I need to live with and be mindful of. I get that. But I want to be more. I want to be better than that." I squeezed Erik's hand. "I want Erik to know there'll be bad days but there will be more good ones, I promise you."

He smiled.

"And I promise to talk about what's on my mind and if something's bothering me. If I want a drink or even before it gets to that. We'll have plans in place and safe words or DEFCON levels or something."

"And what do you fear?" Saul pressed.

"That I'll fail, that I'll let him down. That he'll put all his trust in me and I'll fall short. Or that ten years from now, we'll be out somewhere and there'll be wine or champagne and I'll forget and take a sip. I worry that it'll be too hard for him. Because I'm asking a lot. I'm asking him to take on a shitload of baggage and issues, and there will be things I can't do or things I can't go to, and that's a lot to take on."

"I know what I'm getting myself into," Erik said, his brow creased.

"You say that now. But in two years or five or ten years from now, you'll be sick of it. I have to live with this disease forever, but that doesn't mean you have to."

"Monroe, if you had diabetes or cancer, would I leave you?"

"Well, no, you wouldn't." I sighed. "But it's still a valid concern."

He smiled, almost laughed even. "Look at you, talking like an episode of Dr Phil."

I chuckled. "You can blame Dr Saul for that."

He shot Saul a look. "Or thank him."

Saul's smile slowly faded. "My main concern about your newly established relationship at this stage of Monroe's treatment is that if an unfortunate turn of events sees you parting ways, what that would do to Monroe."

"That's not fair to put that on him," I said. "That's like saying he has to stay with me whether he wants to or not, or any possible relapse will be his fault. And that's not fair at all."

"No, I get it," Erik said. "And it's not an unreasonable concern. He's your doctor, Monroe. He's worried about what could happen to you. And he should be." He looked at Saul, his brows furrowed. "If we talk and do the Dr Phil shit, we'll be fine, right?"

"The Dr Phil shit," Saul repeated with a smirk, "will

help, yes. But I would also advise we establish a broader support circle." Saul turned his gaze to me. "You can't use Erik as your only support person because he can't be there one hundred per cent of the time. Now, I'm not saying he's going to leave you, but what if he's away for work, or in a meeting, or at the dentist, and you have a bad day? High stress, agitated, freaking out, desperate. And you need to speak to Erik but he can't answer his phone—"

I swallowed hard. "I get it."

"So bringing Erik in early is great because I can see how much you needed him," Saul said gently. "And how much he needed you. But Erik leaving tomorrow is going to affect you more than you realise, Monroe. So we're going to establish some ground rules."

"What about you?" I asked. "I can call you, right? You said I could call you any time."

"Of course you can."

I felt better instantly, and Erik squeezed my hand. "It's okay to be a little scared, Monroe," he murmured. "And to be cautious. I'd probably be worried if you weren't."

"This won't be easy," I said.

"Nothing worth having ever is," he replied. "Isn't that how the saying goes?"

"Erik," I said, seriously. "I feel at peace now you're here. Honestly, I do. And I'm not craving right now. But the rational part of my brain knows if there were a bottle of anything on that coffee table right there, I'd drink the whole thing, right now. Vodka, Scotch, wine, beer, mouthwash. It wouldn't matter. I'd drink it all without a second thought. And I'd be back to square one, taking you with me."

He stared at me. "O...kay."

"Do you get what I'm saying?"

He searched my eyes; then he nodded. "Yeah, I do."

"Monroe's right," Saul said. "It won't always be that bad, but there will be days like it."

Erik smiled at him, then turned to me. "We'll get through it, babe."

I raised my eyebrow. "Babe?"

He cringed. "It just slipped out, sorry."

I laughed. "I liked it. I think."

Erik laughed too, scooted a bit closer to me, and nudged me with his shoulder. But he gave his attention to Saul, like a kid in class intent on learning. And he was. In true Erik Keston style, he was focused on everything Saul had to say. Saul spoke about trust and communication and honesty and knowing when we needed space and how to read the signs. He gave us exercises to do, to encourage and open discussion, and Erik listened and questioned, verified and contributed. He truly was committed to doing all he could to help me, and his wanting to learn how to live with and how to love a recovering addict proved just how committed he was to me.

"You okay, Monroe?" Saul asked.

"Oh yeah," I replied. "Sorry. I got sidetracked, lost in my own head. What were you saying?"

Saul sighed with a smile. "Okay, I know when you're done. We've been at this a while." He checked his watch.

He stood, stretched his back. "Why don't you two have some downtime before Elektra gets back. I'll give you some privacy."

He disappeared out the door and Erik stood and stretched as well, then helped me to my feet. "It's pretty full-on, isn't it?" he said. "I mean, it makes sense, and if we promise to talk to each other, we'll be fine. I'll admit, it felt a little bit like the shit therapists say in movies and on TV—"

"Thank you," I blurted out.

He tilted his head. "What for?"

"For trying. For knowing what you're getting into and wanting to do it anyway. For being here."

He put his hand to my cheek, sliding his thumb along my jaw. "I don't want to be anywhere else."

"I love you," I whispered.

His smile was beautiful. "And I love you."

I leaned into his palm and he pulled me into his arms. I fell against him, into him, and sighed. "You tired?"

I nodded against his chest. "I always am after sessions with Saul."

"Come on," he said, taking my hand and leading me back out to the main living room. He planted himself on the sofa, lying lengthwise, and shoved cushions behind his back, then motioned for me to join him.

I'd never wanted anything more. I dove right in as the little spoon. He pressed the remote control and the TV came on, but I didn't want to watch anything. I rolled over so I could hold him, to be held, and nestled into his chest. I was more interested in his hand on my back, his fingers in my hair, and the sound of his heart at my ear.

"Thought it'd be best if we didn't go to the bedroom," he murmured. "Or we'd miss dinner for sure."

I smiled and closed my eyes... and woke up to the feeling of being watched.

"Do you think he'd let me pluck his eyebrows?"

Erik tightened his arms around me. "Leave his eyebrows alone."

"Depends if you bought pizza," I mumbled. Opening my eyes, I hadn't expected Elektra to be so close. She really was studying my eyebrows.

"Hello, Sleeping Beauty," she replied. "Or should I call you Rapunzel?"

Erik rolled us over, tucking me into his arms, hiding me between him and the back of the couch, and shielding me from his sister. "Leave him alone. You're not touching him."

My laugh was muffled by Erik's chest. I loved that Elektra treated me no different to how she always had. I poked my head up. "I was serious about the pizza. Do you know how long I've lived on grilled meat and salad and wholemeal bread?"

Elektra grinned at me. "Of course I brought pizza. I got your favourite."

"Then my eyebrows are all yours."

Erik groaned. "Ugh. Don't let her win."

"No, I'm serious, babe. Let me up." I tapped his arm. "There's pizza."

"'Babe'?" Elektra said. "Did you just call him babe?"

We both turned to face her. "He said it first," I replied.

She laughed as she walked to the dining table. "Well, it's ridiculously cute. And while we're being all mushy, I'm very happy that you two worked everything out. Monroe, just so you know, he's been truly insufferable without you. And Erik, you'll be pleased to know I spent an hour on the phone to Mum and Dad and told them all the details to save you from the four thousand questions you would have gotten if I hadn't taken one for the team. So, you're welcome."

"Thank you," Erik said, unfolding himself from me and standing up. "You're the best sister ever."

"And I also told her you guys had sex in the dunes out the back. So good luck with that." She grinned, took a pizza box from the table, and held it out. "Pizza?"

We sat on the veranda, pizzas demolished and empty boxes cleared away, drinking our Sprites and talking and laughing long after the sun had set. Yes, I was keen to go to bed—with Erik—but doing something as mundane as chatting and talking bullshit with people I cared about was kinda nice too.

Elektra filled me in on all the trash Sydney gossip columns had said about me, and I didn't even care. What they thought about me, I didn't give one toss about. The only opinions that mattered to me were from the people at the table, including Saul.

He stood, thanked Elektra again for dinner, gave Erik and me a nod and smile, then said goodnight. "If I'm late calling my wife, she'll worry," he said, waving us off.

Erik waited until he was gone. "He's actually a nice guy."

"He is," I agreed. "He calls his wife every night."

"That's sweet," Elektra said. "You know, he talked a lot about you today, Monroe."

"Oh?"

"Yeah, in a good way," she furthered. "Without any specific details, he's good with the confidentiality thing. But he likes you, I can tell. He respects you. And he thinks you two are the real deal." She shrugged. "He said you have a very strong bond."

Erik reached over and rubbed my back. "He's not wrong."

Elektra stood up. "And on that note, I have a report that I need to look over. I'll see you both in the morning. What time are we leaving?" she asked Erik.

"Flight's at 9:00am."

Shit. Our time together was almost up. Knowing he was leaving sent a stab of longing through me. Christ. How was it possible to miss him already?

"Night," she said, leaving us alone and flicking off some lights as she went. It left us in a soft glow.

The waves crashed on the shore, seemingly louder in the absence of conversation. My heart was beating at too fast a tempo, and a nervous, panicky feeling began to creep up on me. In my brain, the countdown to being without Erik again had just started... and I needed a drink. Like he somehow knew, like he could hear my heart trying to beat its way out of my chest, he stood and held out his hand. "Let's go to bed. If I have to leave in ten hours, I don't want to waste a minute."

I stood up, so close to him our lips brushed in an almost-kiss. "You read my mind."

He took my face in his hands. "Tell me what you want, what you need."

The dark made it a little easier to answer, but I needed to get used to telling him these things. I looked down at his chest though. If I had to see my truth in his eyes, I'd never get the words out. "I don't like the idea of you leaving. As soon as I realised just now that you were leaving in the morning, I started to feel a bit on edge and panicky. And that makes me want to drink. I know you've got to leave, and I know I'll see you again soon, but I need..." I licked my lips and tried again. "I need you to distract me. And I need you to prove to me, show me... I don't know, Erik." I looked up into his eyes, seeing only concern and patience there. "I want to say that I need you to leave a mark on me, but Saul would be back out in a flash talking about why I felt I deserved pain and self-harm or whatever, and that's not what I mean at all. I just want you to give me something to get me through until I see you again. Something in here," I said, putting my hand to my heart. "Fuck, I don't even know."

His nostrils flared and he made a weird groaning sound, then took hold of my hand and led me to my room, his room. He closed the door behind us and turned to face me, and there was enough light from the ajar bathroom door that I could see the determination in his eyes.

It was fierce and fire, heat and need. My heart rate kicked up a notch; my skin felt flushed all over.

He kissed me, deep and slow at first, with gentle hands on my back and his tongue in my mouth. He took my shirt by the hem, pulling it over my head, then ran his hands over my chest, thumbing my nipples, and I gasped into his mouth.

He smiled, breaking the kiss long enough to pull off his own shirt. Then he kissed down my neck, under my ear, along my jaw, with his lips, his tongue, his teeth.

"Holy shit," I breathed. My entire body was thrumming, my head was spinning, and my cock was hard, and when he slid my shorts over my arse and down my thighs, I almost swayed.

"Lie on the bed," he murmured. I sat, then scooted up, lying with my head on a pillow. Erik undressed and he stood, fully naked, watching me. "You're gorgeous," he whispered, almost to himself like he didn't mean to say it aloud.

His long, lean body outlined by the muted bathroom light looked almost ethereal. His cock jutted out and he gave himself a stroke before kneeling on the bed. "Erik," I murmured, not sure what I was asking for. Just needing him to do something, anything. "Please."

He moved in between my legs, kissing up my thigh, until he nudged my cock with his nose, then licked up my shaft, tonguing the slit.

Oh fuck.

Then he took me into his mouth, all the fucking way, and I almost came. He pulled off and grinned, then kissed up my body, my stomach, my chest, my neck, my jaw, my mouth. Then he pressed his weight on mine, our cocks almost aligned, and he kissed me, hard.

I drew my knees up and he groaned, bucking and thrusting, and I clung to him, holding him tight and rolling my hips. He hooked his arms under my shoulders and we rocked and thrust together, slowly and fiercely. He arched up and I slid my hand between us, taking us both into my fist. Slick with pre-come, slippery, and oh so good.

He shuddered and his hips jerked. "Fuck, Monroe. I'm gonna come."

I squeezed our cocks and he grunted, long and real low in his throat, and he swelled and surged in my hand before he shot come between us. He shuddered and thrust as his orgasm rocketed through him. But his face... his beautiful face as he came...

My own orgasm detonated inside me, and he kissed me and held me as I fell apart in his arms. And as we lay there in a sweaty and sticky mess, the way he held me and traced patterns on my skin and trailed soft kisses over my shoulder and under my ear, there was no doubt, not a single one, that he loved me.

"Should we shower?" he whispered gruffly.

"No," I mumbled sleepily, tightening my arms around him. "Stay."

"I think Saul said separate rooms," I murmured, as I closed my eyes and snuggled in even closer. He chuckled and kissed the side of my head, holding me even tighter. There was no way we were letting go of each other...

I sighed, basking in the warmth of his body. In the gift he'd just given me.

I'd asked him to give me something, a part of him, anything, to make his leaving easier, and he'd given me exactly what I needed. We fell asleep in each other's arms, and in the morning, he gave it to me again.

So much so, that when Saul met us at breakfast, he innocently asked if we'd slept well, and I blushed and giggled.

I fucking giggled.

Erik laughed, Saul sighed, and Elektra stuck her fingers in her ears.

And when it was time for them to go, Erik kissed me soundly. "I will see you soon."

I smiled, feeling good, positive, hopeful for the first time in a long time. "Yes, you will."

We watched them drive off and Saul put his hand on my shoulder. "I'm happy for you, Monroe," he said.

"But?" It sounded like there was a but coming.

"But we still have work to do, and you're not going to like it. I'm afraid to ruin your good mood."

"Then don't."

"We have to. It's the last stage of your recovery." He took a deep breath. "And we're starting today. It's time to say goodbye to your parents, Monroe."

"Things were strained between you after you told them you were gay," Saul said.

I nodded. "Yeah."

"Did you fight?"

I frowned and shook my head. "Nope. They said nothing. It was like radio silence. Like they didn't know what to say to me." I shrugged. "And I didn't know what to say to them either."

"And you worked at Wellman Corporation during that time?"

"Yep. I was on the board of directors, but I don't know what for. My dad never took anything I said seriously. I think he just liked making everyone else feel outnumbered. You know, two Wellman votes every time."

"Could they not see that you and your father weren't close? Did they not know?"

"Jeffrey knew."

"He was good friends with your father, yes?"

I gave a nod. "Yeah." I looked at Saul then. "I let him down too. He tried to help me, and he did everything he could, but I..." I sighed. "I threw it back in his face. He was my fixer, my man to make all the legal trouble disappear. And I'm sorry for that. I never meant to use him like that. I hurt him, and I'm sorry."

Saul nodded slowly. "I think he'd appreciate hearing that. And I think when we go back to Sydney, he'll be on the list of people you need to apologise to."

I wanted to sigh, but instead I used that breath to bolster my resolve. "You're right."

"Where were you when your parents died?"

"Um..." I swallowed hard. "At home. Sydney. I'd been to work that day and the police came to the house before dinner. Erik was there because... well, because he was always there. I thought it was the food delivery guy and I asked Erik to grab the door..." I stared out at the ocean while the memory replayed in my head. "They said there'd been an accident. A plane crash. In Macau, China, of all fucking places."

"Did your parents always travel together for business trips?"

I flinched. "Not always."

"Monroe," he said slowly, calmly. And I knew what he was going to ask. I just knew it... "Who was supposed to be on that plane?"

I swallowed hard and suddenly found it really fucking hard to breathe. "Can we just...? Do I have to...?"

He put his hand on my shoulder. "Take a deep breath for me, Monroe. That's it. Let it out slowly."

We did that a couple of times, until the constriction around my chest eased up.

"Were you supposed to be on that trip, Monroe?" he pressed.

I nodded. "Me and Dad."

"Why didn't you go?"

"Because we'd had a fight. I wasn't a good enough son and they weren't good enough parents, and I told him considering I wasn't good enough at any fucking thing, even though it was my contract, he could fuck off and go without me. So they did. We'd not spoken for a week before they left." Tears ran down my cheeks and my chest burned. "It should have been me."

Saul took my hand and squeezed. "No, Monroe. Fate

doesn't work that way. You're here because you're meant to be."

I shook my head and sobbed. "My mum is supposed to still be here. She took my place because I was a fucking brat. She's meant to be here. Not me. I hate myself for it. I hate myself."

Saul slid over and put his arm around my shoulder and he held me as I cried and cried. I cried for everything I'd held back, for everything I'd repressed. I'd cried for the lives my parents should have had, that they were robbed of because of me. I cried for the agony that was now painfully, painfully open and fresh, raw and exposed. I wanted it gone. I wanted to be numb, and I wanted darkness to come and take it all away.

"I want a drink," I mumbled when my tears began to dry up.

"You're better than that," Saul said calmly. "You don't need to drink any more hurt or any more hate. You've begun to let it go." He pulled back and made me look at him. "You've been drinking your hate for long enough. You don't need it anymore."

Chapter Seventeen
Erik

SAUL'S NAME FLASHED ON THE SCREEN OF MY PHONE. "Hello?"

"Hey."

"Monroe," I breathed. God, I only saw him three days ago, but the sound of his voice squeezed painfully around my heart. "I've missed you."

I heard him swallow. "I've missed you too." He sounded upset. "It's been a hard few days."

"Oh, baby," I whispered. "Did you want to talk about it?" I was at work, but I didn't care. I got up and closed my office door. "What happened?"

"My parents died," he whispered.

Oh shit. "I know."

"Erik, I was supposed to be on that plane."

"Oh, babe," I whispered. I'd always suspected as much. I knew of the fight they'd had before they left, but it never really clicked that Monroe was supposed to be on that flight.

"I wish you were here."

I nodded though he couldn't see. "I wish I was too."

He groaned and it sounded as though he wiped his face. "I'm coming home on Friday."

"You are?" I was not expecting that. "Really?"

"Yeah," he said with a sigh. "I have to say goodbye to my parents. Properly. So I get past this or so I can deal with it. Or something."

"Oh, babe. I'll be there with you, every step of the way."

"Thank you." He cried a little. "I was hoping you'd say that."

"I wouldn't be anywhere else."

"I thought we could have a proper memorial," he mumbled through more tears. "You know, like I should have done three years ago."

"I think that's a great idea."

"Can you ask your parents to be there?"

"Of course they will be." Even if Dad had to fly back from Melbourne. I knew he would if I told him why. "Of course we'll all be there."

He cried again, and I gave him time to collect his thoughts. "I need to speak to Jeffrey."

"Okay."

He let out a shuddery breath. "I need to do this. It's time. It's been time for three years."

"You weren't ready then."

"I am now. I want to do this, Erik. I need to do this."

"I'll be there with you. I promise." His determination

made me smile, though hearing how upset he was hurt my heart. "I'm proud of you."

"I've never wanted a drink so bad as I did this week," he admitted. "Saul talked me through it, and it was a bit of a breakthrough for me. I wanted you here so much, and I begged Saul to call you, but he said I needed to get through this. It was awful, but he was right. He's always fucking right. Then I remembered our night together... God, this sounds so stupid, I can't believe I'm saying this to you. But the way you held me and the way you loved me." He sobbed again. "Fucking hell, I'm a mess. Sorry."

"Don't apologise," I whispered. "I'm here. I'm listening."

"I remembered how much you love me. And it gave me strength to get through it. I know that sounds corny. Believe me, it's fucked up."

"It's not fucked up. It's not corny."

"I knew I wasn't alone," he said. "Even though you weren't here. And I was strong enough to do it. I mean, I had Saul, and I got through it because I have you too, but I did it. I went through the steps Saul had taught me, and I coped."

"I'm proud of you, baby."

He barked out a teary laugh. "Baby?"

"Well, yeah. Sorry, it just slipped out. I can stop with the terms of endearment if you want."

"Please," he whispered, "promise me you won't ever stop."

My heart swelled and I realised we were turning a

corner. We still had a long way to go, but we getting there. "I promise, baby."

***

Oz-E News

Happening now! Erik Keston was seen pacing at the domestic airport arrivals terminal. A far cry from the private airfield he's used to, witnesses said he appeared anxious but happy, and a small crowd had gathered to see who he was waiting for. Rumours began to surface that Monroe Wellman was expected to fly in, so stay tuned for this Oz-E News exclusive!

Friday couldn't come around fast enough. It was going to be a trying day, an emotional day, but one we needed to get through. For the last three years it felt like we'd walked on eggshells, waiting for the eruption of grief. But Monroe had never exploded with rage and anger. He'd imploded instead.

I had no idea what to expect. But I had faith in Saul and the process he used. I also had faith in Monroe.

He was ready, and so was I.

And so, despite my nerves, I stood at the airport waiting for them to walk through the lounge. I'd offered the Keston jet, but Monroe had said it was fine and that he needed to put himself in normal situations. Like being surrounded by people, in crowds, walking past bars, being offered glasses of wine or beer, and declining. It was all part of the recovery process.

And so I waited for what felt like forever.

And then he was there, walking through the gates with Saul at his side. He scanned the crowds, but I saw him first. I called out his name and he turned just in time for me to crush him in a hug. I knew there was a good chance someone was taking photos, but I didn't care.

I gave him a kiss and said hello to Saul and asked which carousel their luggage would be at. "We only brought carry-ons," Monroe said.

Which meant he wasn't staying. He wasn't coming home for good...

"Okay then," I said, trying not to let my disappointment show. "Let's get out of here." I led the way to my car and we made our way back toward the city. "Where to first?"

Monroe, who was sitting in the passenger seat staring at the passing buildings, turned to me. "My place. I guess." He didn't sound overly happy about it.

"I told my parents three o'clock," I said. It was the time he'd suggested, so he nodded.

Saul was in the back seat. "Thank you."

"Yeah," Monroe echoed. "Thank you."

I gave him a smile, and as traffic slowed down to a crawl, I held out my hand. He quickly took it and kept our joined hands on his thigh. He was quiet, in a reflective kind of way, and given what he was here to do, I wasn't surprised.

Pulling up to his house felt weird. The security gates were familiar, the house was familiar, but something felt different. Alien. And I wasn't the only one to feel it. I stopped the car near the front door and turned the engine off, and Monroe made no move to get out. He just stared at the front door, and Saul never moved or spoke, giving Monroe the time he clearly needed, so I did the same.

His hold on my hand tightened, just a fraction. He let out a slow breath. "I'm ready," he said.

So we got out and Monroe led the way inside. The house was exactly as he'd left it. The cleaning staff had been in, but apart from that, everything was as it should be. Though it still felt weird and wrong in a way I couldn't quite explain.

There was a pile of mail on the kitchen counter which Monroe ignored for now. He opened up the glass sliding doors and walked out to the pool. The view out to the ocean was clear, the sky an eternal blue. Monroe took a deep breath in and let it out slowly, then he did it again and finally he looked to me. "I don't know how I feel about being here," he admitted quietly. "It's different now."

I didn't want to tell him I felt that too, so instead I nodded so he'd know I understood. I put my hand on his arm, his shoulder, and he instantly turned into me, wrapping his arms around me.

I held him tight, and for the longest time, he simply hugged me back and breathed.

I could hear Saul doing something inside, pottering about, boiling a kettle, and doing whatever Saul did, but Monroe and I stood by the pool in each other's arms as the world went on around us.

Monroe laid his head on my shoulder and sighed. "I missed you."

I rubbed his back. "I missed you too."

He pulled back and met my gaze. His arms were around my lower back and I kept my hands on his hips, and I could feel his half-hard dick pressing against me. And as much as I liked it, as much as I loved knowing I turned him on, this wasn't about sex. His blue eyes searched mine, with an almost-smile on his face, and he leaned in and kissed me. It was soft and sweet, and it was still so new between us. It made my heart do crazy things, and when he pressed his cheek to mine, then pressed his forehead to my chin, I slid one hand into the hair at the back of his head and held him close.

"I love you, Monroe Wellman."

He sighed and snuggled in closer, held me tighter. "And I love you. And I love being loved by you. I don't know if I'll ever fully deserve it, but I will never take you for granted again."

I pulled his face back and put my forehead to his. "You do deserve it. You probably deserve more than I can give, but I'll never stop trying."

He crushed his mouth to mine, a deep and passionate kiss. So heady and potent, I was considering taking him into his bedroom or bathroom and letting him do what he wanted to me.

Saul cleared his throat. "Excuse me, guys, you're making me miss my wife, so if you could stop any second now, that'd be great."

Monroe chuckled into the kiss and pulled back, his lips wet and plump, smiling. But he curled his hand around mine and we went inside to where Saul had poured three cups of coffee.

Monroe did a double take. "Coffee?"

Saul rolled his eyes. "Thought you might appreciate it today."

Monroe picked up one cup and sipped it and sighed. "Oh, blessed are the gods of mercy."

I chuckled. "He likes the tea. He just doesn't want you to know."

Monroe shot me a look. "I've been betrayed!"

Saul laughed, and we drank our coffees in a comfortable silence. Monroe didn't seem so out of place now; the coffee had been a touch of familiarity in this house for him, and I briefly wondered if there was anything Saul was ever wrong about.

"Are you ready?" Saul asked when our coffees were gone.

Monroe nodded. "Yeah." Then he shot me a look before turning back to Saul. "Can Erik come with me?"

Saul gave him a nod. "Of course."

I had no idea what they were talking about, but

when Monroe held out his hand, I gladly took it. He threaded our fingers together, held on tight, and led the way to his parents' end of the house. He went into their bedroom first, unsure initially, but he took a breath, and then another and another, and finally relaxed. I had no doubt this was hard for him, and that he was drawing on the core strength he never knew he had. The strength that Saul had perhaps sieved to the surface. Much like panning for gold, with the right tools and patience, by clearing away the broken earth, all that remains is gold.

The room was as they'd left it. The bed was made, there was a book on one bedside table, lamps, and a painting on the wall above the bedhead. It was a large room, the bed only taking up a portion. There were two doors, one that led to a wardrobe, the other to a bathroom, and a large window with the curtains drawn. Saul opened them and sunlight filled the room, bringing with it light and warmth.

Emotions flickered across Monroe's face, but he remained silent.

Unlinking our hands, he walked to the walk-in robe and flicked on the light. There were rows of suits and shirts in a range of blues and greys on his dad's side of the wardrobe, dresses, stripes, and florals on his mother's side.

Monroe sighed and traced his fingers along the sleeve of one of his dad's jackets, and then he touched a rose-coloured blouse that I remembered his mum wearing. No doubt he remembered them all...

"What do you feel?" Saul asked.

"Sadness. Loss. And I remember when Mum bought this dress in Paris." It was striped black with bright flowers: bold and gaudy enough to be ridiculously expensive. Monroe smiled. "She was so happy. I thought it was hideous, not that I told her that. She glowed every time she wore it, and I never really appreciated it until now."

He turned to face Saul and me, a little teary but smiling.

The fact he was even talking about his parents, in their room, and remembering happier times spoke volumes as to how far he'd come. When Monroe went deeper into the wardrobe, I clapped Saul lightly on the arm giving him a nod.

Monroe had made so much progress.

He was holding a tie, feeling it between his thumb and fingers. It was blue, striped, very business-like, and nothing like the gaudy dress. "I bought this for my dad's birthday when I was about fifteen. He wore it all the time." Then he lifted the sleeve of a light blue business shirt, just staring at it, before he lifted it to his nose.

And then he went into their bathroom. It was a modern, stylish double-sink. Sleek and white with blue Moroccan tiles. He took another deep breath, then picked up a bottle of perfume that sat atop the counter. He brought it to his nose and closed his eyes.

It was his mother's.

And when he looked up at me and smiled, a tear ran down his cheek. But he nodded and swallowed hard. He was doing this.

He was finally letting them go.

Next was his father's office. This was going to be the most difficult. The cabinet was still broken. It had been tidied, the splintered wood and shards of glass gone; the cleaning staff were efficient.

He ran his hand along one intact glass panel, frowning. His gentle touch now was miles different to the man who, just weeks ago, had smashed it. The pent-up anger, guilt, and rage were gone.

His father's desk still felt ominous and looming, too large and too empty. Monroe trailed his finger along the mahogany and frowned when there was no trail of dust. He sighed, walking to the window that overlooked the pool and the ocean, and he stood there, his face a myriad of expressions and emotions.

"What are you feeling?" Saul prompted.

Monroe looked at him and his brows drew in as he turned back to the view. It was another while before he spoke.

"I know I'm supposed to make peace with it," he murmured. "But how can I make peace knowing I wasn't good enough? How can I reconcile the difference between us when the divide was too great?" Monroe shook his head and whispered, "I wasn't what he wanted... for a son or for a legacy for his company."

"Are you good enough?" Saul asked. "Are you the man you want to be?"

Monroe's gaze shot to Saul, then to mine; then he turned back to the ocean. "I'm becoming him. I never used to be, and I'm certainly not perfect, but I'm closer now than I've ever been."

Christ. My heart was about to explode with pride.

Saul smiled. "Then you have made peace, Monroe. You have reconciled the two conflicting men in your mind."

"My father still wouldn't agree," he replied. "I'm still gay."

"Monroe," Saul said evenly, and Monroe looked at him. "It was never your father's lack of acceptance that was keeping you held under. It was your own." Monroe's chin wobbled a little and his eyes shone. Saul went to him and put his hands on Monroe's shoulders. "You are good enough. And you are exactly who you were born to be."

Monroe began to cry and Saul pulled him in for a hug. It was a fatherly hug; a paternal embrace that Monroe had never had, that he'd longed for. After a while Saul transferred him over to me, and he came willingly. I tucked him into my side and he clung to me.

"I'll give you two a moment," Saul said. "I'll be in the living room waiting, when you're ready." He slipped out of the room.

I kissed the side of Monroe's head. "You okay?"

He nodded. "I will be. It's just... rough, facing all this." He pulled back and looked into my eyes. "I should have faced it years ago. I let it control me, and taking back that control is scary as fuck."

I dried his face with my thumbs. "You're doing great."

His eyebrows narrowed and something akin to pain flashed in his eyes. "One day at a time."

"That's all we can do," I whispered.

He sighed and leaned against his father's desk, pulling me with him so I stood between his legs, his face to my chest. I rubbed his back until he was ready to talk. "What am I supposed to do with their things?" he asked. "I can't keep all of it. I don't want to. I mean, I'll keep some stuff, of course. But their clothes, and God, my mother's taste in art was terrible."

I chuckled and he finally smiled.

"It really was," he mumbled. Then he sighed. "When someone dies, no one ever tells you what you're supposed to do with their stuff."

"You could give it away," I suggested. "Or you could auction it off and give all the proceeds to charity."

"Hmm."

"To a charity for LGBTQIA+ kids. Or you could start your own foundation."

He pulled back to look at me. "A foundation?"

"Sure," I said. "For at-risk kids or education programs for homeless queer kids... There's a hundred possibilities."

He tilted his head and made a thoughtful face. "I like that idea. It's productive, and it turns a negative into a positive. Getting rid of their stuff is gonna be hard, but if I know it'll help someone else..."

I kissed him with smiling lips, just a peck. "I think it could be a great thing."

"I'll speak to Jeffrey when he gets here," he replied, happier now he'd chosen a direction.

I could already see the cogs turning in his head, so I

lifted his chin and kissed him again. A little softer, a little slower. "One day at a time, babe."

He hummed, an optimistic sound. "We should go find Saul."

I stood back and held out my hand. He took it easily, confidently, and together we walked out to the living room. Saul was sitting on the sofa, the coffee table pulled in close where he had a smallish white box. It looked to be recycled cardboard or something similar, a little bit artsy, but only big enough to maybe hold a few postcards. Beside it sat a pile of paper squares and a pen.

Monroe put our still joined hands on his thigh as we sat opposite Saul. "Been shopping on Etsy, I see."

Saul smiled. "Not quite." He pushed the box toward Monroe and then the pile of paper, or notecards as they turned out to be. "Monroe, over these last few weeks, we've done a few word clusters." He looked to me and clarified, "Just single words to describe emotions. Sometimes it's easier to just say random words about how we're feeling, particularly if we're trying to describe something we haven't talked about much."

Monroe chewed on the inside of his lip and glanced to the pen and paper. "Yeah."

"What I'd like you to do is take some time to write down those cluster words. All the things you feel about your parents, good and bad, all of them. Then we can put them in the box. And, if you think you're ready, when everyone arrives later, we can light a fire. It's a good way to let go, taking all the words, all the emotions, and saying goodbye."

Monroe looked at him like he'd gone mad. "By setting them on fire?"

Saul almost chuckled. "By absolving them. By taking them from here." He put his hand to his heart. "And releasing them out into the atmosphere."

Monroe chewed on his lip again and his brow creased. "Okay." He let go of my hand and took the pile of notecards and held the pen in his right hand, but he stopped short of actually writing anything.

"Do you want some privacy?" I asked quietly. "What you write down is yours and yours alone."

"I, um." He made a face. "I don't know. I don't know where to start."

"When you think of your parents, what do you feel?" Saul asked. "What did you feel when they first died? What do you feel now? What would you tell your parents if you had the chance? Write as much or as little as you need."

Monroe stared at him for a second and then, with a nod to himself, he began to write. I leaned back on the sofa so I couldn't see the words he chose, but I rubbed his back and Saul made us all some tea. After a while, Monroe leaned back against me and I put my arm around his shoulder. He kind of curled up into himself, but he kept on writing. He took his time, obviously giving each word, each line the time and consideration it deserved. Sometimes, for a few minutes at a time, he didn't write at all. He just leaned the side of his head against my chest, and I kissed the top of his head and held him that little bit tighter.

I don't know how long we sat there for. Long enough for Saul to potter about by the pool, make more tea, disappear, come back again, clean up the cups and saucers, and potter about some more. Then, eventually, Monroe put the last piece of paper into the box and put the pen down. He turned around and snuggled into me, and we ended up lying down on the sofa, his face in my chest, our legs entwined, and my arms wrapped tight around him.

Saul smiled when he saw us, but he never interrupted. He just did whatever it was he was doing. Until I think I'd dozed off and woke up to see Saul reappear, wearing different clothes. "You have half an hour until people arrive," he said.

I sighed and stretched, as much as I could with Monroe still snuggled into my side. I put my hand to the side of his face. "Hey, baby," I whispered. I kissed his eyelid, his cheek, his forehead. "Monroe, baby. Wake up."

His eyes opened slowly and it took him a second to focus on me, but he smiled as soon as he saw it was me.

"It's half two. People will start arriving soon."

He groaned out a sigh and rolled off the couch. I followed him into his room, but it was too late. Saul called out, "Erik, your parents are here!"

I sighed, took Monroe's face in my hands, and kissed him. "I'll only be out there with them, okay?"

"Okay," he replied. "I'll just get changed. I won't be long."

I left him to it and met my parents as they were walking into the foyer. Mum and Dad both had their arms full. Mum was carrying a massive bouquet, and Dad was juggling two trays of something that smelt good. "Here," I said, intercepting him and taking one of the trays.

Mum put the flowers on the kitchen counter, turned, and kissed my cheek. "How is he?"

"He's okay. Just getting changed," I said. "What did you bring food for?"

"Because that's what you do for memorial services at people's houses," she said, like I should have known. Then she looked me up and down. "Erik, you're all crumpled. You can't wear that."

I looked down at my navy trousers and light blue button-down shirt. It was kinda crumpled... "We fell asleep," I mumbled, trying to press down the crinkles in my shirt with my hand.

"Take it off," Mum said. "I'll go iron it. I assume Monroe has an ironing board somewhere."

Saul entered at the right time. He'd walked in with Elektra, both carrying more flowers and more food. "It's in the laundry, second door on your right up the hall."

"That's everything out of the car," Elektra said as she slid a foil-covered tray onto the kitchen counter. "Have you seen the YouTube videos of you at the airport? It's ridiculously romantic and has about a million views already. I think it's viral on Instagram." She stopped talking, eyed me unbuttoning my shirt and taking it off. "What are you doing?"

"Living an unacceptably crumpled life apparently," I

said by way of explanation and passed my shirt over to Mum, who was waiting with her hand out.

Dad laughed as he slid the trays of food into the oven, and Elektra went scouting for vases for the flowers, then arranged them. Saul gave me a bit of a smirk as the Kestons took charge: Dad in the kitchen, Elektra in the living room, and Mum when she returned with a freshly pressed shirt. She handed it to me, then inspected the oven, then the flowers. Saul and I stood aside and let them do their thing. "You learn to accept it," I whispered, redoing the buttons on my shirt. "It quicker and easier that way."

Monroe appeared, wearing black pants and a charcoal shirt. His black hair looked a little damp, and he froze when he saw Mum and Dad and rubbed his hands down his thighs. I immediately went to go to him, but Saul put his hand on my arm. "Let him do it," he murmured.

And maybe Saul was right. Maybe it was my instinct to rush in and save him, and maybe I needed to let Monroe fend for himself.

Monroe licked his lips and took another tentative step when my mum spotted him. "Oh, my! Look at you," she said, crossing the room and pulling him in for a hug. "My darling, you look wonderful." He smiled awkwardly but it was obvious he liked it. She held him at arm's length and inspected him. "You really do look amazing."

It was true. He had a healthier glow now; gone was the pallid skin and dark circles under his eyes. "Um, it's the obscene amount of healthy food Saul makes me eat," Monroe said.

Then it was Dad's turn. He gave him a hug too and Monroe hugged him right back, then Dad said, "So I hear you and Erik are a thing now." Monroe's eyes went wide, but before he could speak, Dad gave him a nudge and said, "If he pisses you off, you let me know. I'll sort him out for you."

Monroe laughed, purely with relief, I'm sure. "Um, thanks?"

I laughed and Monroe spun at the sound. He sighed and walked over to me, and like he'd done before, straight into an embrace. He held me tight, his face pressed into my neck, and my arms slowly went around him. Mum smiled, a little teary, and Dad patted her arm. She nodded and shook her tears off.

"You okay?" I murmured into Monroe's hair.

He nodded. "Yeah. I will be."

I kissed his forehead just as Jeffrey walked in. I hadn't even noticed Saul was gone, but he was beside Jeffrey, who stopped when he saw me with Monroe. Monroe looked around my shoulder, and seeing who was there, he straightened and pulled away. He took a deep breath and walked over to Jeffrey, his hand extended. "Thank you so much for coming."

Jeffrey couldn't hide his surprise or outright shock. "Uh. Yes." He shook Monroe's hand. "Of course I would be here. Monroe." He paused. "I must say, you look like a different man."

Monroe laughed, and maybe I imagined it, but he

stood a little taller. "That's because I am. Well," he allowed, "I'm still me. Just without the drunken arsehole routine."

Jeffrey laughed but he shook his head, still staring at Monroe. "You look... good, Monroe," he said.

"So everyone keeps telling me," he replied, a little embarrassed. Then he turned to face everyone. "I'd like to thank you all for coming. And I have some things to say, that I need to say. It's not easy, so forgive me if I get it wrong or if it doesn't make sense. But it's gonna get real Disney for a minute...," he trailed off. Saul gave him a nod and Monroe took a breath and let it out. "I've made a lot of mistakes. A lot. Jeffrey, I owe you a huge apology. Actually, sorry probably doesn't begin to cover it, but I am sorry. I really am. I was entrusted with responsibility I was not prepared for or mentally or emotionally equipped to deal with. You stepped up when I failed, and I'm grateful for you and your dedication to the Wellman Corporation. Without you..." He sighed. "Well, without you, I'd be broke and I'd probably be in jail."

Jeffrey bowed his head. "Thank you, Monroe. Your acknowledgement means a lot."

"We have a lot to discuss when you have time," Monroe said to him. "I'm not sure where I fit in the company or if I fit at all. I don't know yet, and I don't want to make any decisions until I'm more comfortable with myself."

Jeffrey looked so proud he could burst. "Whenever you're ready."

Monroe gave him a nod, then turned to my parents.

He let out a shaky breath. "Mr and Mrs Keston. I owe you so much. You've been understanding and patient and supportive. I haven't been the best thing for your son these last three years, but you've never once lost faith in me. Having a parent's support—" He got a little choked up and my mum burst into tears. Monroe sniffled and his eyes were glassy, but he nodded and almost laughed when my mum dabbed her face with a tissue with one hand and waved him off with her other. Monroe continued, "Your family is kind and generous, and you all love with such abandon."

"Thank you, Monroe," Dad said when it was pretty obvious Mum still couldn't speak.

Then Monroe turned to me. "And Erik." He let out a deep breath. "I owe you everything. Everything. When I was downright awful and when I felt like I was drowning in a sea of guilt and grief, you never gave up on me. I'll never be able to thank you enough. For not giving up on me. I'm still not sure I know what love is or if I deserve it." He swallowed hard and wiped away a tear. "But then I see you and I know."

I knew I was supposed to probably give him space and time to finish his speech, but I couldn't help it. I had to go to him. I walked to him with my arms outstretched and he laugh-cried as he stepped into my embrace. He squeezed me tight. "I love you," he mumbled into my neck, just for me to hear.

"Love you too," I whispered into his ear before pulling away and giving him the floor again. "Sorry. I just had to..."

Monroe laughed, his cheeks red. He shook off his tears and took a deep breath. "Elektra, thank you for being a constant source of support for Erik and for me as well. You don't treat me any differently now to how you always have, and I really appreciate that."

"You're welcome," she said, fondly.

"And you brought me pizza," Monroe said. "And I'll always love you for that."

She laughed. "And you still have to let me do your eyebrows. That was the deal."

Everyone laughed and the mood was a little lighter. Then Monroe turned to Saul. "Saul. You have seen the worst of me." Then Monroe shook his head. "Erik, if you thought you'd seen me at my worst, I can tell you, you've got nothing on poor Saul."

Everyone chuckled, and Saul nodded, smiling. "It's true."

Monroe bolstered himself to continue. "And I know I probably cursed you out more than was completely necessary, but every single thing you have said to me is the truth. Everything you put me through, made me face, and went through with me has made me a better person. You're the reason I'm here. And I can probably tell you now that your god-awful tea isn't *that* bad."

Saul gave him a sad, proud nod. "You did good. It wasn't easy, but you did it."

Monroe nodded and took a deep breath. Then he looked at everyone in turn and raised his chin. "I have a long road ahead of me. It won't be easy, and there's no quick fixing me," he said, getting a little teary again. "I'm a... I am... an alcoholic. It's my truth and I have to own it. And own my past wrongs, and I'm not asking for forgiveness today. I just need you all to know that the mistakes I made were mine and mine alone." He shrugged. "That's it. That's what I needed to say. Apologies fall far too short, and I have more faults than a tectonic plate, and I promise to you all that I will try—with everything I am—to be the person you all deserve."

Chapter Eighteen
Monroe

I knew it wasn't going to be easy, and it was one of the hardest things I'd ever done. But there was nothing but love and acceptance in that room, and telling them I was an alcoholic was tough. Owning it was tough.

It felt like I had barbed wire wrapped around my insides.

But I needed to face them, and I needed to apologise to them. I needed to own my wrongs and call my disease what it was.

I was an alcoholic.

Owning and acknowledging it didn't make me any more comfortable with that label and I doubt I ever would be. But it was the truth and it was my truth, and it was mine whether I liked it or not.

But everyone hugged me, including Jeffrey, and even Saul. Mrs Keston hugged me the longest, and Mr Keston a close second longest. They were all proud of me, and they all loved me.

Lord knows I didn't deserve it. But like I'd told them, I would never stop trying.

Erik's parents brought out the food and we toasted with mineral water, and Erik was never far from my side.

He was ridiculously handsome, laughing at something Saul said, and I would never—ever—know why he loved me. But he did. And I'd never take him for granted, and I'd never stop trying to be a better man for him.

I promised myself that, right then and there as I watched him laugh in the fading afternoon sun.

"He is kind of handsome," Mr Keston whispered beside me.

My face burned so hot I thought it might catch on fire. "Oh."

He bumped his elbow into mine. "I won't embarrass you too much," he said, smiling. "But I meant what I said. If you need advice or if you want to vent because he pisses you off about something"—he leaned in and whispered—"all the bad traits he got from his mother, by the way." He winked. "You can talk to me. I mean that. Don't ever feel you're alone. You have a place in our family, Monroe."

I found it hard to swallow. Talking wasn't much better. So I nodded instead.

"And to be honest," he continued, "I thought you two had been together for years. I just thought it was kind of low-key. Because he has never had eyes for anyone else."

I blushed again. "Oh, yeah, well. I was too blind to see. And too stupid, apparently."

He laughed. "Love does that to all of us. Makes us all blind and stupid. Don't be too hard on yourself."

I chuckled. "Glad to know it's not just me."

Saul gently interrupted. "Monroe, should I light the fire?"

He'd stacked up the fire pit when Erik and I were dozing on the couch earlier, apparently. I glanced at it, and what it symbolised. Was I ready to say a final goodbye to my parents? Would I ever be? But with these people around me, there was no better time.

I met Saul's eyes and nodded.

He put his hand to my shoulder and smiled. "Good lad."

Saul left and Erik took his place, sliding his arm around my shoulder and tucking me into his side. "My dad isn't being too embarrassing, is he?"

They bantered back and forth and I just basked in it all. My heart was full despite knowing what I was about to do, or maybe because of it. I was completely surrounded by people who cared for me, who were still beside me after everything I put them through. It was humbling and empowering, and it gave me a strength that somehow came from within.

When the fire was well alight, Saul came back with the white box, and he handed it to me. Everyone was watching us, curious, cautious.

"I um," I said and had to start again. "I have one last thing to do. I said this was going to be a memorial for my parents, and it is. I never said goodbye. Not really. I carried their deaths around with me for three years, and the weight of it almost killed me." I let out a shaky breath. "It's time for me to say goodbye."

I walked over to the fire pit and everyone gathered around. Erik was right beside me, his hand on my back. I resisted leaning into him. I needed to stand on my own two feet for this.

"Saul suggested I write down everything I wanted to say to my parents and all the things I've carried around for far too long and put them in this box." I lifted the lid and took out the first slip of paper. "But I didn't just carry them around with me. I drank them. Lost. Alone. Orphan. Pain. Anger. Grief." I threw the slips of paper into the fire and watched them burn, drifts of smoke disappeared into the air. I pulled the next one out and read the word written on it. "Oh boy, this is a big one. Hate. I drank so much hate that I became it." I held it above the fire and met Saul's gaze. For the first time since I'd known him, he was teary. I knew this one was a painful one for him too. I nodded because we both understood this one the most, then I threw it into the flames. "No more hate. No more self-loathing."

Erik squeezed my shoulder and scraped his fingers through the hair at the nape of my neck. It was all the comfort I needed to keep going.

"And this one is for my parents," I said, taking out the last paper. I swallowed hard and read the words I'd written earlier. "I'm sorry. I'm sorry you're gone, and I'm sorry it was supposed to be me on that plane. That anger and grief lit a fire in me that burned far too hot. It almost razed me to the ground. But that fire now burns a light that guides me.

"I need to let it go. I need to live because you were taken away; I need to live for the three of us.

"I love you and I will miss you forever. But it's time to say goodbye."

I put the paper to my lips, kissing them farewell, and placed it into the flames. I threw on the box and watched as the fire consumed it and the smoke drifted upward into the sky above.

And maybe it was crazy, and maybe it was all in my head or some psychobabble placebo thing, but I actually felt lighter. As though the weight of grief had shifted, lessened.

I looked up to see how far the smoke had gone, and Erik kissed the side of my head. "You okay?"

I looked at him and smiled. Genuinely, honestly. "Yeah. I think I am."

EVERYONE STAYED A WHILE LONGER. The night was cool and we'd moved inside. Jeffrey and I spoke a little. He was proud of me, so very proud. And he said my dad would have been proud too. I wasn't sure if that was true, but it felt nice to hear. The fact was, Jeffrey knew my father better than anyone else on the planet. So maybe he did know.

"I'm sorry you lost your friend," I said. "I'm sorry you

were hurting too and I was a selfish brat. I was too consumed in my own self to see you were grieving too."

Jeffrey got a little teary and took my hand and squeezed it. "Thank you."

He left not long after that, and Elektra and Mr and Mrs Keston did too. They hugged me again, told me they loved me, they were proud of me, and when it was just Erik and Saul and me left, I collapsed on the sofa, exhausted.

"Been a helluva day, huh?" Erik said, sitting beside me.

My head was resting on the backrest and I turned to look at him. "I feel like I've climbed a mountain."

"Want me to run you a bath?" he asked.

I couldn't believe it. "You would do that for me?"

He rolled his eyes and made a tsk sound. "Of course I would."

Saul sat down opposite us. "You did great today, Monroe. I'm very proud."

I took his compliment. I didn't refute it or play it down. His praise meant a lot. "Thank you. I couldn't have done any of this without you."

"You did the hard yards. Not me."

"Do we need to have a few sessions on your ability to take a compliment?" I asked, smiling tiredly.

Saul laughed. "Perhaps."

Erik patted my leg before he stood. "I'll go run that bath and give you two a minute."

I watched Erik disappear and turned back to Saul.

"What happens now? I'm not sure I like not knowing. It feels... I dunno. Weird."

"What's weird?" Saul asked.

"That your time with me is coming to an end." I shrugged and picked at my trousers at the knee. "I don't know if I'm ready to leave the nest yet. Like I'm a baby bird and I'll either fly... or plummet to the ground below."

Saul gave me a smile, like he expected me to say that. "We have a few days left together, and we need to do a few more tests so we can go back to the beach house. But Monroe, you're ready."

I wasn't sure I felt it.

"How did it feel coming back here?" Saul asked. "Being in this house?"

I shook my head, uncertain. "I'm not sure. I um... it feels wrong. I can't explain it. I mean, it's my house, but I don't feel at home here. There are no ghosts or anything like that, but sometimes I still expect to see my mother's bag on the table or a whiff of her perfume." I sighed. "I don't know, but it's like a heavy weight and I don't know how long I can carry that, ya know?"

"Yes. I get that." Saul nodded slowly. "Do you think you'll stay in Sydney?"

My gaze shot to his, and I whispered. "I don't know."

"You need to talk with Erik about that."

I sighed again, exhaustion rolling over me. "I know."

"Go have your bath," Saul said. "I'll see you in the morning."

I managed to get to my feet, my bones feeling like

concrete. I found Erik in the bathroom, adding something to the water. He smiled when he saw me and held up the bottle. "Shampoo. It was the only kind of bubble bath I could find."

I snorted and closed and locked the door behind me, then turned back to him and began to unbutton my shirt. "Thank you for being here today."

He stood up tall and looked a little perplexed. "Of course. I wouldn't be anywhere else."

I let my shirt fall to the floor, then toed out of my shoes. "You need to be naked too," I said, taking in his still-dressed body. "You're getting in this bath with me."

He cocked his head. "Am I?"

I nodded. "Absolutely."

He grinned and began unbuttoning his shirt. "Well, it is a big tub."

I was undressed before him so I got in first. I sat forward enough so he could sit behind me. As soon as he sat down, I leaned back, squirming between his legs until my back was against his chest. Water splashed everywhere, but I didn't care. And for a few moments, neither of us spoke. I pressed my head against his neck, and he would give me sporadic kisses to the side of my head. The water was hot and the bubbles were a nice touch. I hadn't had a bubble bath since I was a little kid and I hadn't expected to like it.

But if I was tired before, the bath almost put me to sleep. I felt heavy and my mind was weary, and Erik's warm body, being between his long legs and having his arms around me, his hardening dick at my back, made me feel loose all over.

"I could stay like this forever," I mumbled, my eyes closed.

Erik cupped some water and let it run over my collarbone. He kissed behind my ear. "Feels good, huh?"

I nodded and turned in his arms so I could kiss him. Water sloshed everywhere, and it probably wasn't graceful and I think I elbowed his thigh, but he never complained. He took my face in his hands, kissing me with equal fervour, then ran his hands down my back and over my arse. He lifted his body for contact, friction. Our kiss deepened, our hands roamed, gripped, teased. The room filled with steam, with the sound of water splashing, with groans and grunts and heavy breathing.

I came first and Erik followed soon after, shuddering and gasping, kissing and holding.

"Christ," I mumbled, almost collapsing on top of him.

He chuckled and eventually got me out of the bath and into bed. He wrapped me up in his arms, and the last thing I remembered was him kissing my eyelid and telling me he loved me.

WAKING up in my own bed felt a little disconcerting. Waking up next to Erik and waking up completely naked felt very right.

I could have snuggled in, pressed my ass against his cock, and begged him to take me. And I wanted it. I was ready for it; my head and heart were finally aligned and I wanted to give myself to him.

But there was something about doing that here in this house that felt wrong.

I didn't know why.

These walls, these memories weren't good for me. They felt wrong, like I was being held back here.

I slid out of bed and pulled on some jeans and went to the kitchen to make coffee. Saul was already up, drinking his tea in the morning sun. When he spotted me making coffees, he came inside. "Morning," he said brightly. "How'd you sleep?"

"Like the dead. You?"

"Very well, thanks."

"What time do we leave today?"

"Five."

I nodded. "Okay."

He sipped his tea. "I'd like to ask Erik to come up on Wednesday, if that's okay with you?"

Today was Saturday. "Sure!"

"That should give us enough time and he can spend a day or two with us before I leave."

I stopped stirring the coffee and glanced up at him. "That soon?"

He nodded. "You're ready, Monroe."

"I have to decide what I'm doing, where I go from here," I said. "And I don't know if I can do that by myself."

He looked to the hallway, making sure we were alone. He whispered, "Does that include Erik?"

"One hundred per cent," I replied immediately. "Always."

"Then you need to work on plans that include you both." Saul gave me a serious nod. "You need to be certain on where you stand, what your limits are, and which direction you want to go in."

I nodded. "I know. That's what scares me."

"Be honest and be open, that's all you can do."

Easier said than done. I picked up Erik's coffee, fully intending to deliver it to him in bed, but he walked out from the hallway. He had bed hair and a sleep-rumpled face; he wore nothing but an old pair of my grey tracksuit pants. He had blond stubble, one eye still half squinted shut, and he had a whopping hickey where his neck met his shoulder.

Fuck. I would have laughed if it didn't turn me on.

I held up his coffee and he took it with a grateful hum, sipping it when Saul noticed the love bite. He turned to me, wide-eyed. "Jeez, Monroe. Did you break the skin?" He stood up and checked Erik's skin. "It looks like he's been hit with a baseball. At close range."

"What?" Erik mumbled, rubbing his skin where Saul was inspecting it.

"You have a haematoma," Saul said.

I snorted and bit my lip. "It's a hickey. That I don't remember giving you in the bath last night, but it's hot as fuck."

Erik blushed bright red and put his hand on his neck, not really over the hickey at all, and Saul shot me a look. "I've seen injuries from rubber bullets that left less of a mark."

I tried not to grin, and hid behind my coffee cup. "I'm not even remotely sorry."

Erik snorted out a laugh and came and stood behind me, his forehead on my shoulder. "You guys leaving today?" he mumbled.

"Our flight's at five," I answered.

Erik sighed and planted a kiss on my shoulder. "Then we better get started."

"On what?" I asked.

"Whatever it is we need to do."

I turned and got another good look at the mark on his skin. "I really like that I marked you," I murmured. Erik stepped right in close, backing me up against the counter. Our coffees splashed out as we both tried to put them down, spilling over the floor and the cupboard. I laughed and Erik kissed me, hard.

"Clean that up," Saul ordered as he was walking out. "And be ready to leave in an hour."

We broke apart to laugh, and I led Erik to the bathroom where he saw the hickey. "Christ," he mumbled, running his fingers over it.

I stood behind him, sliding my hands under the elastic of his track pants, and I pushed them down. He turned to face me, and not breaking eye contact, I dropped to my knees and took him into my mouth.

He was delicious.

He returned the favour in the shower, and after I'd come down his throat, I pulled him to his feet and directed his mouth to my neck. "Mark me. Leave your name on my skin."

So he did.

And I went back to Queensland taking that with me. The mark, his mark on my body and in my heart.

It wasn't easy to leave him at the airport, but I would be seeing him again in a few days. And I was on the home straight now. I was almost at the finish line. And if I wanted to spend my life with him, I needed to finish this.

I was almost excited.

Saul said I was ready, and I believed him.

We did all sorts of tests and things. Dining out, grocery shopping, going into liquor stores, going to bars. Immersing myself in locations and situations where alcohol was not only available but offered and offered multiple times, upsell, upsell, upsell.

I was surprised by how easy it was to say no. I knew it wouldn't always be easy, and some days it would be downright fucking hard. But I was prepared. Saul had given me all the tools to live a balanced life, and I was ready.

And Wednesday couldn't come fast enough.

I was up early, like most days now. But I was excited to see Erik and nervous, knowing what I had to tell him.

I made tea for Saul and myself and cut up fruit to go with his granola and yoghurt. Saul made some phone calls, and I couldn't stare at the time any longer. I changed into my swimmers and dove into the pool. I'd always loved doing laps. It cleared my head, and it was a productive expenditure of energy.

I don't know how many laps I did. I swam, lap after lap, until my mind zoned out and my body took over.

Muscle memory, repetitive—back and forth, back and forth—until my lungs couldn't take another lap.

I came up at the end, breath ragged and my chest heaving, to find Erik crouched down by the end of the pool, smiling at me like sunshine personified. "Hey."

I almost spluttered. "What time is it? Did I miss your flight?"

"No," he replied, still grinning. He leaned down for a kiss, which I happily supplied. "I got in earlier. I think I drove everyone so crazy they were glad to get rid of me." He stood from his crouch and offered me his hand. "Need some help getting out? You've done so many laps you'll be chasing down Michael Phelps soon."

I rolled my eyes, but it did make me smile. I could haul myself out of the pool with two hands tied behind my back, but I wasn't going to knock back his offer. His hand was warm, his grip firm, his smile wide, and he pulled me out of the water. "Thanks."

Then I threw my arms around him, making him laugh. "Argh," he grumbled at now being as nearly soaking wet as me. But he cupped my face and kissed me soundly before pulling back to inspect the hickey he'd left on my neck. "Hmm, it's faded," he noted.

"Then you better do it again."

His eyes shot to mine, dark with desire, and it sent a shiver through me.

"Boys," Saul called out. "Can I speak to you both for a second?"

I shot Saul an incredulous look. "Did you know he was arriving early?"

"No," Saul replied. "Not until he called from the airport, but you were busy swimming your laps. I thought the surprise'd be nice. And I have to say, I'm pleased that you swim to counteract stress and not—" He paused to smile. "—do lines of coke like other clients I've dealt with."

I snorted and jokingly asked, "You mean, that was an option? All this time I've done the cold-turkey, healthy-eating, balanced-lifestyle shit and I could have been snorting coke?"

Saul rolled his eyes and Erik chuckled. I wrapped the towel around my waist and joined Saul at the table, Erik in the seat beside me, his hand over mine.

"Okay, boys, I just want to say something..."

Oh God. This didn't sound ominous at all.

"I'll be heading out for most of the day," Saul said. "I have things I need to organise and finalise, but it will give you both some time to talk. And I do mean talk. Before anything else." He gave me a pointed look. "I'll be home in time for dinner tonight. And because it's my last night here, I'll bring home pizza."

I could have hugged him. Both for mentioning his leaving tomorrow and for the pizza. And also for giving Erik and me some much needed time alone.

"Now, go and get changed," Saul ordered. "I'll wait until you're dressed at least. Otherwise I know what will happen if I leave now and you need to get out of wet clothes..."

I laughed. "I don't know whether you sound like a headmaster or a dad."

Erik laughed, then coughed to cover his laugh when Saul shot me a look. "Okay, okay," I said, getting up. I left them to it, got changed into dry clothes—a pair of comfy shorts and one of Erik's T-shirts—and found Erik and Saul on the balcony, talking quietly. "My ears are burning," I said as I got closer. They weren't but I had the feeling they should be.

"I'll be off then," Saul said. "And I'll be back about six."

"With pizza," I prompted.

He rolled his eyes but he grinned as he left.

And that just left Erik and me. And all jokes aside, I did need to talk to him.

"You're in good spirits," he said. His blue eyes shone like the sky and the ocean behind him.

"I am. I feel good. Better than I've felt in a long time." I held out my hand and he took it, and I led us down the few steps onto the sand. "But Saul's right. We do need to talk."

Erik made a face. "Oh. Is everything okay? Between us, I mean..."

I stopped at the ridge of dry sand that sat a little higher, waiting for the tide to come in, and I plonked myself down on it and patted the sand beside me. "Everything between us is perfect," I said, and he visibly relaxed. "But we do need to talk about where we go from here. Saul leaves tomorrow..."

"How do you feel about that?"

"Mixed. I'm excited to start living again, ya know? And I *am* ready. But I'll miss him. He's a total pain in the arse," I said fondly, "but he knows what he's doing. He saved my life. And doing this every day without him is a little scary."

"Are you worried about going back to your old routine? Your house?"

I glanced sideways at him. "My house. Why would you say that?"

"Because you didn't seem comfortable there. Like you were tense or anxious. Not like you are here. I don't know, maybe I imagined it."

"No, you didn't. I can't believe you picked up on that." I stared at him, almost disbelievingly, but then again it was Erik... He knew me best. "I was expecting to feel weird when I got there, but... It's not my home. Not anymore. There's just a bad energy there for me now."

He took my hand and threaded our fingers. "I felt that too. Not like there were poltergeists or anything, but just that you'd moved on."

"I want to sell it," I told him.

He nudged me with his shoulder and smiled. "Lucky I know someone at Keston Realty."

I felt lighter just having even admitted that I wanted to sell the house. There was no judgement, no questions, just complete understanding. "I'm still not too sure what I want to do with the company," I said, looking out to the ocean. "I don't think I'm in any place to make a decision yet. I'll need to speak to Jeffrey about a lot of things, and I know he'll give me an honest opinion."

Erik looked at me for a beat too long. "You don't want to go back to Sydney, do you?"

I stared straight ahead at the waves coming in. "I don't know. I... just don't know. The house and the company, I don't care for. But you're in Sydney, and your family. So that's where I'll be." I looked at him then. "I can't live without you, Erik. Not now I've finally figured it out. I finally pulled my head out of my arse long enough to realise it's with you that I belong, and I'm not giving that up. Not until you're sick of me."

His eyes softened and he leaned in to give me a quick kiss. "That's never going to happen."

I leaned my head on his shoulder, and for a little while, we watched the ocean. "I could stay here forever," I mused.

Erik was quiet a second, then said, "We should."

I hummed. It was a nice dream.

"I'm being serious, Monroe. What have we got waiting for us in Sydney?"

I sat up straight, my gaze shot to his, narrowed and searching, as if looking for a flicker of humour or truth. "Um, your job. Your family. The entire Keston empire. My company..." That I'd just said I didn't care for...

"We have a home here. This holiday house," he said, squinting at the sunlight. "Mum and Dad have been talking about branching out for years. You know they have. Melbourne or the Gold Coast. So why not the Sunshine Coast? I could set up an office here, no worries. Flights to the Gold Coast from here are like forty minutes long."

Holy fucking shit. "You're being serious."

"I am. Very serious."

"What would I do?" I shook my head.

He shrugged. "Work something out with Jeffrey. Work from an office set up here. Or we can fly back to Sydney once a fortnight, or weekly if we need to."

Holy crap. He was really serious. "You make it sound easy. I'm sure it's not quite that simple."

"It is simple. We can make it as easy as we want." He grinned like he had already made up his mind. "I don't know about you, but waking up to the sound of the ocean, to the bluest water, the whitest sand—waking up with you—sounds pretty damn good to me."

I couldn't help it. I laughed and squeezed his hand. "Sounds pretty damn good to me too."

"So let's do it."

"Just like that?"

"Hell yes. Just like that. Going back to Sydney at this point feels redundant." He shrugged. "Same people, same places, same bullshit. You don't want to go back to that. And I'll be all too happy to leave that behind. I want to take a step forward, with you, and this feels right." He looked a little uncertain. "Doesn't it?"

Life with him, here in this beautiful house, on this beautiful beach. No crowds, no media, no tabloids. I nodded, relief and excitement bubbling up inside me. "It really does. It feels so right."

He leaned in and kissed me again with smiling lips. "I'm actually really excited!" he said with a laugh. "Mum's gonna flip her shit, but she'll come around. And I can take a few days to look around for a suitable office space. I'll need to research some market trends and..."

Erik rambled on for a bit, talking real-estate jargon and statistics. His whole face lit up, he spoke with his hands, the way he did when he was really excited, and all I could think was *This man loves me. He loves me enough to move here with me. For me.* He was amazing and thoughtful and kind and attentive. And he was mine.

"You okay?" he asked. I hadn't realised he'd stopped talking real estate. "You're looking at me kinda weird."

I laughed. "I think we need to go inside," I said. My eyes went to his lips... his pink, wet lips. "And I want you to show me..."

"Show you what?" he whispered.

I met his eyes. "You told me... before. You told me you'd show me what it felt like to be loved. To make love. You said you'd show me and make it good for me, and well, I want you to show me."

His nostrils flared and he jumped to his feet and held out his hand. I gave him mine and he wasted no time in leading me inside and into the bedroom. But then he stopped and let out a shaky breath. "God. I need to calm down or this is going to be over really fast."

I laughed. "Shut the door."

He did that and I pulled off my shirt, then my shorts, and I crawled up the bed and lay face down with my arms and legs spread wide. "Condoms in the side drawer," I said.

He didn't move or say anything, so I looked over my shoulder. He was standing there with his shirt almost pulled off, frozen in place, staring at me. His shorts were nicely tented, but he was stuck still.

"Uh, Erik? Something wrong?"

His eyes went from my arse to my face and he let out a pent-up breath. "Absolutely not," he whispered. "You're... God, you're so perfect. Fuck."

"Well, only if you get over here," I said, raising my hips off the bed and taking hold of my cock. "Or I'll have to start without you."

The taunt spurred him into action. He quickly stripped himself naked—so gloriously naked—and he ran to the bedside table. He threw some condoms onto the bed and the bottle of lube and followed them. First, he kissed the back of my thigh, then up to my arse cheek, trailing his tongue. He covered me with soft lips, little nips of teeth, and long strokes of his tongue.

And then he was between my thighs, spreading me wide, and he licked me. "Oh fuck," I gasped.

He hummed and he did it again. Then he flicked his tongue at my opening and pushed inside, just a little. His hands kneaded my arse, my lower back, and he tongue-fucked me, then added lube and a finger until I was writhing, moaning, begging for more.

He crawled up my back, kissing the line of my spine and pressing his hot cock in between my arse cheeks.

I lifted my hips, trying to guide him, trying to get him inside me. He pushed my hips back down to the mattress and pressed his entire body weight on mine. He spread my legs with his own and traced his hands along my arms above my head. He kissed the back of my neck, gently biting me, and it drove me fucking wild.

I tried rolling my hips. I could feel him right there.

He was so close. He was so fucking close... "Erik. I need you. In me. More."

He scraped his teeth along my neck and whispered into my ear. "You're so fucking hot."

I groaned, though it sounded more like a whimper. "I can't take much more."

He pulled back and flipped me over, ducking my leg and settling himself back between my thighs. My cock was hard, as was his. He took me in his fist and leaned down to tongue the slit, and I bucked my hips. He let go and leaned forward to kiss me. "Do you want to come before you take my cock in your arse or after?"

His words sent a rush of warmth through me, curling low in my belly. My cock jerked, and fucking hell... "You'll make me come just by talking if you keep that up."

He grinned and kissed my belly, my chest, my neck. Spread me wider so my cock was aching and in desperate need of friction. He nipped at my ear and whispered, "Before or after?"

I was almost too far gone to speak. "After."

He sat back on his haunches, took a condom, and rolled it down his shaft, then slicked himself with lube. He winced as he did. "Fuck, I don't know how long I will last."

"We have hours until Saul comes back," I whispered. "Pretty sure once won't be enough."

He bit his bottom lip, then he added lube to his fingers and rubbed my hole again with them and pushed them in. He lay over me, his hand still working me, stretching me. My knees were pushed up to my chest and he kissed me harder, deeper, with more passion and love...

Then his fingers were gone and in my hair, holding my face, as his blunt cock pushed against me, into me. I gasped and he shuddered and groaned, our kiss frozen with sensation as he pushed slower, deeper.

I gasped again and his eyes shot open. He saw the shock of it in my eyes, the pure pleasure of it. "Fuck, yes."

He shuddered again but pushed until he could go no further. He kept his elbows beside my head and one hand on my head. His other hand found mine, and he threaded our fingers, gripping with every ounce of restraint he had.

I rolled my hips and he began to move, in and out, slow and deep; kissing me, his tongue moving in time with his cock.

We moved as one. We became one.

He had said he would show me what it meant to be loved, what making love was like, and I knew. There was no doubt. He loved me, he took me, and he owned me.

And it was magnificent.

His kiss became strained, and his thrusts became erratic, his gaze bored into mine, and he murmured against my mouth. "You feel too good, baby. I'm gonna come inside you." He held me, held me so damn tight when he thrust in so fucking deep. I could feel him pulse as he groaned through his orgasm.

It was the most beautiful thing I'd ever seen.

"Holy shit," he breathed into my neck. "That was so intense."

He began to pull out of me, but I gripped his arse to keep him inside me. I was right there, right at the edge... "I'm close," I whispered.

He thrust in again, kissing me deeper, and slid his hand between us and pumped me, once, twice... and I came. Every part of my body, every cell bloomed with pleasure, and he squeezed every ounce out of me.

When he finally pulled out of me, we collapsed into a tangle of limbs and panting breaths, tender touches and lazy kisses.

"Just so you know," I mumbled. "I'm not getting out of this bed for the rest of the day. You can have me as many times as you want. I will not object."

He rumbled with laughter and snuggled in. "You might regret that offer."

"Highly unlikely."

He hummed and kissed my chest. "How long until Saul gets back?"

It couldn't even be lunchtime yet. "Dunno. Hours."

Erik smirked and kissed up my jaw, sending a shiver through me, which made him laugh. But he pushed me down and he slid onto my back, kissed my shoulder, and I spread my legs for him, groaning into the mattress.

He ran his hands up my sides and along my arms, his cock pressed into my arse crack. "Can you feel how much I love you?" he whispered gruffly behind my ear, kissing down to my shoulder.

"Hmm."

"I will worship your body." He grinded his hips. "I will worship every inch of you."

A curl of pleasure rolled through me, making me stretch like a cat in the sun underneath him. I lifted my hips, offering myself, needing him to be inside me.

Erik did worship me. For hours. Until I couldn't think, I couldn't move. I was boneless, utterly spent, and feeling very loved.

Adored.

Everything he promised, he delivered. We napped, we ate, and we made love again. When I'd said I wasn't leaving the bed, it was my promise to Erik. He helped me keep it, though. No questions asked.

By the time Saul came back, we were in the pool. I was on the step with my back to the edge, Erik was between my legs, and we were laughing, kissing, still unable to stop touching. Saul came in carrying two pizza boxes. He slid them onto the table and lifted his sunglasses. "I see the talking went well," he said. "Well, I hope it did."

We climbed out, thankful we'd opted to actually put on some board shorts. I was also thankful for Erik's persistent semi that he had to wrap a towel around his waist to hide. I wasn't thankful, per se, but not entirely sorry for the new hickey I had on the back of my neck, nor the scratches down Erik's back.

Saul took one look at us and sighed. He gave me a look that was almost humorous. "Do we need to talk about the marking?"

I laughed and opened the first pizza box. "Nope. We've got it covered, thanks."

"You do know there is no such thing as a magic dick,

right?" Saul asked, and Erik almost choked on his first bite of pizza.

I laughed and nodded as I swallowed my food.

"I know it's all new and exciting," Saul added. "But you still need to work on your steps and your processes, okay?"

"Yes, I know," I replied. I was so thoroughly happy, I couldn't even be mad. "So, his dick might not be magic, but what he does with it sure is."

Erik sputtered and coughed, almost choking again. Saul laughed, shaking his head at me. "Okay, stop it or he'll rupture something."

So we sat on the deck as the sun set and ate glorious pizza and told Saul of our plans for our future. It all began tomorrow. Saul would leave, and I was ready for that. Erik would call his family and put the proposal of opening a Queensland office forward. I'd call Jeffrey and we'd discuss options for me remaining on the board of Wellman Corp but stepping back. I wanted to look at options. Options for something I was passionate about, something I could call my own.

And I was ready for that too.

Saul looked at us like a proud dad and held up his bottle of mineral water. "To tomorrow."

We clinked our mineral waters to his. "To tomorrow," Erik repeated.

I felt the hope of it, the drive, the love, and the dream in my chest. "Tomorrow."

EPILOGUE
ERIK

THREE YEARS LATER

SYDNEY TIMES

Monroe Wellman and Erik Keston are to be married on the beach fronting their home on the Sunshine Coast. Wellman and Keston dropped out of the social media spotlight three years ago, leaving behind the bars and nightclubs of Sydney, opting for a quiet, private life in Queensland. The wedding will be small and private; close family only to attend.

.   .   .

Monroe was nervous. He fixed the cushions, again. Then he went to touch the flower arrangement in the centre of the dining table. "Touch those and I'll break your fingers," Elektra said from the couch. She didn't even look up from her laptop.

Before I could calm him or chip my sister for threatening bodily harm, the doorbell rang. Monroe stared at me. "He's here."

"I'll get it," I said before he had a meltdown.

It was hard to tell if he was pacing or pulling his hair out, or both, when I reappeared with our two guests.

Monroe stopped and sagged, smiling as he quickly crossed the floor. He hugged Saul hard, only pulling back to be introduced to Saul's wife, Marcia. She was in her fifties with a greying mop of wiry ringlets that gave her a halo as it fell past her shoulders. She wore a white linen dress, red lipstick, had a lovely free-spirit energy, and I honestly couldn't picture a more perfect partner for Saul. Saul made quick introductions. "Oh, I've heard so much about you," Marcia said, taking Monroe's hand in both of hers.

"Same. Thank you for coming," he replied. He quickly turned back to Saul. "It's so good to see you."

Saul hugged him again. "You too. And you look great. I can see the beach life agrees with you."

"Uh, yeah. Love it. Would never move back to a big city again, for the shoe factor alone, really." He looked down at his tanned bare feet. "I haven't worn shoes in weeks."

Saul laughed and turned to me, offering his hand to shake. "You look good also," he said. "Very happy."

"I am." And that didn't even come close to describing it...

Saul looked around the living room. "You guys really made this your own."

The house was different now. Our furniture, our art on the walls, our things. The colour scheme had changed, there was more of Monroe's driftwood art dotted around, and the kitchen had had an upgrade. It'd been a busy three years.

The truth was, everything was different.

It was better.

Elektra was now behind us, and she gave Saul a kiss on the cheek, then did the same for Marcia. "Please come in," she said to them. "Can I get you a drink? Coffee or tea?"

"That'd be lovely, thank you," Marcia said, and she and Elektra made their way into the kitchen.

"Thank you for coming," Monroe said again. "It really means a lot."

"Wouldn't have missed it," Marcia said, turning back to smile at him. "Saul speaks of you often."

Monroe beamed at that. He and Saul had chatted over the phone every chance they got. Saul worked all over the world, weeks at a time. So while they'd talked, they hadn't actually seen each other for over a year.

Monroe had spoken to Marcia several times on the phone but they'd never met, until today.

"Come sit down and tell me all about everything," Saul said. We made our way to the back deck, pulling seats out at the table. "Tell me what's been going on? You're still ridiculously in love, I see," he said with a smile.

"Yeah, it's disgusting." Monroe laughed, giving my knee a squeeze. Saul already knew about Monroe's drink driving court case. He'd been put on a two-year good-behaviour bond. The judge said she could see he'd made changes to his life and let him off, all things considered. So Monroe didn't have to relay any of that, but there was something he'd wanted to tell Saul about face-to-face.

"I handed control of Wellman Corp over. Well, that's not really true," he corrected. "I'm still the majority owner, but I have a CEO now, and I'm more focused on my work here. I started a new venture. It's a community organisation that's doing some good things for the local addictions support centre here on the coast. It's low-key but it's hands-on and I love it. I contacted them a few days after you left and went in, and over the next few weeks, I made some lists of what was missing and decided to do something about it. I work from home most days, and it's mostly sourcing and networking, but it's great. I love it."

"He's never been happier," I declared. "And he talks himself down all the time. He's doing some fantastic work and making real progress."

The truth was, Monroe wanted Saul's approval. He'd probably never admit it, but I knew him. I knew how much his work meant to him, and how much Saul had influenced him.

"Oh wow," Saul said. "Monroe, I'm seriously impressed. That is... incredible!"

Monroe's grin was instantaneous, as was his relief. He put his hand to his forehead and glanced out over the water. If he hadn't realised just how much Saul's approval had meant, he did now.

"If you're staying for a day or two, I'd love to show you around the centre," Monroe said.

Saul nodded, a little teary, a lot proud. "I'd really like that."

Elektra brought out a tray and slid it onto the table. There was a jug of fruit punch, filled with diced strawberries, oranges and sprigs of mint, and a pot of tea. "Summer punch for we normal folks, and that healthy green tea swill for Monroe." She put a teacup in front of Monroe and handed one to Saul as well.

"Yes, I still drink it," Monroe said before Saul could say a word.

Marcia brought out a plate of cake and sat it in the middle of the table. "This smells delicious!"

"Monroe makes it," I said, looking firmly at Saul. "It's a cold hummingbird cake loaf thing. And it's amazing."

Saul's eyes went to Monroe in disbelief. "You bake as well?"

Monroe rolled his eyes. "Shut up. You started it."

Saul laughed, and we chatted for a while, and I could

see Saul marvelling at Monroe. At the changes in him, the differences, the growth. He still swam every day, and he kept to Saul's eating plan, with the exception of pizza for special occasions. He was the picture of health. Sure, he'd had bad days, even downright horrible days, but he recognised them, saw his faults, and relied on his strengths. He never missed a support meeting. As much as he'd give other people the credit, Monroe got himself through. And not once did he ever look back.

And not long after that, Mum and Dad arrived. "Look who we found pulling up!" Mum said.

It was Jeffrey Kwon. Monroe got to his feet and went to hug him. They embraced for a long time and had a few quiet words, then Jeffrey joined us at the table. "I hope I'm not late," he said.

I checked the time. "Not at all. Perfect timing, actually."

"Time to get ready!" Elektra said, taking Monroe by the arm, and they disappeared down the hall.

An avalanche of butterflies collapsed in my belly. "Yep," I tried to say. "Time to get ready."

"Do you need me to help you?" Mum asked.

I almost laughed. "Nah, I got this."

"He's thirty years old," Dad said. "He can get dressed on his own."

I excused myself from the table and went into the spare room. It was crazy, but Elektra had insisted we get ready sin opposite ends of the house, and I wasn't to come out until she said.

I pulled on my trousers and neatly pressed white

shirt. We'd agreed on navy pants and white dress shirts, no shoes. It was a beach wedding after all.

We'd planned this whole thing together. Not that there was much to plan. We had invited three guests each. That was it. There was no fancy fanfare, no expensive church wedding, no extravagant dinners or reception halls. I'm sure we could have flown to Bora Bora or the Swiss Alps and made one helluva fuss about it all, but that wasn't us.

All we needed was two wedding bands, an officiant to call us husbands, and we'd call it good.

We wanted it simple. We wanted it private.

A quiet knock on the door surprised me. "Come in."

Elektra poked her head in, then sighed. "Aww, you look so cute!" She came in, fixed my shirt button, my collar, my hair. "He's waiting for you out there," she said softly.

I let out a breath that belied my nerves. "Then I best not keep him waiting."

Elektra gave my hand a squeeze and slipped out of the room. I took another deep breath, one hundred per cent ready to do this, and went out the back.

There, just off the back deck, on the sand before the gorgeous azure-coloured ocean, stood the only people in the world we needed. Mum, Dad, and Elektra on one side, Saul, Marcia, and Jeffrey on the other. A celebrant, and Monroe.

There he stood, with the cuffs of his pants rolled, and navy braces over his white shirt. A small touch I'd known nothing about, and it made me smile. Our families stood to the sides holding flowers like a bridal party; another touch I'd known nothing about.

And I was surprised by how emotional it made me.

I walked straight for Monroe, grinning, and he held his hand out, waiting for me to hold it. Then we stood there before the ocean and in the light of the summer sun and promised our hearts to one another.

"I have something to say," Monroe said, taking my hands. We'd agreed on no vows, so this was also a surprise. He raised his chin and looked me right in the eyes. "Someone once said to me that if you drank hate, it would get to a point where that's all there was inside you," he said. "And that's very true. But the same can be said for love. If you drink it in, if it's the only thing you let in, then love is the only thing in your heart. And I owe that to you, Erik. The love you give me is without limit, undiluted, and the only intoxicating thing I will ever need. You gave me purpose and family, and I will spend every day of forever being the man you deserve. That's my promise to you."

His eyes were a little glassy, so I let go of his hands to cup his face and I kissed him.

"Uh, we're not up to that part yet," the celebrant whispered.

"Yes we are," I replied and kissed him again.

"Then I now pronounce you husbands!" she said, and our families clapped and cheered and Monroe laughed into my kiss.

I pulled back so we could exchange rings, and then Monroe took hold of my face and kissed me again. I rested my forehead on his. "And I will spend every day of forever being the man you deserve," I said back to him. "My promise to you."

THE END

About the Author

N.R. Walker is an Australian author who loves her genre of queer romance. First published in 2012, she now has over 70 books, many which are also audiobooks, and numerous translations done in nine different languages.

She loves writing and spends far too much time doing it but wouldn't have it any other way.

nrwalker.net

Cronin's Key

Cronin's Key II

Cronin's Key III

Cronin's Key IV - Kennard's Story

Exchange of Hearts

The Spencer Cohen Series, Book One

The Spencer Cohen Series, Book Two

The Spencer Cohen Series, Book Three

The Spencer Cohen Series, Yanni's Story

Blood & Milk

The Weight Of It All

A Very Henry Christmas (The Weight of It All 1.5)

Perfect Catch

Switched

Imago

Imagines

Imagoes

Red Dirt Heart Imago

On Davis Row

Finders Keepers

Evolved

Galaxies and Oceans

Private Charter

Nova Praetorian

Second Chance at First Love

Outrun the Rain

Into the Tempest

Touch the Lightning

EWB - Enemies With Benefits

Holiday Heart Strings

Bloom

The Men from Echo Creek

Method Acting

The Bait

Nothing Left to Lose

Deck the Fire Halls

Benji

Fitch

TITLES IN AUDIO:

Cronin's Key

Cronin's Key II

Cronin's Key III

Red Dirt Heart

Red Dirt Heart 2

Red Dirt Heart 3

Red Dirt Heart 4

The Weight Of It All

Switched

Point of No Return

Breaking Point

Starting Point

Spencer Cohen Book One

Spencer Cohen Book Two

Spencer Cohen Book Three

Yanni's Story

On Davis Row

Evolved

Elements of Retrofit

Clarity of Lines

Sense of Place

Blind Faith

Through These Eyes

Blindside

Finders Keepers

Galaxies and Oceans

Nova Praetorian

Upside Down

Sir

Tallowwood

Imago

Throwing Hearts

Sixty Five Hours

Taxes and TARDIS

The Dichotomy of Angels

The Hate You Drink

Pieces of You

Pieces of Me

Pieces of Us

Tic-Tac-Mistletoe

Lacuna

Bossy

Code Red

Learning to Feel

Dearest Milton James

Dearest Malachi Keogh

Three's Company

Christmas Wish List

Code Blue

Davo

The Kite

Learning Curve

Merry Christmas Cupid

To the Moon and Back

Second Chance at First Love

Outrun the Rain

Into the Tempest

Touch the Lightning

EWB

Holiday Heart Strings

Bloom

The Men from Echo Creek

Method Acting

The Bait

Deck the Fire Halls

Benji

Fitch

SERIES COLLECTIONS:

Red Dirt Heart Series

Turning Point Series

Thomas Elkin Series

Spencer Cohen Series

Imago Series

Blind Faith Series

Missing Pieces Series

The Storm Boys Series

Gay Sex Club Stories

FREE READS:

Sixty Five Hours

Learning to Feel

His Grandfather's Watch (And The Story of Billy and Hale)

The Twelfth of Never (Blind Faith 3.5)

Twelve Days of Christmas (Sixty Five Hours Christmas)

Best of Both Worlds

TRANSLATED TITLES:

ITALIAN

Fiducia Cieca (Blind Faith)

Attraverso Questi Occhi (Through These Eyes)

Preso alla Sprovvista (Blindside)

Il giorno del Mai (Blind Faith 3.5)

Cuore di Terra Rossa Serie (Red Dirt Heart Series)

Natale di terra rossa (Red dirt Christmas)

Intervento di Retrofit (Elements of Retrofit)

A Chiare Linee (Clarity of Lines)

Senso D'appartenenza (Sense of Place)

Spencer Cohen Serie (including Yanni's Story)

Punto di non Ritorno (Point of No Return)

Punto di Rottura (Breaking Point)

Punto di Partenza (Starting Point)

Imago (Imago)

Imagines

Il desiderio di un soldato (A Soldier's Wish)

Scambiato (Switched)

Tallowwood

The Hate You Drink

Ho trovato te (Finders Keepers)

Cuori d'argilla (Throwing Hearts)

Galassie e Oceani (Galaxies and Oceans)

Il peso di tut (The Weight of it All)

Pieces of You - Missing Pieces 1

Pieces of Me - Missing Pieces 2

Pieces of Us - Missing Pieces 3

Code Red

FRENCH

Confiance Aveugle (Blind Faith)

A travers ces yeux: Confiance Aveugle 2 (Through These Eyes)

Aveugle: Confiance Aveugle 3 (Blindside)

À Jamais (Blind Faith 3.5)

Cronin's Key Series

Au Coeur de Sutton Station (Red Dirt Heart)

Partir ou rester (Red Dirt Heart 2)

Faire Face (Red Dirt Heart 3)

Trouver sa Place (Red Dirt Heart 4)

Le Poids de Sentiments (The Weight of It All)

Un Noël à la sauce Henry (A Very Henry Christmas)

Une vie à Refaire (Switched)

Evolution (Evolved)

Galaxies & Océans

Qui Trouve, Garde (Finders Keepers)

Sens Dessus Dessous (Upside Down)

La Haine au Fond du Verre (The hate You Drink)

Tallowwood

Spencer Cohen Series

Thomas Elkin One

Lacuna

German

Flammende Erde (Red Dirt Heart)

Lodernde Erde (Red Dirt Heart 2)

Sengende Erde (Red Dirt Heart 3)

Ungezähmte Erde (Red Dirt Heart 4)

Vier Pfoten und ein bisschen Zufall (Finders Keepers)

Ein Kleines bisschen Versuchung (The Weight of It All)

Ein Kleines Bisschen Fur Immer (A Very Henry Christmas)

Weil Leibe uns immer Bliebt (Switched)

Drei Herzen eine Leibe (Three's Company)

Über uns die Sterne, zwischen uns die Liebe (Galaxies and Oceans)

Unnahbares Herz (Blind Faith 1)

Sehendes Herz (Blind Faith 2)

Hoffnungsvolles Herz (Blind Faith 3)

Verträumtes Herz (Blind Faith 3.5)

Thomas Elkin: Verlangen in neuem Design

Thomas Elkin: Leidenschaft in klaren

Thomas Elkin: Vertrauen in bester Lage

Traummann töpfern leicht gemacht (Throwing Hearts)

Sir

So Unendlich Viel Liebe (To the Moon and Back)

THAI

Sixty Five Hours (Thai translation)

Finders Keepers (Thai translation)

SPANISH

Sesenta y Cinco Horas (Sixty Five Hours)

Los Doce Días de Navidad

Código Rojo (Code Red)

Código Azul (Code Blue)

Queridísimo Milton James

Queridísimo Malachi Keogh

El Peso de Todo (The Weight of it All)

Tres Muérdagos en Raya: Serie Navidad en Hartbridge

Lista De Deseos Navideños: Serie Navidad en Hartbridge

Feliz Navidad Cupido: Serie Navidad en Hartbridge

Spencer Cohen Libro Uno

Spencer Cohen Libro Dos

Spencer Cohen Libro Tres

Davo

Hasta la Luna y de Vuelta

Venciendo A La Lluvia

En la Tempestad

El Toque del Rayo

Corazón De Tierra Roja

Corazón De Tierra Roja 2

Corazón De Tierra Roja 3

Corazón De Tierra Roja 4

ECB (Enemigos con Beneficios)

Floral

CHINESE

Blind Faith

Bossy

JAPANESE

Bossy

To the Moon and Back

PORTUGUESE

Sessenta e Cinco Horas

DUTCH

De Strafbank

Vijanden met Voordelen

Perfecte Vangst

De Gluurder 1 - 3